Praise for the
Red Dog Conspiracy

"The story is rich in intrigue, Family politics, social conflict, and dangers to the very existence of the City of Bridges."

— MARY BOWERMAN

"This is definitely noir, including the traditional breaking of the narrative timeline. People are doing nasty things for sometimes known, and sometimes not yet uncovered, reasons. It's what makes the world turn for the Families, who are in an uneasy alliance with shifting loyalties, cease fires, and outright aggression."

— MARGARET FISK, *TALES TO TIDE YOU OVER*

"Crime families. Corruption. Kidnapping. Murder. Betrayal. What more could a reader ask for ...?"

— CHERIE JUNG, *OVER MY DEAD BODY*

"Think Victorian/Sherlock in a dystopian world. Think Victorian manners with gangs of the new World. Think reserved, hidden Victorian wives and you will find that Jacqui is exactly the opposite. A strong character who knows exactly how to manipulate the males in her world. Add to this the wonderfully inventive extended metaphor of the pack of cards and you have a thriller that keeps you glued to the pages."

— THALIA SIMPSON

"… the political intrigue in this story is unrivaled …"

— TANGO WITH TEXT

"Beautifully written."

— GABRIEL CLASON

For more reviews, visit JacqOfSpades.com

FICTION BY PATRICIA LOOFBOURROW

RED DOG CONSPIRACY

Part 1: The Jacq of Spades
Part 2: The Queen of Diamonds
Part 3: The Ace of Clubs
Part 4: The King of Hearts
Part 5: The Ten of Spades
Part 6: The Five of Diamonds

THE PREQUELS

Gutshot: The Catastrophe
The Alcatraz Coup
Vulnerable

THE COMPANIONS

Drawing Thin

OTHER FICTION

Weird Worlds: Science Fiction and Fantasy Flash Fiction

The Five
Of Diamonds

Part 6 of the Red Dog Conspiracy

Patricia Loofbourrow

Copyright © 2020 Patricia Loofbourrow
Cover design © 2020 Patricia Loofbourrow
All rights reserved.
ISBN-13: 978-1-944223-34-2

This is a work of fiction.
No part of this work may be reproduced or transmitted in any form or by any means without the express written consent of the publisher.

Published by Red Dog Press, LLC
Printed in the USA

The Thief

Darkness lay in the opulent bedroom, save for a beam of moonlight which streamed from the open window to display the wide dressing-table and the contents there. Perfumes, makeup, all the trappings of a wealthy woman — including a decorative tall box of fine jewelry.

I crouched in shadow beside this table, waiting.

We'd been hired to solve a string of burglaries in this fine set of apartments: a collective in Spadros quadrant, 177th Street East.

The members met together every Wednesday. Over the past few weeks, a different woman returned to her rooms after each meeting to find her jewels missing. Guards had been set in the hallways, yet the thefts continued.

A puzzle, and I so loved to solve them.

Pale bluish light ruffled the edges of sheer curtains billowing in the faint summer breeze.

I glanced back to the doorway: all was quiet.

I never asked why these people didn't first go to the Spadros Family for help. Yet I did understand turning next to an investigator. Going to the police in a city ruled by the Four Families would have been their last option. Life could become most unpleasant should Roy Spadros learn they'd crossed him.

A grating noise at the window startled me.

A hand appeared, gloved in black leather. A form clothed in black perched upon the windowsill briefly, then entered, one stealthy motion at a time. Then the figure approached, falling into and out of shadow.

The way this person moved seemed familiar.

My heart pounded so loudly I feared the thief might hear it. I dared not even breathe. I also was clothed in black, but any motion would bring notice.

Like some moth reversed, the shape moved away from the moonlight's glow to what it illuminated. More to the point, the jewelry box.

A dark hand reached for the lid.

That was far enough. I grabbed the wrist. "Got you!"

A shriek came from the intruder, who tried to pull away. But I'd anticipated this; my grip was firm.

Lights came on.

Morton lounged against the door frame, finger still on the light switch. "Well, well, well … what do we have here?"

The black-clothed intruder tried to pull away again more forcefully, glancing between us both in fear. The sudden move wrenched my wrist, and I let out a cry.

The thief tried to run, but Morton (or as he was known in Bridges, Master Blaze Rainbow) crossed the room to lay hands upon the burglar's shoulders. He wrestled the prowler, shrieking and kicking, back to me.

The figure was almost as tall as I, but lithe, boyish. Black trousers, a loose tunic which hung to the upper thigh, and a finely-knitted, tight-fitting mask covering all but a bit of pale skin around deep blue eyes. Trapped, the intruder said nothing, staring back and forth, eyes wide.

Morton grabbed the mask at its crown and yanked it off, a few strands of black hair coming along with it.

The intruder grabbed — her — head. "Ow!"

I stared at the girl in astonishment. "**Katie?**"

The Girl

My sister-in-law Katherine Spadros had changed in the two years since I'd last seen her. Now fifteen, her face had lost its baby fat, and although she'd not developed much of a womanly form, she'd grown taller, and strong. I blinked at her, stunned. "What on earth are you wearing? And what have you done to your hair?"

She touched her formerly long auburn hair, now dyed black and cut to her chin. Then she flung her arm to her side. "It's how I want it," she said defiantly. "It's certainly none of your concern."

Morton smirked, his hands still firmly grasping Katherine's shoulders. "I take it you've been introduced."

I sighed. "Indeed." We had to get her out without the entire quadrant knowing. "Put your mask back on."

Katie frowned. "Why?"

A door opened and shut from far off, and voices rang in the hall.

I leaned closer and whispered, voice shaking. "You want your quadrant to learn you've been stealing from them? You'll have everyone trying to kill you."

Katie shook off Morton's grasp. "I'm Katherine Spadros. No one would dare kill me!"

Grabbing her shoulders, Morton spun Katie around, then drew his revolver. "Put it on, or I'll shoot you right now."

Katie scowled. But she put on the mask.

Morton grinned at me. His gun's hammer wasn't cocked; I hadn't seen him even load the thing.

Morton and I each took an arm, leading Katie past the apartment's astonished owners. We ignored their questions and exclamations as we took her down a flight of stairs and out to my "plain" carriage parked around the corner.

Without markings, in the dark it looked remarkably like a taxi. My former day footman Skip Honor and my butler Blitz Spadros stood beside it, dressed in street clothing.

I handed her over. "Don't take your eyes off her."

I turned to Katie. "And don't you say one — single — word."

Katie looked angry, but she stayed silent. Morton and I returned to the homeowners.

After several burglaries, the collective's Board went to our mutual lawyer Doyle Pike for help. Mr. Pike sent them to Mr. Jake Bower, his main investigator. Mr. Bower, who'd sent us cases from time to time, contacted me.

The past year hadn't been kind to me: my reputation had been all but ruined amongst the high-card quadrant-folk. Did I care? No — except in instances like this.

The Board wasn't entirely pleased to see me at our first meeting. But after much discussion, they agreed to our plan. And to my surprise, when the plan was presented to the entire membership, this elderly couple volunteered to leave their window open for the night's exercise.

Their butler let us in, showing us to the parlor. When the pair saw us, they rushed over. The woman said, "You've caught the thief, then?"

Her husband's face turned amused. "I'll let the Board know."

I held out my hand. "Payment's due in full, sir."

"Oh, yes, quite right." But he hesitated, I suppose, to pay a "Pot rag" woman. Instead, he glanced at his butler. "Pay the gentleman, and send a notice to the Board for our reimbursement."

"Very good, sir." The butler turned to Morton. "Follow me."

Morton gave me a wry smile, then went into the hall.

The old woman said, "But who was it? Why would anyone steal from us?" She drew back, palm to her chest. "And how did they climb all the way up **here**?"

The fact that none of the burglaries had been on the bottom floor of this large complex gave me the idea that this might be a climber. "We'll take care of it."

Morton stood in the hall, putting an envelope into his brown tweed jacket's left inner breast pocket.

I gestured at the envelope with my chin. "All in order?"

"It is."

So we returned to the carriage. But rather than sitting quietly, the carriage rocked from side to side. Blitz stood at one door, Honor at the other, blocking the way.

Angry words came forth: "Scoundrels! Traitors! My father'll have you killed!"

I pushed past Blitz, into her view. "Will he now?"

Katherine looked abashed.

I sat beside Katie; Morton climbed in to sit across from us.

"Lock the doors," I told Honor. "And take us to Spadros Castle."

He disappeared from view. The locks clicked into place.

Katie scowled, pulling off her mask, her hair wild. "Now I'm to be locked into the carriage like an infant?"

"If you act like one," I said. "Now be silent, as I asked."

Katherine turned away in a huff.

She used to be a sweet little girl; now she'd become a royal brat.

I rested my arm upon the window's edge, staring through the pane to the sights beyond. Most shops were closed, their windows dark and quiet. Few were on the streets, which was fortunate, given the circumstances.

I glanced at Morton, grateful for his help. With him, I could take on many more cases, without the constant struggle clients gave to a woman alone.

He looked up from winding his pocket-watch and winked.

Katie's head drew back, and she glanced from Morton to myself, suspicion in her eyes.

I peered out of the window. The arrangement was perfectly reputable, or I suppose it would have been, were I a man.

Morton hired me more than a year earlier to find his informant, a former Detective Constable turned Spadros Family man named Albert Sheinwold. Over time, though, Morton and I ended up working together, as we'd done to find young David Bryce a few years back. With little other income, we took these jobs for one reason: to get paid.

At the time, I was in a unique situation. I'd been a private investigator twelve years, with many a reference. I was still technically married to the Spadros Heir, which at times helped. Yet over the past two years, I'd separated from both my husband Tony and the Family. In some minds, that made me more trustworthy.

Whatever the reason, Morton and I had no shortage of clients. We split the proceeds, and where we could, looked for clues as to what might have happened to Albert Sheinwold.

His family and friends knew nothing. The police were baffled. The Spadros Family had scoured the city. It was if Mr. Albert Sheinwold had vanished without a trace.

Personally, I believed the man to be dead.

The Rebellion

A lot of people had died. And I don't mean those murdered by the Red Dog Gang because of me.

Almost at once, protests rose in Diamond quadrant against their second Purge, this particular one instigated after discovering spies in the quadrant. Young toughs on either side, emboldened by the disorder, tried to cross the river and infiltrate. In the year since, many had died in the fighting, or if captured on our side, in the torture rooms Katie's father Roy kept underneath Spadros Castle.

Our carriage passed a magnificent restaurant, the chandelier inside twinkling through plate glass windows. It reminded me of those glorious chandeliers inside the back hallways of the Ball-house on Market Center.

The situation for the most recently-held Grand Ball must have been perplexing. The Diamond Family was in line to host the Grand Ball that year. Yet Mr. Julius Diamond — the quadrant's Patriarch — was being held incommunicado by his oldest son and Heir, Mr. Cesare Diamond.

I heard the party inside went well. They say Cesare's wife was responsible for much of the preparation. But many died outside the Ball-house that night as police and protesters clashed.

I didn't attend. For many months after the battle with the rogue Spadros men outside the Old Plaza, I didn't go much of anywhere.

But when they caught the Bridges Strangler right after the Grand Ball, I began to feel as if things could get better. If, as I'd suspected, those scores of murders had been the work of Frank Pagliacci, or whatever he was calling himself at the trial, then executing him was a major blow to the Red Dog Gang's operation.

Maybe, just maybe, I was safe.

The carriage stopped. Honor appeared at the door. "Spadros Castle, mum."

I smiled at him as he opened the door. "Thank you." Some call it bad manners to acknowledge or even thank servants. But in my view he was a free man, and I'd be damned if I treated him like some object.

I glanced back. Katie sat arms crossed, face angry. Beyond her, Blitz stood outside, his hands firmly pressed upon the door; Morton had hold of Katie's arm. I said, "Is something amiss?"

"No," Katie snapped, flinging Morton's hand away.

"Then let's go. I'm sure your parents await you."

Her eyes widened in fear, but she came out willingly.

I turned to Honor. "Drop Blitz off and return home; they'll send us along once we're done."

Spadros Castle was a huge pile of white stone on East 192nd Street, a good ten miles from my former home, Spadros Manor.

Outside, Spadros Castle seemed to have been created more for defense than for any artistic quality. Inside, the front hall was cold. The butler never spoke, only gestured towards the parlor.

The decor was white, trimmed in pale blue, floored with light gray stone. Above the fireplace hung a stunningly lifelike pencil portrait of a much younger Katherine, spanning four feet by three. According to Katherine's mother Molly, her father Roy had drawn it by memory.

Molly Hogan Spadros entered, wearing a red dressing-gown. Raven-haired and buxom, even at her age she was beautiful. Yet her makeup was smeared, as if she'd been crying. She rushed to Katie, taking the girl into her arms. "Oh, dear gods! You're safe!" She turned to me, still clasping her child. "How did you find her?"

Chagrin crossed her face. "I didn't think to send a messenger." Molly turned to the butler. "Send word that she's here."

The man bowed and left, shutting the door behind him.

Molly cupped Katherine's face in her hands. "Daddy's gone looking for you. Where have you been?"

"Well," I said, "that's what we're here to talk about."

* * *

We sat, and the picture emerged. From the start of my trial almost two years earlier, Katherine had become sullen, withdrawn. She'd dyed her hair black, flying into a rage at the slightest provocation. She'd been caught smoking, drinking, stealing wine from the cellar.

"Lately she's been disappearing," Molly said. Then she turned to Katie. "And your poor hair! It'll take years to grow back. How could you?"

Katie scowled at her mother.

Morton's face turned surprised, and he leaned forward. "She's just now cut her hair?"

Molly's eyes narrowed. I'd introduced Morton as my business partner, but I believe she felt suspicious as to his motives. "Just."

I turned to Katherine. "Why are you doing this?"

Katie crossed her arms, face angry. "You smoke, and drink, and do whatever **you** want! Why do you care when I do?"

Molly said, "However did you find her?"

Morton leaned back, arm along the sofa. "Caught her pilfering a jewelry box on East 177th. On the second floor."

Molly stared at her daughter, aghast. "What if you'd fallen? You could have been killed!"

Katie smirked.

I said, "There's been a rash of burglaries in the apartment collective there. We were hired to catch the thief." I gestured at Katie. "I caught her with her hand on the box!"

Molly appeared completely dumbfounded. "But Katie, why?"

"Daddy never gives me anything. I can't have a horse of my own, I don't have my own money —"

"For shame!" I said. "You live in luxury to make the King blush. Why grasp for more? Why steal from your people?"

Katie's face turned angry. "Why should you care about them? They tried to kill you!"

"Yes," I said, "some in Spadros did try. But not those ones. They just want to live in peace."

Katie had nothing to say to that.

Morton said, "Say you did take those jewels. Where would you sell them?"

The girl seemed to withdraw into herself, face guarded. For a few moments, she said nothing as we watched her. Then she blurted, "There's a guy in the Pot, okay?"

Molly gasped.

Katie didn't seem to notice. "I give him the jewelry, and he gives me money."

"Hmph," Morton said, his face amused. "Likely a fraction of what it's worth."

Katherine Spadros had no idea what things cost, of that I felt sure. "And then he'll sell it for twice that." Which would still be a bargain for the party-goers streaming to the brothels who fancied a bit of jewelry to appease the wives waiting for them back home.

For once, Katie seemed less sure of herself. "You mean, they cheated me?"

I smiled at her. "For certain. You've been played."

The Difficulty

Morton and I left before Roy might arrive, neither of us wishing to see him that night. As we rode home in Molly's carriage, I felt dismayed at what I'd learned. Smoking … drinking …?

I'd been a bad influence on her, it was clear.

And she couldn't go on like this for much longer. If some homeowner didn't shoot the girl, whoever she'd gotten involved with might. I hoped her parents could talk some sense into her.

By the time the carriage pulled up to my apartments, the normally dark, narrow street was bathed so brightly that I could read the sign beside my door:

Kaplan Private Investigations

Discreet Service For Ladies

Below it hung another:

Studio For Hire — Inquire Within

Blitz answered my knock, and we walked past him into the front hall. Not nearly as large or grand as that at Spadros Castle, but much more pleasant. Morton handed over the envelope, then the three of us went through the parlor and into the kitchen.

Blitz counted out the money onto the kitchen table, took off ten percent for our Family fees (he'd bring that to our street's Family man in the morning), and split the rest between me and Morton.

Morton pocketed his share. "Good night, then." He went into the back hall, closing the door behind him.

At the time, Morton was renting the back room. I felt glad that someone reliable stayed there after all that had happened.

Blitz said, "Was there much trouble?"

I sat at the table. "Roy and all his men were out looking for her." At least we'd been able to keep this out of the public view. "Maybe she'll settle down once her father's done with her."

Blitz sat heavily. "Good gods."

I smiled to myself. "I don't think he'll hurt her. That girl might be the only thing the man's ever loved."

Blitz stared at the table for a moment, then abruptly raised his head. "Did you see the evening news?"

I shook my head. "What happened?"

"Helen Hart didn't die naturally. She was poisoned."

Poisoned? "Who — why would anyone do that?"

Blitz shrugged. "Just one more problem for the Families."

"What do you mean?"

Blitz leaned back. "Well, you've been targeted. And the Spadros Family's had its own share of trouble — "

Interesting, that he no longer placed himself in the Family. When my husband Tony ordered his men to beat Blitz a year ago, it must have affected Blitz more than I'd thought.

" — and from what you've told me, the Clubbs are in a turmoil. Plus the mess Cesare Diamond's gotten himself into. And now this." His eyes narrowed. "But it's a good question. Who benefits from Helen Hart's death?"

"Surely not the Harts. They have no heir, unless someone can be persuaded to marry that weird old Etienne."

Blitz chuckled. "He's an odd one."

I leaned an elbow on the table. "Are they sure it was murder?"

Blitz gave a one-shoulder shrug. "The coroner sent tests to Azimoff. I'm pretty sure they're sure."

I went to my room, stunned, appalled. Why would someone murder the Lady of Hart?

I hoped no one thought **we** did it.

The Spadros Family had no alliance with the Harts: Roy Spadros hated Charles Hart as much as I'd ever seen any man hate another.

Technically, we weren't even at cease-fire with them. With the position of our quadrants, though, we couldn't mount an effective attack on Hart without the aid of the Clubbs, who apparently didn't want war.

Blitz softly played my piano in the hall. He'd do that, nights. He said it was to help us sleep, but I think he just loved to play.

I tried to sleep, yet something bothered me. Tony and I had gone into Hart quadrant many a time. We'd been made welcome.

Why?

* * *

Early the next day, my housekeeper Mary brought in the morning edition of the Bridges Daily, my mail, and my tray — toast, jelly, the tonic for my liver ailment, and my "morning tea."

My Ma told me this was actually called blood tea, but of course I couldn't let anyone know that. The tea kept me from bearing children — these days, a precaution against attack more than anything else.

I'd never wanted any man besides Joseph Kerr.

Except the night I'd gladly bedded my husband Tony.

I should never have let myself love him.

"My husband thought you might want to see this too." Mary handed over the front section of the evening news.

"Thanks. I hope you're well?"

Mary Spadros was two and twenty with light brown hair, married to Blitz and nine months with child. She patted her belly. "We're both quite well." She twitched a bit. "Keeps kicking."

"That's a good sign." Growing up in a brothel as I did, I heard many bits of baby lore over the years.

Mary patted her belly. "You'll be out soon enough."

I snorted. Yowling at all hours wasn't what I had in mind when I moved here.

"I know, mum. A baby, now ..."

I reached up and took her hand. "I'm only ever happy for you. Truly. I never meant to make you think otherwise."

Mary gave me a warm smile. "Think nothing of it." Then she said to her belly, "We best get back before our breakfast burns!"

I lit a cigarette, then drank my bitter tonic as I read the article about Mrs. Helen Hart. It seemed ghoulish to test the poor woman so long after she lay dead.

Inventor Etienne Hart seemed a strange man. Yet his determination to learn what happened to his wife impressed me. If I'd been murdered, I'd want someone to learn who did it.

Setting down the paper, I stretched lazily, surveying my room. I'd become so sick after stripping the wallpaper from Blitz and Mary's room after their misdeal that I decided to paint instead. The white walls were now a rich forest green. I'd sanded the furniture, moldings, and banisters in the hall and stained them to match the dark cherry-wood desk in my study. The silver fixtures had been sold, one by one, and replaced with brass.

It'd taken me months. But it helped me not to think of that dreadful night outside the Old Plaza.

I don't think I shall ever forget it.

Setting aside the previous night's news, I raised the morning paper. Spadros Inventor Maxim Call held a shovel in his wrinkled brown hands, apparently engaged in digging!

TRAIN CRISIS: DAY 35
Dismay And Turmoil

The Inventors and their Tinkerer's Guild have worked around the clock to learn why the trains slowed to a stop thirty-five days ago. Vast amounts of digging has taken place to learn the exact location and structure of the train's power lines.

Yet the fact that this must be done has led to dismay.

Mr. Valentine Lahire of Hart quadrant said, "Why didn't they know how the trains were run in the first place? Were we being put into danger?"

The outage has caused more than dismay. Whilst usage of taxi service is at an all-time high, not enough taxi-carriages exist to move workers to and from the zeppelin station, much less care for our usual tourism. Many station workers now sleep in the station, or camp upon the premises. The last of those vacationing families stranded in the countryside have been brought home, yet many vow to sue the city for damages.

The availability of taxi-carriages throughout the city proper has dropped, leaving quadrant-folk high and low unable to travel to their destinations. Commerce has suffered. Unemployment has risen. Transportation of goods continues, yet many drivers complain of hangers-on and harassment by those begging to ride.

Your Families urge you to remain calm. Please contact your neighborhood official if you need assistance. Those wishing to aid in the effort should contact your local Tinkerer's Guild office.

    The situation was worse than I'd thought. That the *Bridges Daily* should mention the Families was unprecedented. Not even the *Golden Bridges*, a notorious tabloid, dared to do so.

The *Golden Bridges* had collapsed after Tony's speech a year prior. A dozen sprung up in its place, all competing for attention. No story seemed too wild to print these days.

One of my informants sent this one, the *True Story*, with an article circled:

ONE HUNDREDTH DIAMOND PROTEST
Citizens march outside Diamond Manor

Protesters marched in Diamond quadrant today, marking one hundred in recent history. Signs with slogans such as "Fear Imperils Commerce," and "Security Has Gone Too Far," urged an end to the isolation from the rest of Bridges. Yet others such as "Die Before Ally" show the depth of animosity between Diamond and Spadros quadrants.

The Constabulary have kept the protesters at safe distance from Diamond Manor. Yet this challenge to their Heir suggests Diamond rule over the quadrant may be weakening. What this means for the stability of the city as a whole is uncertain.

Had one of the members of the *Golden Bridges* fled to this paper after Major Blackwood's murder? The writing seemed similar.

A knock at my bedroom door startled me. Mary said, "Breakfast is ready."

When I entered the kitchen, Morton was already eating. I sat across from him. "Early day?"

He swallowed, nodding, then wiped his mouth. "Something that butler said last night. He used to know Sheinwold."

"Oh?"

"He hasn't seen him. But what he said reminded me: Sheinwold used to take his kids to the river for the summer. Up in Clubb quadrant, near Bath. Chances are someone there knows him. I think I can get an invitation into the quadrant."

"Karla Bettelmann might be willing to speak for you."

Karla Bettelmann and I had spent some time together over Yuletide. She'd been entirely unaware that her father led a group agitating against her grandfather Alexander Clubb, Patriarch of the Clubb Family. More to the point: they planned assassination, of both Mr. Alexander and his son, Master Lance.

Mr. Alexander had eliminated Karla's father, along with several other of her relatives. Yuletide had been dismal for us both.

Morton smiled to himself. "I don't think that'll be necessary." He took a long drink of his tea and set the empty cup down. "What are your plans today?"

"I need to understand how Katherine Spadros, of all people, is fencing jewelry in the Pot. Who her contacts are. What hold they have over her." I let out a breath, feeling shaky. What Katie did was incredibly dangerous. "And I need to find us another case."

Since our bargain the year prior, my lawyer Mr. Doyle Pike had been sending us both cases and letters of recommendation. When I brought him his cut of my earnings to help pay what I owed him, I'd see what he or his investigator Mr. Jake Bower (who lived close by) needed done.

The front bell rang; Mary went to answer it.

I speared some scrambled eggs with my fork. "You say Sheinwold took his children to Bath for the summer. How does a police detective have money for that?"

Morton let out a short laugh. "He'd been working for the Spadros Family on the side before he became an Associate. The man had all kinds of money."

He probably had all kinds of enemies as well. "And you're sure he's still alive."

"I have to hope, Mrs. Spadros. He trusted me. I told Zia about him, and now he's on the run. I have to help him if I can." He stared at the table, face grim. "If he's dead, I might as well be."

The Feds thought Morton killed Zia. Albert Sheinwold was the only witness to the truth: the former Federal Agent Zia Cashout had been turned by the Red Dog Gang. So far, she'd killed everyone who might be able to identify her as a Fed except Sheinwold and Morton.

Zia and Morton had worked together as private investigators for years. It was only when the Feds accused Morton of killing her did he even know she worked for the Bureau. "The last time I saw Zia was a couple years ago on Market Center. If I see her again —"

"Bring her in. She's only good to me alive."

That might be difficult to do. The last time I saw her she'd tried to kill me. She came close to succeeding.

Yet she claimed he tried to kill her. Perhaps she meant to ruin Morton as well. "What could she possibly have against you?"

Morton shrugged, glanced away. "Whether because our parents knew each other, or what, I've always thought she felt compelled to work with me, rather —"

"Than it being her idea."

"Yes."

"What of her parents? Where are they? Have they seen her?"

Mary came in and began washing pots.

Morton wouldn't meet my eye. "They died some time back."

Dread rose within me. "Did you kill them?"

He faced me, eyes wide and startled. "Of course not! What sort of man do you take me for?"

Mary's face turned disapproving.

I raised my hand. "If I didn't trust you, you wouldn't be here. It's just ... I want to understand what happened between you. Why she's trying to kill you. Ruin your name. If I could understand that, perhaps I might know how to make her see reason."

As a child in the Pot, I'd been trained to kill Federal Agents on sight. And the Feds were no friend to the Spadros Family. But Morton needed Zia alive. If I could stop their feud, perhaps more death might be avoided.

Morton spoke slowly, head down. "Men like Frank Pagliacci seem to be able to put — if I weren't a rational man, I'd say a spell — on people. He can say anything, do anything, and she'll follow. I've tried talking to her." He pushed his plate aside, put his elbows on the table, his face in his hands. "I don't know if anything will stop her, short of death."

And it grieved him. "I'm sorry."

He lowered his hands, turned his head away. "I'm sorry, too." Then he turned to me. "Mark my words: I'm good. But Zia Cashout is very good." He glanced at Mary, then back at me. "She frightens me. Unless I'm extraordinarily lucky -" he let out an ironic chuckle, "— or perhaps, unlucky — she'll be the one who kills me."

The Quarrel

Morton rose. "I'll be back by nightfall."

Talk of his death brought all my fears up again. But though my stomach churned and my hands shook, I kept my voice light. "Stay out of trouble, will you?"

He laughed. "I'll try."

Once he left, Mary said, "I put your mail on your desk."

Should I involve myself with Katie's business any further? What if it drew the attention of the Red Dog Gang? I pictured Maria Athena Spade lying dead, and as the face turned into Katie's, tears came to my eyes.

"You worry yourself too much, mum," Mary said. "It'll only lead to melancholy."

Since that terrible night in the Pot a year past, for a long time all I saw was the horrible empty look in Maria Athena's eyes as I pulled that trigger.

I wept for days in my room, wracked with grief. My hands shook. Even so much as to put my shoes on caused me to doubt my judgment, my decisions.

When the afternoon sun hit the large windows upstairs, I'd go there, in desperate hope that the sun would bring me peace. I felt unable to do much else than lie upon the bare wooden floor.

After some days of this, Mary bought me a long, wide rug of many colors. My best friend Jonathan Diamond came to visit then, at first sitting beside me, then he lay upon the floor too, his feet going one way and mine another, his face beside mine. He always brought an extra handkerchief, for which I felt grateful.

We'd lie there, Jon and I, and talk of our days, our pain, our troubles. I told him what I'd done, how I'd caused the deaths of so many people. He'd reach up to take my hand, and console me. He'd tell me of his fears: of dying, leaving me without a friend in the world, his family and quadrant falling into ruin. I don't know if anything I said helped, but I gave what encouragement I could.

As the months passed, though, Jonathan could lie upon the rug for less time, and eventually he sat beside me once more. Yet after many months the sun worked its charm upon me, and I regained my strength. I only wish it could have done the same for him.

Looking back, I think those days with Jonathan were the most terrible, yet also the happiest time of my life. I shall never forget it.

I gave Mary a weak smile, feeling shaky.

Mary patted my hand. "Things'll get better, you'll see."

Though she was almost three years younger than I, Mary had an unfailing optimism which seemed quite the accomplishment. I took a deep breath. *I can do this.* "What's on the schedule?"

A wooden clipboard hung from a hook on the wall: she handed it to me. "Mr. Lag Hilton will be doing photography from eleven to noon. Then we have a Mr. Shuli Palmer who wishes to paint the skyline from your window from two until four."

"Never heard of that one."

"I checked his credentials, mum. Lives with his maiden aunt on West 89th. No ties to any paper."

"Make sure Blitz answers the door." We'd had more than one pose as an artist to score an "exclusive story" for some news rag.

Blitz opened the door from the hall. "Did I hear you speak of me?" He only needed a few hours' sleep, so he'd gone to bed when Mary rose.

Mary beamed, going over to kiss him. "Only good."

He glanced at me. "Morning, Mrs. Spadros."

"Good morning, Blitz. We were discussing today's schedule."

"You're still having luncheon with Master Jonathan?"

"I am." I handed the clipboard to Mary. "Not too many today."

Mary said, "I don't schedule too many anymore, mum. And I don't let them come back if they leave a mess."

I rose, trying to sound cheerful. "It sounds as if you have the matter entirely under control! Carry on."

The door to my study now held a small sign:

Kaplan Investigations

The room was much the same as my bedroom, but it only held one window, high upon the wall, and the bed had been sold long since. Instead sat my cherry-wood desk and matching chairs, a small bookcase, and a wooden file cabinet.

Becoming an independent woman with a recognized business would have made me happy, if it weren't for all that had come before. But now I must hourly put aside the horrors I'd seen.

Mail sat upon my desk: notes from my informants, a request for payment. But there was a note from — of all people — a bartender in Spadros quadrant.

> My dear Mrs. Spadros,
>
> It's come to my attention that you've sought a drink known as the chocolate martini. I can now assure you that the ingredients and proprietary knowledge has been attained at some cost from the racetrack. Please visit at your convenience to enjoy.
>
> Yours most sincerely,
>
> Mike Valdez, Proprietor

I set the note down and lit a cigarette, hands shaking. A year, even six months past, I might have rushed to the call. But drink didn't interest me as it once did.

Few things interested me back then.

The kitchen door jingled. Amelia's voice came in from the alley.

Amelia Dewey had been my lady's maid since before my marriage. She was married, with children at Spadros Manor, so she'd arrive mid-morning and leave before dinner. I'd learned to run my bath and do enough to get by, so it worked.

Those days, I mainly used her for help with my street clothes and to accompany me when likely to be recognized in public.

I completely despised most of the quadrant-folk's "traditions." But I'd learned through bitter experience that defying their ways left me open to attack.

A knock on my study door: Amelia poked her head in. "Ah, there you are, mum!" She stood in front of my desk and curtsied. A bit stout and of a middle age, her dark brown hair was gray here and there under her hat. "You'll be using the carriage early today?"

I smiled to myself. Amelia's husband was Spadros Manor's stable-man: of course she'd know I'd called for the carriage early. "We'll visit Mr. Pike before luncheon."

I'd had Blitz send for the plain carriage. In daylight, of course, it wasn't much of a disguise. But at least it wouldn't have a Family seal on the doors. And if hangers-on did try to approach, my men would be able to point to the Spadros horses — and their holstered guns — to dissuade them.

"So your case went well, then."

I chuckled, recalling the shock on Katie's face when we caught her. "It did. I hope your younger daughter's well?"

Amelia curtsied. "She's well today, mum, you're too kind for asking. Would you like to dress now?"

I checked the clock. "Yes, I'd better."

I wore one of my four charcoal gray walking dresses. Atop my head, a hat with a veil which hid my face well. The rest of my wardrobe had been sold two years back to pay for my trial.

Amelia accompanied me, still dressed in her street clothes. We meant to attract as little attention as possible.

Blitz opened the door for us. A woman down the street sweeping her upstairs porch waved and smiled. I waved back. People finally seemed to tolerate my living here.

Our street's Family man Mr. Eight Howell keeping the entire block under strict scrutiny might have had some bearing upon it, but at any rate, my walk down the steps was pleasant.

Honor opened the door to the carriage. He also had dressed for the street, if somewhat better than the night prior.

I took his hand. "Good morning."

Honor smiled to himself, giving me a slight bow. "Good morning, mum. Market Center?"

"Yes, Pike and Associates. Thank you." Amelia and I got into the carriage, and it set off.

Amelia drew an envelope from the pocket of her coat. "A letter from the boy."

"The boy" was her twelve-year-old son Pip, but I'd stopped chiding her long ago for how she spoke of him. Katie's father Roy had attacked Amelia, which is how Pip came to be born, and I don't think Amelia ever forgot it.

Pip's writing had progressed so much in the past year it was almost like night and day: nicely addressed, neatly written, spelled correctly, and without even so much as a blot. He wrote about slicing veal and hauling lettuce and pickling the early peppers — thirty jars' worth!

I never realized how much food needed to be prepared for a mansion the size of Spadros Manor. Reading Pip's letters had been quite the education.

At the end, he wrote:

    Monsieur and Miss Anne send their regards.

I put the envelope into my pocket with a tinge of melancholy. I missed Monsieur and Mistress Anne and little Pip. I missed my garden. And I missed my little bird, who now lay under a flat stone in front of my apartments.

"Is all well, mum?"

I thought for a moment upon that. "Do you ever wish you might have the good without the bad?"

Amelia chuckled. "Many a time. But the deck holds low-cards for a reason."

Her words dismayed me. "Low-cards" was the term used here for servants. Menial laborers. People like her.

Did she really equate her very existence with calamity and pain?

The carriage turned onto the Main Road towards the island of Market Center, more or less neutral territory for the Four Families. Most government offices were upon the island, including the Courthouse, so attorneys tended to congregate there as well.

The streets held little traffic. At this hour, taxi-carriages were bringing tourists from the zeppelin station into the city. But an occasional police wagon, ambulance, coroner's horse-truck, or rider on horseback passed us, the latter likely a Family man.

Not many traveled the sidewalks; with the trains out of service, only those who owned their own carriage — or lived nearby — might visit the shops.

As we drew closer to the Pot, the buildings became shabbier, the traffic more its usual. None of these people had money for carriage rides. Then came the Hedge: eight feet tall and thick, yew and holly twined through wrought iron.

A cage for my people. Their only crime? The misfortune of being born there.

According to these quadrant-folk, we "Pot rags" were the discards. Some even thought us ruined cards, soiling all we touched, destined for the Fire.

But I refused to be used and cast aside, no matter what these people thought of me.

"I'm sorry, mum."

Shaken from my thoughts, I turned to her. "For what?"

"Being late, mum. The downtown taxi-carriage ran behind."

"Wait. You took the taxi?"

"Mr. Anthony hasn't let his men bring me here for over a year."

"Do they compensate you for the cost?"

She glanced down. "No, mum."

Yet they commanded her to wait upon me. Was this some new torture of Roy's? "Tally up what you've spent. I'll pay you."

"But, mum —"

"It's not fair for you to spend the little they give you going to a place you don't want to go to do a job you don't want to do."

"Begging your pardon, mum, but I'm happy to be here."

I turned to her, raising my veil. "Are you really? Your little one is ill most days, you have to be away from your home —"

But she'd reached the highest level a servant-woman might. And she'd do or say anything, no matter how false, to keep her position.

Amelia straightened, faced me. "Yes, mum. I am."

"Then do as I ask and tally your spending on my behalf."

She turned away, arms crossed in front of her.

We crossed the mile-wide river and rode onto Market Center. The carriage turned onto Promenade. The usual high-cards strolled along, yet few tourists could be seen, even fewer of the middle-cards and none of the low. When workers had trouble getting to their jobs, coming here on a lark would be impossible for those without the means to hire — or own — a private carriage.

Soon we arrived at Pike and Associates. I lowered my veil over my face: someone seeing me enter my lawyer's office could lead to gossip in the tabloids.

A thin brown-skinned young man stood behind the podium. "May I help you?"

"Mrs. Spadros for Doyle Pike."

He pressed a button, then spoke into a brass tube. "Mrs. Spadros, sir."

Mr. Pike's high quavery voice came forth. "Send her up."

A second young man approached us. "This way, mum."

The building was paneled in fine wood. The direct way to Mr. Pike's office never showed the dozens of young men — like his own grandson Thrace — toiling for a pittance in their dank closet-like workrooms to bring him his money.

Our guide opened the office door and stood aside.

Mr. Pike's office held a mahogany desk beside wide windows overlooking the island. Books of law lined fine wooden shelves. Mr. Doyle Pike, a man in his eighties, seemed intent upon writing.

I turned to Amelia and raised my veil. "Please wait outside, if you will."

Amelia curtsied. "Yes, mum."

I went in, the young man closing the door behind me.

Mr. Pike glanced up, then resumed work, golden pen in hand. "So the case went well?"

I placed the envelope with his money before him. "It did. I'm ready for another."

"Well, I'm not sure I'll have another for some time."

This wasn't entirely unexpected. "May I sit?"

"I don't think you'll be here that long." He put his pen down. "I want the rest of my money."

Now this **was** unexpected. "Have I offended you in some way?"

"I've given you more leniency than any other client. You have the means to pay me, yet you choose not to."

"What do you mean?"

"I mean it's high time you went to that husband of yours, got my money, and paid me."

A few months back, I'd asked Mr. Pike's grandson Thrace to calculate the debt I owed. He'd secretly gone to his wife, who had a better head for numbers than he, and asked her to do it — without telling her who he needed the calculations for.

She was no admirer of mine, by any means.

To my horror, the sum came to over nine thousand dollars. So to say I felt dismayed was a vast understatement. "Mr. Pike, I promised I would pay you. And I have. On time, every time, since I understood our agreement. Now you wish to change the terms."

"Which I have every right to do. You think I'm a fool? You pay me the entire sum, or I'll make you wish you had."

"What's that supposed to mean?"

"A certain secret about your mother would make the Court quite interested, don't you think? You won't beat another perjury charge, Missy, not if I have anything to say about it."

"You scoundrel! You've already spread that one around, and it's cost me everything I hold dear." I'd been banished from the only real home I'd ever had because of his betrayal.

Mr. Pike's head drew back, eyes widening. "If someone's learned of this, it wasn't from me."

I crossed my arms and turned towards the windows. "I've paid you all I can and more." I faced him. "You could make twice this if you let your 'interest fees' ride. Why do you harass me now?"

Mr. Pike's cheeks flushed, and he glanced away. "That's none of your concern."

"It is, if you'd stoop to blackmail."

His face grew fierce. "Does your husband know of your lies?"

Tony still thought Ma was dead. More importantly, I felt sure his father Roy thought so as well.

But that wasn't what really frightened me. I saw no way to escape the Prison — where my old enemy Jack Diamond ruled — if the Spadros Family turned against me.

And I didn't know how much more they'd be willing to forgive.

"As I thought. I'm quite willing to drag him into scandal. If he thinks he can shirk payment because of your lovers' quarrel, he's got another thing coming."

I stared at him, horrified. What did he know? Tony had all sorts of secrets he'd not wish to come to light.

Mr. Pike let out a self-satisfied "hmph," then leaned back, arms crossed. "I'll find out what he's hiding if I have to." His smile was unpleasant. "But I'd rather have my money."

I rushed to the door.

Amelia jumped to her feet. "Is anything wrong?"

I lowered my veil. "We're leaving."

The Life

Every day we might, my best friend Jonathan Diamond and I met for luncheon on Market Center. We tried to go different places each time to escape the chance of reporters.

I'd eaten at this day's restaurant often. It was a favorite with the police, which made for an occasional awkwardness. But the reporters never tried to force their way in as they did other locales.

The restaurant had fine wood paneling and a patio in the back with small round tables, a large umbrella covering each. That day, the weather being nice, Jonathan had chosen a table outside near the back wall.

Jonathan was eight and twenty, a tall man with very dark skin and fine-coiled black hair. He wore his navy blue uniform as Keeper of the Court. Yet he also wore a black boiled-wool overcoat and black leather gloves, which seemed rather too much, past midsummer as we were.

He had his cane with him today, black tipped with silver, yet used the arms of his chair to rise. He spoke quietly enough so no one might overhear. "Jacqui!" He held out his hand, beaming. "How wonderful to see you today!"

I took his hand briefly, then let Amelia seat me to his right, our backs to the crowd.

An armed man wearing the navy and silver livery of the Court stood along the wall before us. This man faced the crowd, yet stood far enough off not to overhear.

Once seated, I raised my veil. "Have you ordered?"

"Just tea."

I turned to Amelia. "That'll be all."

She curtsied. going, I suppose, to the servants' room downstairs.

I said to Jon, "How are you feeling?"

"Better, now that the weather's nice." Jonathan had suffered rheumatic fever as a child, and took tonics for his health several times a day. The fever had affected his heart, and his joints as well.

I smiled fondly at him, taking a small package from my pocket. "I got this for you."

"For me? Why, thank you!"

He opened the package, then stared at it, an edge to his voice. "What's this?"

"Just some liniment I found."

"Jacqui —"

"The advertisement said it was new and improved. I thought it might make you feel better."

Jon didn't answer for a time. "I know you want to help, but —"

I felt chagrined. "You don't want me to."

"It's not that." He turned towards me. "You know how many liniments I've tried? I —" He stopped himself then, took a deep breath, let it out. "I'm sorry. You're just trying to help."

My eyes stung. *I just want you to be well.*

But he never would be. How could I pretend otherwise? "Don't give up, Jon. There's still hope. I know it."

Jon smiled to himself, then sat silent, eyes downcast.

I didn't know what to say, so I said, "Any news?"

Jon shrugged. "Still no word from Gardena." Jon's sister, two years younger, wrote to him every day.

A year ago, Jon's five oldest brothers had seized him, their parents, Jon's twin brother Jack, his younger sister Gardena, and her son Roland in the dead of night and taken them by force to the countryside. This caused many a problem, the first being that Master Jonathan Diamond was Keeper of the Court.

By Merca Federal Union law, major Court cases couldn't proceed without the Keeper's supervision. Since only Jon's father Julius (who was being held incommunicado) could appoint another, the docket began to back up.

After two weeks of this, protests from City Hall led to a compromise: Jonathan's oldest brother Cesare expelled Jon from Diamond quadrant. Jonathan now lived in the Keeper's quarters on Market Center.

This made things easier for Jonathan on the days his health was bad, as he had much less further to travel. But Cesare's action only split the Diamond Family further.

The doctors had just told Jon they could do nothing more for his condition. When Cesare banished Jonathan, his four brothers became furious, and their anger turned to rebellion.

They secretly met with Jon many a time, giving him information on doings inside the quadrant. When Cesare learned of it, he barred them from going to the countryside to see their parents and sister, claiming they'd turned against him.

I considered the article in the *True Story* which warned of the situation in Diamond becoming unstable. "Do you think Cesare's gone mad?"

Jon considered the matter. "No. I think he's afraid."

The waiter poured our tea and left.

Jon added milk to his, blew on it, and took a sip. "My brother's in an impossible situation of his own making. If he admits he was wrong, he looks weak. If he continues, Diamond may end up fighting Diamond so fiercely it may end with the quadrant open to the takeover he most fears."

I recalled the terrible time Tony had with the rebellious Spadros men. "Are things that bad?"

"My father's men have been fighting Cesare's for months already." Jon let out a breath. "Some good men have died." He shook his head. "And for what?"

The waiter returned. "Are you ready to order?"

Jon asked for lamb chops. I ordered chicken pie.

I'd been recognized. But other than the occasional curious glance, we were left alone. "Is your sister unwell?"

"Not that I know of. But it's been too long since she's written." He seemed to ponder this a bit, then smiled to himself. "Sometimes, Roland writes too."

Roland was my husband Tony's son "under the table," from time in a closet with Gardena at the Grand Ball a year and a half before we married. Not "the" reason I left Tony: I wasn't in love with the man — it'd all been arranged. But the fact he hid his son from me still hurt.

The boy was innocent. Gardena and I had resolved our differences. I wished no harm upon either of them. "Is there no way to learn of their well-being?"

"Cesare said she might write to me, so unless he's gone back on his word —"

Men who are afraid do things outside their nature. I'd said that to Mary once. If Jon were right ... what might Cesare do out of fear that he otherwise might not?

"— it's not that. None of my letters have come back, so someone's getting them." He let out a breath. "It just worries me."

"Has Tony heard from them?" Tony's agreement to visit his son had been made with Gardena's father Julius, not with Cesare. I wondered how well Cesare had been honoring it.

I hadn't seen Tony in a year: my monthly allotment and an occasional mention in the paper were all that told me the man still lived. He'd made it clear the last time we met that he wanted nothing to do with me.

"Not a word in twice that."

According to Jon, Tony visited him often. But he never revealed what they spoke of.

I didn't expect him to. My brief tryst with Joseph Kerr had not only ended my marriage but upset them both, for different reasons.

I understood Tony's hurt, his anger. He once did love me, and I betrayed him.

Jonathan, on the other hand, believed Joseph Kerr to be a scoundrel and a cad. He'd presented evidence of the man's wrongdoing which even I couldn't deny.

But I'd known Joseph Kerr since I was born. I'd been in love with him for so long that he seemed part of me. Though his abandoning me to scorn, danger, and death hurt deeply, I hoped one day to get his side of the story. I owed him at least that much.

Yet no one had seen him in over two years.

"Jacqui," Jonathan said softly, "does something trouble you?"

I shrugged. "Just thinking about Joe."

Jonathan snorted. "You really must stop that."

I had a sudden flash of memory: trying to kiss Jonathan, drunk, and him pushing me away. Feelings of shame, remorse. Then gratitude, that I hadn't driven him away entirely.

He watched me, a curious expression upon his face.

I took a deep breath, trying to focus. "I actually do have a matter which troubles me." Leaving out the issue of my Ma, I told Jonathan about the meeting I'd just had with Mr. Pike.

Jon gave a slight frown. "I wonder what that's about."

"I have no idea. He seemed both agitated and distressed."

Jonathan shifted in his chair, then his face changed, as if he'd come to some decision. "Let me see what I can learn. It sounds as if some calamity has befallen him. Yet I can't see Mr. Doyle Pike, of all people, being **that** in need of money."

* * *

After we ate, I summoned Amelia and went to see Mr. Jake Bower.

Mr. Bower's home was on the ground floor, near Pike and Associates. His rooms, which doubled at his office, opened onto a narrow, dead-end street. I had the driver stop a half-block away at the corner; Amelia and I walked the rest.

It took several minutes for Mr. Bower to answer the door. A very dark-skinned man in his early forties, he reminded me a bit of Jonathan's father, Julius Diamond.

Normally, Mr. Bower was dressed nicely and full of good humor. But instead of his usual dark blue suit, he wore a workman's shirt and trousers, sleeves rolled up, and scowled when he saw me. "What do you want?"

"Why, Mr. Bower, have I arrived at an inconvenient time?"

Jake Bower glanced around, then gave a couple of quick gestures: *get in here*. He closed the door sharply behind us. "Were you followed?"

"Not that I know of, sir," I said, "but I wasn't looking."

"Never mind that." He gave Amelia a quick glance, then turned to me. "What do you want?"

His home was full of boxes: on his table, on the bed in the room to my left, stacked in the hall. "Are you moving?"

"That's none of your concern. Either tell me what you want or get out. I should never have helped any of you."

"I came to see if you had any cases I might handle for you. Especially now that you're so busy."

"Well, I don't." He put his fists on his hips, face annoyed. "Is there anything else?"

I felt concerned. "Mr. Bower, are you in some kind of trouble?"

His eyes darted to the side. "I'm perfectly well." He grabbed the door-knob, jerking his front door open. "Now if you'd be so kind?"

In my surprise, astonishment, and shock, I felt a sudden sadness. "Whatever's wrong, sir, I hope it resolves peacefully. If you need call on me, don't hesitate to ask."

This seemed to settle and touch him. "You're a sweet girl. But I must ask you to go, before anyone sees you here."

"Good day, then, sir."

The whole way home, I wondered what could possibly be upsetting the man. Did it have anything to do with Mr. Pike's predicament?

There was no way to tell. But Tony need to know about this situation with Mr. Pike: it could endanger the Family.

I didn't dare write him — the matter was much too delicate. So when we arrived, I asked Blitz to call Tony's right hand man: his first cousin Ten Hogan, who everyone called Sawbuck.

* * *

Sawbuck arrived after dinner. Blitz and I met him in the hall.

A huge man just turned thirty, Master Ten Hogan dressed like a gentleman: fine suit, topper, shoes nicely shined. To my surprise, he smiled and tipped his hat when he saw me. "Thought I'd bring this early." He handed a dollar — my allotment from Tony to live on for a month, the "minimum for a woman of my station" — and his hat to Blitz.

"Let's go into the parlor, then." I directed Sawbuck to the sofa — which I'd re-covered in forest green — and sat in one of the matching armchairs across from him. There I told him about the meeting I'd had with Mr. Pike.

Sawbuck leaned back. "What's he got on you?"

I hesitated. "That's not your concern. What I'm concerned about is ... I think I let it slip that my husband has something to hide."

Sawbuck laughed. "Mrs. Spadros, we all have something to hide. What we need to know is what Pike's trying to hide. That we can use."

"Jon said he might ask around —"

"Master Jonathan Diamond?"

"Yes, I saw him at luncheon today."

Sawbuck snorted. "I know."

Sawbuck seemed to know altogether too much for one man. I suppose that came with being responsible for Tony's part of the Business — which those days spanned much of the city proper. "Well, if you can learn anything more," I said, "be my guest."

"You need anything?"

This was surprising. "What's happened, Ten?"

"What do you mean?"

"You seem in a good mood. What's going on?"

He grinned, but his cheeks colored. "Just decided — after you saved my life last year — that you only get but the one."

Ah. "And Tony?"

That seemed to touch him. He spoke so softly I had to strain to hear him. "I will always love your husband, Mrs. Spadros. But —"

he leaned forward, then let out a sigh. "And I will always, always be by his side. I will give my life for him. But …"

"You only have one." It was why I left Tony in the first place: I only had one life, and I needed to be free to live it.

"Yes."

Sawbuck had been in love with Tony for decades. Tony thought of Sawbuck as a father. "Then I wish you well."

"Thank you, Mrs. Spadros." He rose. "I'll pass this along."

"I need his help, Ten. That's the message. I'll pay him back, every cent. But right now I need him to pay this man before matters get worse."

"He's not gonna like it."

Tony vowed never to give Mr. Pike one dime. And I promised he'd never have to. "I don't care whether he likes it." I stood, feeling weary. "But he's determined to stay my husband, and I have nowhere else to turn."

The Desperation

The next morning, a letter came:

> How dare you involve Ten in this matter? You got yourself into this, Jacqui, and you must find your own way out.
>
> I am the Spadros Heir. I gave you everything I had. Yet it's clear you see me as nothing more than a moneybag.
>
> Your lies and secrets — which appear to be boundless — will trap you until you renounce them all.
>
> Don't contact me again.

Tears came to my eyes, and a lonely grieving remorse lay heavy upon me. I heard Tony's voice, saw his pale stricken face, pictured the anger and hurt in his eyes.

Something had driven Mr. Pike to desperation, and he'd fixed his salvation upon **me**. What was I to do?

A knock at the door. Mary said, "Mum, may I come in?"

I felt weary. "Yes, come in."

She began to open the door. "It's about the temporary housekeeper —" She stopped, staring at me. "What happened?"

I sighed. "My husband is wroth with me." I shrugged, eyes downcast, as droplets fell upon my desk. "I don't know why I let him affect me so."

Mary sat across my desk from me, leaning as far forward as she might. "Begging your pardon, mum, but I think you do know." She hesitated, drawing back a bit.

"You've always spoken plainly, Mary, don't stop now."

She glanced down, swallowed. "It's something my Ma said. The worst is when you don't care, when the anger or hate —" She shrugged. "— just falls away. But if you have feeling still — for each other …" She hesitated. "Then you do."

I peered at her, trying to understand. "You mean -"

Her head lifted, and she looked into my eyes. "I mean there's hope, mum. For you. If you ever could come to love him, and he you. Again." She blushed. "I've known Mr. Anthony since I was born. He did love you, mum, very much."

I wiped my eyes, a lump in my throat. "I know."

"Maybe he still does." Then she sat back, her eyes upon my desk. "I don't know what hateful thing he wrote there, but it's because he has feeling for you. That's all."

I hadn't looked on it this way before. "What was it you wanted to ask me?"

"The housekeeper. To take over when I'm abed. After our child's dealt in?"

"Oh, yes. Have you found anyone suitable?"

She pulled out a list. "There are three I wished to speak with you about …"

* * *

After Mary and I spoke, I had Amelia get me into one of my charcoal street dresses, so I'd be ready for my luncheon with Jon. Then I told Blitz I was going for a walk.

It was half past eleven and the streets were busy: messengers on their bicycles, women beating rugs or sweeping steps.

A couple of Tony's men, dressed in suits, stood in front of the Backdoor Saloon, nodding to me as I passed. I turned left, strolling along. A full taxi-carriage trundled past, men hanging on the sides, a woman sitting beside the driver, three little girls perched upon the back bar. The horses' eyes were wide, lips wet with foam.

I felt sorry for them.

At the end of the block, I turned left again.

Although 33rd Street was wider, few were outside. I approached the back apartments of my duplex building, which looked much like mine. Tony's men stood guard over the entrance to the narrow alley running past my kitchen door.

"Good morning," I said. "Any news?"

The man who answered wasn't much past childhood. An up-and-coming Family man on his first real duty. "Nothing much, mum. Never fear, we got your back."

Literally. "Well, done, sir."

The young man blushed as I continued on.

But as I walked that long row of duplexes, my mind was ever drawn to the mystery of mine.

It wasn't why men spied upon me through that hole we found in back of what became Morton's rooms. Or even why the place seemed to be built entirely to listen to those living on my side.

What fascinated me was what this implied.

Great thought. A plan spanning decades.

At the time, I was only four and twenty. How could the man who led this Red Dog Gang possibly know I might end up there?

I turned left at the corner as I pondered this.

He couldn't, I decided. No arcane knowledge was necessary to create a construct. My apartments had been a tool, nothing more.

But how cunning! I felt the mind on the other side of this game. What did he want? How might I beat him?

I turned left onto my street, not much more than an overly wide alley. A group of boys too small to be messengers played stick-ball, stopping to doff their caps as I passed. "Morning, mum."

"Good morning." I waved them along. "Don't mind me."

Blushing, they returned to their game.

With the destruction of the rogue Spadros men and the more recent execution of the Bridges Strangler (who had to have been their man Frank Pagliacci), the Red Dog Gang had to be scrambling to recover. Sooner or later, the man leading the Red Dog Gang would make a mistake. I had to be ready.

Blitz stood beside my front steps. When he saw me, he sauntered over. "A message came for you."

"What is it?"

Blitz lowered his voice. "Mr. Charles Hart wants to meet today for luncheon."

"But I'm going to luncheon with Master Jonathan."

Blitz nodded. "I sent word to Master Diamond."

I let out a breath, feeling disgruntled. "You should **not** have done that without asking. I don't want to see Mr. Hart —"

Blitz gave me an "I don't believe this" look. "You must! Even if you were not the Lady of Spadros, to refuse an invitation by the Hart Patriarch would insult the entire Hart quadrant." He glanced away for a long moment, then back, lowering his voice. "Our position is precarious at best. We don't dare bring more attention to ourselves than necessary."

I nodded, chagrined. All that kept us safe was the Families' favor. It was why Mr. Pike hadn't sent enforcers to ransack my home for his money. It was why the Red Dog Gang had to use the subterfuge of my apartments to learn what they could instead of dragging me off to some torture room.

It was why my sworn enemy Jack Diamond — Jonathan's twin — hadn't made good long ago on his threat to kill me after extracting as much pain as he could.

A loud crack came from behind. As I turned towards the sound, something round and gray flew towards me. I took a step back, let it ease into my hand.

Shouts of disappointment came from one team, shouts of joy from the other.

Amused, I side-arm lobbed it back towards the boys playing stick-ball.

A boy caught it. The others began to argue.

Blitz chuckled. "That was a good catch."

I grinned at him. "In the Pot, we played stick-ball with rocks."

Blitz grimaced and laughed at the same time. "Ow!"

Amelia emerged. "Mum, the carriage will be here any minute!"

I hurried up the steps and into my bedroom. "Can't I just wear what I have on?"

"For luncheon with a Patriarch?" She surveyed my outfit. "Perhaps. We need to touch up your makeup, shine your shoes …"

I let her bustle about, brushing my dress and wiping my hands. What could Charles Hart possibly want to speak with me about? And why now?

He'd behaved badly in the past. We discussed the matter, and I thought he understood I wished to remain friends. He'd been a great support to me during my trial. Once the trial ended, though … his attentions brought me close to scandal.

After I refused any more gifts or flowers and rejected his offer to move into his home after his wife left, the man had backed off from his pursuit. Since then, he hadn't sent so much as a letter.

Why wouldn't he leave me alone? I'd never done anything to encourage him.

The door-bell rang. A few minutes later, Blitz knocked on my bedroom door. "The carriage is here."

Mr. Hart's white carriage — trimmed in silver and pulled by sorrel horses — stood before my door. All my neighbors were in the street gaping. "Very well."

At the time I thought: perhaps I should never have accepted flowers from Mr. Hart in the first place.

The Search

The inside of Mr. Hart's carriage was entirely lined in red velvet. I felt like a doll inside a music-box as Amelia and I rode along.

I'd never asked where the luncheon was to take place, so I felt relieved when the carriage stopped at a private restaurant on Market Center rather than continuing on into Hart quadrant.

The Kournikova was on the northeast side of the island. It'd been a common meeting-place for the Four Families back when they used to meet together, long before I was born.

Outside, the building looked non-descript, even a bit shabby. But inside, it was lovely: walls in two tones of mustard-brown with golden edgings, thick reddish-brown carpeting, chairs upholstered in Paisley, woven in green, gray, gold, and brown.

The tables in the long, narrow room were set for six and empty except for one in the middle, where Mr. Hart sat facing the door.

Mr. Charles Hart was an overweight pasty-faced man in his early seventies, only a bit of red left in his silver hair. He didn't rise. "Hello, Mrs. Spadros." His warm blue eyes flickered to Amelia, then to me. "Send your servant in back, if you please."

I turned to Amelia, whose face had gone pale. "Go on, Amelia, all is well."

Amelia gave Mr. Hart a fearful glance. "Yes, mum." She hurried through the double doors far behind him and into the white-tiled kitchen beyond without looking back.

I approached the table. Head bowed, I curtsied low. "To what do I owe this great honor, Patriarch?"

Mr. Hart sounded amused; he smelled of alcohol. "That's not necessary." He gestured to the table. "Please, join me."

I sat across from him. A man dressed in dark red slid my chair in. It was then I noticed a man standing in each corner.

Mr. Hart said, "They're here for our protection."

I should have anticipated this. Many people wanted Mr. Hart dead, not least of all Roy Spadros. "I'm sorry about your daughter-in-law."

Mr. Hart nodded. "That's very kind. Would you like something to drink?"

I shook my head, then said, "Perhaps some water."

One of Mr. Hart's men filled our glasses, then set the carafe on the table.

Mr. Hart picked up his water-glass, drank half, then set it down. Only then did I drink, remembering my mother's words: *Never take nothing, food nor drink, unless you trust the hand who gives it.*

Mr. Hart smiled as if he remembered something amusing. "I'm sure you're wondering why you're here."

"I am."

He hesitated. "Do you recall Joseph Kerr?"

I nodded, feeling melancholy. "But it's been many years since I've seen him."

"It's vital that I find him, and soon."

I snorted softly. *Join the club.*

The whole city searched for Joe. No one asked why. But in a city where low-cards were paid pennies a day, Tony's bounty of ten thousand dollars for Joseph Kerr's live and safe capture was an unimaginable fortune.

At first, any man who vaguely fit Joe's description might find himself dragged from the street to be brought in for the reward. It took Tony threatening to shoot anyone who touched a Family man for this sort of thing to stop.

The tabloids held daily odds of when and by who the capture might take place. Bookies had a brisk trade just on this alone. Speculation about where the man was and if he remained alive had persisted to this day.

I used to think of nothing else but finding Joe. But so much had happened: Joe taking my money, consorting with all those women. The little boy who looked like him.

I wasn't sure I wanted to find him anymore.

Mr. Hart set his napkin upon his lap. "I'm no longer able to come to you. It would put us both in a great deal of danger, and I can't allow that."

Now this was interesting. "What's changed?"

No one had asked my luncheon order. Yet good smells wafted into the room. One of Mr. Hart's men brought in our plates. Roast ham, mashed potatoes, and a small bowl of chopped cooked greens sat on mine, grilled fish and noodles upon Mr. Hart's. His food smelled sweet and spicy.

The ham was excellent. "My favorite," I said. "Thank you."

He gave me a fond, gentle smile. "Of course I remember your favorites, my dear." He began to eat his fish left-handed, cutting it with the knife in his right as he went along. "Are you well?"

"I'm well." I took a bite of my mashed potatoes, which was also very good. "My compliments to the chef."

Mr. Hart chewed a bite of food, nodding. Then he swallowed. "I'll pass that along."

He had entirely ignored my earlier question. "Roy no longer gets anything from you visiting me."

Mr. Hart's jaw tightened at the mention of Roy's name. He took a drink of his water, then set the glass down, hand shaking. "You understand the situation quite well for someone so young."

He picked up his fork and knife, knuckles white, and cut precisely. "He believes that preventing me from coming to you tortures me more." He set his silverware down. "But I had to see you, Jacqui —"

I folded my napkin and set it on the table. "Mr. Hart, please. This conversation has become too intimate for my liking."

His face flushed red. "My apologies, Mrs. Spadros. I forget myself." He held up his hand. "Please. Don't go." To my surprise, his eyes were moist. "I don't wish to offend."

"Very well." I opened my napkin, put it on my lap, resumed eating. The greens reminded me of my mother's cooking back in the Pot. "So all you want is to find Joseph Kerr?"

Mr. Hart shrugged, seemingly dejected.

For an instant, I felt sorry for the old man. "If I hear anything, I'll let you know."

We finished the meal in silence. I thought I understood Roy Spadros allowing then forbidding Mr. Hart to come into Spadros quadrant. But Mr. Hart had never been drunk at a meeting between us before. "Are you well, sir?"

He seemed to seriously consider this. "I don't honestly know."

"I don't mean to pry. I only wish to help."

He gave me a fake smile. "I'll be fine. How might I help you?"

I almost laughed. Taking money from Charles Hart was out of the question. Roy Spadros would probably kill me if I did just on general principles. Even if Roy didn't care, even if Mr. Hart would just hand over the money without asking the details, I'd be in a hell of a lot more danger from the Harts if I didn't pay up than I ever was from Mr. Pike.

But there was one area in which Mr. Hart might be of service. "Have you ever heard of a man named Albert Sheinwold?"

Mr. Hart snorted. "Turning me into your informant, are you?"

I shrugged. "I might as well try."

He laughed softly, shaking his head. "Never heard of him. But I can ask around if it's important."

"It's strange. I've always been able to find someone I'm looking for. It's almost as if this man doesn't want to be found."

Mr. Hart leaned back, a wry smile on his face. "Perhaps he doesn't."

The Pot

By the time I returned home, it was mid-afternoon. Amelia went into my bedroom; I went to the kitchen.

Mary stood kneading bread for dinner. "Oh, there you are, mum! I forgot to ask: did you get another case?"

"Not yet," I said. "But I'm sure one'll come along."

Mary smiled, turning the dough out onto the floured counter.

I lowered my voice. "I'll need to go out after dinner."

Mary nodded, eyes flickering to the parlor door.

Amelia reported to my husband Tony. Tony didn't need to know about my outing. If he kept his word and didn't have his men stop me, he'd most certainly have them follow.

And I didn't need that, not tonight.

* * *

Amelia returned to Spadros Manor when Morton arrived. She neither liked nor approved of the man, which amused him no end.

Morton had spent the day in Bath questioning the shopkeepers and hotel staff. Though they remembered Albert Sheinwold well, none had seen him for some time.

Once Morton went to bed, I changed into one of my disguises.

Over the past six months, I'd gone to several poorhouses and selected items from each which would go well together.

I also had Mary disguise herself and get wigs of each color.

Women didn't wear wigs in Bridges unless their hair was falling out. Only a few stores sold them. And since wigs were a major part of my disguise, I didn't want anyone to know I had them.

But with these wigs, the makeup book which Dame Anastasia gave me before her death, and my assortment of low-card clothing, I hoped I'd never be recognized on a case again.

I removed my makeup. Then I braided my thick reddish-brown curls tightly, shoving them under a straight blonde wig. I twisted this into a loose bun, then put on a patterned V-necked dark green dress without a corset. Atop that, my black hooded cape.

Mary turned off the kitchen light and let me out of the side door to the alley.

Trash cans and a few cigarette butts lay there. Twenty yards to my right, three young guards stood blocking the alleyway entrance beside my door.

After the Red Dog Gang got spies right behind my home, Tony had men patrolling at all hours. So if I didn't want him to learn about this, I had to be cautious.

I crept along the alley towards 33rd. One silent step after another brought me closer. I crouched down and peered out, taking care to stay out of the moonlight.

Two men stood in front of the steps. A noise down the street, and their heads turned.

I darted out and away, ducking into the next alley over. I waited several heartbeats, then crouched down, peering out.

The men stood talking; neither of their faces were in view.

I moved down the street, keeping close to the buildings. At the corner, I turned left, crossing the street. So far as I could tell, they never noticed me.

Next was the taxi-stand. Now that the rogue Spadros men were destroyed, taxi-carriages were safe for me again.

Three months after that terrible night, Sawbuck got together the thousand men he said he needed to root the High-Low Split out of the Old Plaza. But instead of sending his men into that U-shaped mile of 'scrapers, he used the men to set charges all round. Centuries-old masterpieces of architecture went crashing down.

And it angered me still.

I hurried to the stand just as a taxi-carriage pulled up to the small crowd still waiting. As I went along in the packed conveyance, I wondered who thought of demolition. It seemed harsh enough for Roy, yet I'd never seen him use that kind of tactic before. And Sawbuck always vowed never to work with him.

By the time the taxi-carriage reached Bryce Fabrics, I sat alone. The moon had moved lower in the sky; clouds blocked it. A group of men stood down the street smoking, but they ignored me as I went to the door and knocked.

Eleanora Bryce-Highcard, a black-haired woman in her middle forties, answered the door with an oil lamp turned low. "I hoped it was you."

Once the door closed behind us, she turned up the lamp.

The shop had changed much since Mr. Trey Highcard arrived from Dickens. Before they married, he'd scraped and whitewashed, both outside and in the front room.

Since then, he'd built shelving along the walls, where the fabrics and notions now lay. Along with the display shelving inside the small room, a wooden table and chairs sat; we edged past them.

During the day, when weather permitted, their tables would be put outside for people to sit and have tea. Eleanora now made as much from selling tea as she did her fabrics.

The once-rickety counter had been rebuilt, sanded, and painted. Eleanora knocked on the new door.

"Come in," a deep voice said.

The tiny room beyond had been curtained into three areas. The center held the other table and chairs, a cabinet, and a pot-bellied stove. Two curtains surrounded the beds along each wall.

A middle-aged man with a straight posture and graying black hair sat facing us; he stood when he saw me. "Good evening, Mrs. Spadros. I must say, with your coloration, the blonde is striking."

I smiled: his accent was still very strong. "Good evening, sir. I brought the news." I handed Eleanora my morning copy of the *Bridges Daily*, which she brought to Mr. Highcard.

He turned to his right. "Davey, she's here."

The curtain to my left opened and David Bryce peered out. A boy of fourteen, he'd grown in height since the day Morton and I found him locked in the windowless basement of Jack Diamond's factory. A few dark wisps shone at his chin, yet he still lacked the beard and strong build of a man.

He ran to embrace me tightly, as if he'd feared never seeing me again. This he did every time I arrived, of late. His eyes had never changed since that horrible day: haunted by what he'd seen, and whatever the scoundrel Frank Pagliacci had done to him during the month David had been his prisoner.

David released me, then huddled close to Mr. Highcard, who put his arm around the boy's thin shoulders.

The ordeal Mr. Highcard had suffered at the hands of the Clubb Family when he arrived in Bridges seemed to have bonded the two, to Eleanora's great relief.

When I told David of Frank Pagliacci's execution, he only nodded gravely, as if this were to be expected. The boy had never spoken since his captivity, other than two words when I told him I planned to leave Bridges: *"Don't go."*

Eleanora said, "Would you care for some tea?"

"No, thank you." I glanced at David. "Any change?"

Mr. Highcard drew David close, kissing the boy's hair. "He's become quite good at helping me fix things." He looked up at me. "Won't you at least sit?"

"I'd love to, sir, but I have an errand in the Pot."

"Nothing too dangerous, I hope?"

He knew I'd grown up there, and of course living so close to the Pot knew much of it. But being an outsider, he didn't have the revulsion to the Pot and its people which the quadrant-folk of Bridges had. "Just visiting a friend."

He rose. "Then if I may, I'll escort you to the Gap."

Mr. Highcard was quite good with people. The quadrant-folk called the main opening to the Pot the Rathole. But once I explained the matter, he'd never called it that in my presence again, rather using the name my people had given it. "I'd be honored."

* * *

Along 2nd Street it was over a mile to the Main Road, almost three to the Gap. The hour was late, and the sky clouded over. But warm: a few unsavory-looking men sat here and there on front steps or curbs, stood smoking on corners.

Mr. Highcard seemed to naturally carry himself with a presence which brooked no mischief: they let us pass without a word.

We approached the Main Road. Lights from the shops still open and from carriages going to and from Market Center lit the way. We waited with a few others until the wide road was clear, then crossed. Once on the other side, I asked, "How's David, really?"

Mr. Highcard kept his eyes in front of him. "Improved, if my wife's account be true. Yet in the past year, I've seen much change as well. I'm glad I came here, in spite of all that's happened."

"What are your plans now that you've recovered? Will you —"

He let out a deep chuckle. "Return to my life as a Constable? That ended the moment I left Dickens. True police in a city ruled by the Four Families are as welcome as a bath to a cat. My only hope is to bring some cheer to my family and the people around me."

My family. "You're a good man."

He shrugged. "I thank you for the honor, madam. To the rest of this place, I'm an outsider, and will be until the end of my days." He smiled to himself. "But I'm alive, with the woman I love, and a boy who means the world to me. I ask for nothing more."

The man's words moved me. "Eleanora's very dear. I'm grateful you hold her in such regard."

Across the street, a couple of Family men patrolled, going the other way. I don't think they recognized me, but they tipped their caps just the same.

Mr. Highcard tipped his in reply. "Those young fellows do come in handy from time to time. If it weren't so — infuriating — to be ruled by scoundrels, I'd almost enjoy living here."

I chuckled softly. One of those "scoundrels" was my husband. "I suppose it must be."

He stopped and bowed. "No offense meant, of course."

"None taken."

We strolled the cracked sidewalk in darkness, the occasional working street-lamp casting a pool of light as we went. After some time, I ventured, "What would you do to change things here?"

Mr. Highcard took time to answer. "Change comes at a price; great change is sometimes too costly to bear." He gestured down Scoop Street, where the Gap stood, two blocks off. "Would your people say change was worth the cost?"

The thought gave me some dismay. "I don't know."

He tipped his cap. "Good night, Mrs. Spadros."

"Good night, sir. And thank you." I left him standing there on the corner. When I glanced back before passing through the Gap, he still stood watching.

The way to the Cathedral was much as always in an evening: quadrant-folk in the street, my people along the sides trying to make a living from them.

On the surface, it was the perfect place to fence a jewel or two. But the fact that Katherine Spadros came to the Pot made me very suspicious, particularly since the High-Low Split (and by extension, most of the Spadros Pot) was now in the hands of the Red Dog Gang.

A woman calling herself Black Maria had taken over the High-Low Split, the only children's street gang in the Spadros Pot. Almost every adult here had belonged to it at one time or another. I felt certain that after Tony blew up the High-Low Split's hiding place at the Old Plaza, Black Maria's men and women had simply melted into the alleyways.

I'd found proof that the High-Low Split, the rogue Spadros men, and the Red Dog Gang were working together. That is, until the Spadros men outlived their usefulness.

I scanned the faces of the vendors: any of them might be part of the Red Dog Gang's plot. Unless I eliminated Black Maria, or whatever name she used now, the thousands of children living here would continue to be used by them as well.

The frightened eyes of Maria Athena Spade when I last saw her alive outside Madame's shop flashed before me.

They'd used quadrant-women, too.

I removed a little hand from my pocket. "Nothing there, dearie."

A pale, dirt-streaked face looked up at me. She pulled away and ran, yellow curls bobbing. She was pretty enough to be at her brothel, this time of night.

When I approached Shill Street, a hand grabbed my arm and drew me into the short, narrow alley. I tried to pull away, but the grasp was too strong.

A man's voice said, "I told you not to come here."

Good gods. "Benji, how else might I see you?"

Benji was a big man, brown of skin and full of muscle, with straight black hair in a braid which reached to his hip. His dark eyes narrowed. "Why?"

"Walk with me."

We moved down the short, narrow alley.

"What I say must not be spoken."

Benji nodded, half-lit in the darkness. "It dies with me."

"Two nights past, I caught Katherine Spadros thieving jewels."

His eyes widened.

"She claims to sell them here. Who does she contact?"

Benji crossed his arms. "Who wants to know?"

I gave a half-shrug. "The information may one day have worth." Information always had worth, especially with the Family.

He gestured back in the direction I'd come. "Could be anyone."

I followed his gaze to the teeming crowds passing by. "It won't be secret for long." Men loved to brag. One who'd been making a fool of a Family member had the brag of the century.

"It shouldn't be secret **now**. Are you sure it's one of us?"

So even though he'd left the Cathedral, he still had access to their sources. "She told this tale."

He gave a quick nod. "I'll learn it true."

Benji turned to go; I placed a hand on his arm. "Is Tim well?"

He gave a nod farther down the short alleyway to a small figure across the street from its opening. The boy held out a tin cup with one hand and a cane with the other. Quadrant-folk were dropping coins in left and right. "The leg hurts him sometimes, but he's good with the cane." Benji patted one of several fat purses under his vest. "Says he makes more now than he ever did a-whoring."

True to his word, Benji had rebuilt the shack they'd moved into after the Cathedral cast Tim out, and made a real home for the boy. I smiled there in the darkness. "Tell him I said hello."

"Until next time." And he was gone.

I made my way back to the Gap, and eventually found a taxi-carriage home. But I wondered at something Benji said. Why would someone pretend to be a Pot rag?

***

Since Morton planned to leave early, the next day I had my morning tea and toast in the kitchen.

Morton said, "I got a lead on Sheinwold over in Hart quadrant. I'll visit with friends there for a few days and check it out."

I'd refused further payments from Morton long ago, as he seemed to be doing more to find Sheinwold on his own than I could. "If you need any help, let me know."

So far, Morton hadn't asked for his money back. But I had it set aside: he was doing all of the work on this case, and I figured it was only a matter of time before he did.

Blitz came in, yawning. "Did you need me to call for a carriage?"

"No," Morton said. He checked his pocket-watch. "I have one arriving any minute."

The doorbell rang. Blitz said, "I'll take your bags for you."

"That's very kind." Morton downed his tea and set the cup aside. "See you in a few days."

Mary poured herself some tea and sat across from me. "It's good to get off my feet."

I smiled at her, pulled up the sleeve of my robe, and reached for another slice of toast. "Just relax. I'll finish the dishes."

"That's very kind of you, mum." She took a sip of her tea. "The interviews for the new housekeeper are today, so we won't have anyone upstairs until two. The first woman should be here soon."

"Where will you be holding the interviews? In the parlor?"

Blitz came in, holding a letter. "Nowhere, unless you want to do them upstairs." He brandished the note. "Roy Spadros is on his way here."

The Request

Alarm spiked through me. What could he possibly want to come **here** for? "Have the first woman reschedule. And tell Amelia when she arrives." A dozen years after Roy had violated her, the woman was still terrified of him. "Don't let her go through the parlor."

Amelia normally didn't arrive for many hours. But I had no idea how long the man would be here. I didn't want her to be confronted with him. "We'll seat him there."

"Yes, mum."

I rushed to my room to get into a house dress and fix my hair. Roy Spadros, here?

* * *

Once done with my hair, I returned to the kitchen. But Mary refused to let me do the dishes. "What if he finds out?"

She seemed genuinely afraid. So I went back to my room and forced myself to read the paper.

RIOT AT ZEPPELIN STATION
Over A Hundred Arrested; One Dead

> The zeppelin station train terminal was the scene of a disturbance at Platform B. As reservations for taxi-carriages and other hired transportation filled for the day, a worker fraudulently charging tourists for train

passage left a large number stranded, including women and children. An equally large number of workers joined them, following a rumor that the train would soon be made operational.

When made aware of the falsehood, angry men stormed the platform, attacking workers and causing damage to train windows and doors. One man was killed; his relatives have yet to be notified.

Station Police quelled the melee. One hundred and three were arrested, and are being held for assault, disturbance, and property damage.

On the financial page, I found this:

RACETRACK REPORTS RECORD LOSS
"Not enough carriages"

Mr. Ivey Zipai, spokesman for the Hart Family, cites insufficient transportation as cause for a loss in financial operations for the first recorded month since the Coup. "There aren't enough taxi-carriages, yet we can be of no assistance. Our racehorses would be damaged were they to pull carts."

Workers without families have been offered free room and board on the racetrack premises in an attempt to solve the manpower shortage. However, despite the Hart Family pressing numerous rickshaws into service for travel around the city and offering free drinks for all who visit, the lack of sufficient carriages to transport visitors to the much more distant racetrack has been cited as the cause of its financial shortfall.

The Hart Family, whilst undergoing its own — more discreetly presented — turmoil, was fabulously wealthy. They'd survive a down month or so.

At the time, I felt no stake in the matter. The Inventors were on the job: eventually the Four Families would settle the problem one way or another.

But this was on the third page:

SPADROS INVENTOR MISSING

The Spadros police have been called by the Apprentices of Inventor Maxim Call, who failed to return to his quarters last night. Anyone having information about his whereabouts please contact Precinct Station 8.

This should have been front page news!

When I turned the page, a roughly printed flier on cheap paper had been slipped inside:

THE BRIDGES STRANGLER IS BACK TO WORK

The body discovered in Ensley Park yesterday morning shows all the signs of the villain.

The Families' declaration that the scoundrel's dead is an evident LIE.

No amount of COVER-UP will keep OUR BOYS from MURDER!

WHO WILL PROTECT US IF THEY WON'T?

I sat staring at the flier, heart pounding.

When they caught the Bridges Strangler six months back, I felt sure that the Red Dog Gang had suffered a fatal blow.

And I remembered it all: the man's confession, the trial. The police said he knew details that only the killer might know.

Was it all a lie?

The door-bell rang.

I crumpled the flier and shoved it into my pocket.

Blitz strode to the door, which squeaked just a bit as he opened it. I detected a hint of fear in his voice. "Good day, sir."

Roy's cold, barely-suppressed fury was unmistakable. "May I come in?"

"Of course, sir! Let me take your hat, sir. Right this way." A few minutes later, Blitz knocked. "He's here."

Wrapping my shawl around me, I followed Blitz into the parlor.

I expected to see Roy already seated, yet he stood in the center of the room, facing away, hands clasped behind his back. "You've done a great deal with this place." He turned towards me and nodded. "Mrs. Spadros." He glanced at the door, and it clicked behind me.

It had been over a year since I'd seen Roy Spadros. His hair had gone mostly white. He seemed thinner, much older somehow.

But the last time I'd been alone with the man in a parlor, he'd hit me. I curtsied low, feeling shaky. "Mr. Spadros. To what do I owe the great honor of your visit?"

He gazed at me, unmoving. Then he gestured to the sitting area. "Please. We have much to speak of."

I sat in an armchair, as I usually did. Roy hesitated an instant, then sat upon the sofa. Somehow, having my coffee table between us made me feel better.

Roy said, "I thank you for your discretion with Katherine."

I smiled to myself, a fond image of the girl in mind. I'd always cared about her, even as a baby. "Think nothing of it."

His eyes widened. "Then perhaps I might trust you with another matter."

This interested me at once, but I stayed silent.

"I'd like you to speak with Cesare Diamond."

I quite unintentionally let out a short laugh. "I believe on our last meeting, he referred to me as a 'Pot rag wench.' Assuming he'd deign to speak with me now, on what topic might we speak?"

"Spadros quadrant wishes cease-fire with Diamond."

I felt so surprised that for a moment, I had no words. Finally, I said, "Why ask **me**?"

Roy grinned, letting out a small snort of amusement. "If you must know, Anthony and I have been barred from entering."

This made sense. Cesare Diamond seemed close to paranoia on the topic of security. Over the past year, he'd driven anyone not "Diamond-born or Diamond-sworn" out of the quadrant, both high and low. He'd even killed three of his own Associates he suspected of spying for one of the other Families.

Which I imagine made for an uneasy time. "Why now?"

Roy leaned forward. "Why are you always so inquisitive? I'm giving you an honor above all men, much less women, yet you continually question."

I shrugged. "If I — of all people — am to represent the Spadros quadrant, I must know all that the topic entails. The conflict's been underway for a year; you could have done this at any time. Why am I to go there **now**? What is it you really want?"

Roy's eyes narrowed. "Very well. It's about the trains."

Inventor Maxim Call had been asking Tony to let him meet with the other Inventors for years. When the train system failed and Tony continued to ignore him, Inventor Call went to Roy.

Roy told the Inventor to get back to work. But then Inventor Call did something unexpected. "My men caught him trying to sneak onto Market Center yesterday against my explicit orders."

"And where is he now?"

"Oh, he has a nice, comfortable room as my guest." Roy leaned back, an amused grin on his face. "He was quite ungrateful until I described some of the less pleasant accommodations below."

I could only imagine.

Roy rested one ankle on his other knee, obviously pleased with himself. "But the old geezer might for once have an idea of merit."

"You think the Inventors should meet."

He gave a quick nod. "They might actually come to some solution. And yet I dare say young Mr. Cesare would fall into apoplexy should we — of all people — suggest such a thing."

The thought made me laugh. "Indeed."

He stretched an arm along the sofa's back, gazing at it. "I've seen this before. The Diamond's made a rash move. His people aren't behind him. Now he can't retreat without looking weak."

"Don't you like it when people are hurting?"

Roy smiled to himself. "I take no pleasure in the misfortune of others, particularly when they affect those close to me."

I felt astonished. "You're worried about Roland!"

Roy scoffed, shaking his head, but his eyes never met mine. "Nonsense." Then he uncrossed his legs and leaned forward. "The train system must be repaired. Our incomes from the casinos are suffering. Our people can't travel the quadrant. And I want no more violence. If our people start to believe the Spadros Family can't take care of their problems —"

The flier flashed before me. "They may turn to others for help."

"Exactly." He clasped his hands together, head turned aside. "We've lost too many men already to that Red Dog Gang. I won't let everything the Spadros Family's accomplished over the past century slip away because of a young man's fear."

The connection he made startled me. Could the Red Dog Gang be behind the train stoppage?

He looked up at me, face weary. "I won't be here forever. And I won't leave Anthony a quadrant in shambles."

Something about the way he said it touched me. "Why would Cesare Diamond listen? He hates me."

This truly seemed to surprise him. "Oh?"

"You should have seen him the night his brother Jonathan rescued me from the assassin outside the Courthouse and brought me to their Manor. The man is rude, dismissive, and holds me nothing but disdain."

"So why did he testify for you?"

I considered the matter. "I didn't know about the bomb until we met with Gardena's blackmailer. Well, fake blackmailer. He stood next to me when I realized it. To him, not speaking would be worse than allowing me to die."

"Why was that?"

"I told him if he didn't speak, he could no longer claim to be impartial. He'd be siding with those who wanted me dead."

♣

"Floorman help us! An honorable man." He laughed. "We may be able to use this. As to why he'd listen to you? Why, you'd be my formal emissary, with letter of introduction."

"Yet he's already refused to speak with you or my husband."

Roy glanced away. "He doesn't trust us. For various reasons." Then he faced me. "But you have no chips in this round."

This might work. And it would ease Jonathan's mind if I were to verify that Gardena and little Roland were well.

But I now had the trust of the Spadros Patriarch, and I intended to gain all I could. "Tell me what you know of the Red Dog Gang, and I'll consider it."

"What's your interest in this?"

"They've been tormenting me and my husband from the night you hosted the Grand Ball. People I love have been murdered." I leaned forward, raising a finger to point at him. "Don't pretend ignorance, sir: it's clear you've been searching for them as well."

He drew back a bit, head tilted to one side, eyes thoughtful. "And what would you do with such information?"

"When I find the bastards, I intend to kill them."

His eyebrows rose. "Well, then." He hesitated a moment. "Here's what I know: this so-called Red Dog Gang operates in all four quadrants, with the goal, it seems, of creating strife. They've clearly been using old hatreds and fears to cut communication. To keep us fighting each other rather than them."

I'd thought much the same thing.

"This is no group of young ruffians: their leader knows too much about things they ought not."

Such as Tony not being Roy's son. And quite possibly the dreadful rumor Sawbuck had heard, about how a much younger Roy had been treated by his mother.

I glanced up: Roy sat watching me. "Go on."

He didn't move. "All the evidence we have so far points to the Kerr family —"

"What?"

He leaned forward, elbows on his knees. "— more to the point, your young Joseph Kerr."

"This is ridiculous. Talk about using old hatreds! You people have hated the Kerrs from the beginning. And now you want to plant this all on them? Two years ago, they were barely making ends meet. Where would they get the money? The connections? The men?"

"It's not as difficult as you might think," Roy said. "Jacq, you gotta admit, them splitting you up from Anthony then running off looks bad."

I stood. "I'm done listening. I won't believe Joe — or Josie, for that matter — would be involved in this sort of thing."

Roy just sat looking at me.

"You're not interested in getting rid of the Red Dog Gang, after all they've done to you, to me, to my husband?" At the time, it seemed incredible. "You're just looking for someone to blame! An almost ninety-year-old man and a couple of 'Pot rags' — easy targets, right? Frame them, string them up, and sweep it under the rug —" I grabbed the crumpled flier from my pocket and threw it at him. "— like you Families always do. Then you can have your *Bridges Daily* headlines and brag about how mighty you are. I'm serious about finding these men. When you are, let me know."

Then I realized what I'd just done. Heart pounding, voice shaking, I pointed to the door. "Now if you'll excuse me, sir, I have work to do."

Roy shook his head, let out a sigh, picked up the crumpled flier, and stood. "Then good day to you."

Once Roy left, Blitz rushed in. "Are you mad? He could have killed you!"

Frank Pagliacci was still out there. My vision blurred. "I almost wish he would have."

Mary came in. "You don't mean that, mum." She put her arm around my shoulders. "Let's sit in the kitchen."

Despite what I told Roy, I didn't have much work to do. Feeling shaky, I let Mary sit me at the kitchen table with a cup of tea.

Blitz leaned his fists on the table. "What happened?"

I tried my best not to cry. "You remember the Bridges Strangler? Catching him, the trial, everything? It was all a scam."

Blitz went pale. "The execution was just last month!"

"Some 'Pot rag' dressed as quadrant-folk, no doubt." I felt bitter. "He's back. Back killing young men."

"That's upsetting," Mary said. "But I don't truly understand."

I sighed. "Sit down, both of you."

They sat, the two of them clasping hands upon the table.

"Remember the Red Dog Gang?"

Blitz nodded; Mary peered at him, confused, then nodded.

So Blitz told her more about Family business than I'd thought.

I took my handkerchief from my pocket and wiped my eyes. "A man named Frank Pagliacci went between the Red Dog Gang, those rogue Spadros men we eliminated last year —"

Mary glanced away. She likely knew those men.

"— and another gang in the Pot. He set that whole thing up."

Mary blinked at me, a slight frown on her face. Blitz nodded, but I could see he wasn't following me either.

"I'm almost certain this man is the Bridges Strangler."

Both their mouths fell open.

"Do you remember when Mr. Anthony was taken abed? It was a couple of years ago, before the troubles with Duck and Crab."

Mary nodded.

"Well, at the time, I was on a case to find a missing little boy. You know his mother: Mrs. Bryce. She was here for the auction."

Mary's face turned horrified. "Her little boy was taken?"

"He was, by this same man, and his older brother was strangled when he went a-searching."

Blitz seemed as horrified as Mary. "That was when it all began. The murders."

"Yes." Frank had done much more: had men follow me, my husband, my informants. Three of my informants now lay dead because of him. "And it stopped for a time after I shot him. When I rescued the boy, and —"

"Wait," Blitz said. "You shot this man? Did you get a good look at him?"

"I'm amazed I even hit him. Master Rainbow can tell you the whole story; he helped find the boy."

"So that's how you came to know him," Mary said.

I stared at my hands. "Defeating the Spadros rogues was important. It was a true blow. But when they caught the Bridges Strangler, I thought maybe we could beat this Red Dog Gang. Maybe I was safe from him finding me. But it was all a lie!"

I rushed to my study, and my despair turned to anger.

Out of all the possible reactions to what was going on, Tony and Roy chose to **ignore** the Red Dog Gang? To murder scapegoats in some bizarre attempt to save the Families' reputation? These responses seemed at the bottom of any sane man's list.

After all Roy had done to me over the years — the beatings, the torments, the humiliation — now he wanted me to be part of framing three of the few friends I had in Bridges?

Assuming they still were alive.

Demoralized, I slumped into my chair.

A new pile of mail sat before me on the desk. But I didn't really see it. My eyes burned, my vision blurred, and I began to weep, putting my head on the desk.

I felt so alone. I needed someone to hold me, to tell me all would be well. I wanted someone to talk to that truly understood me.

But Joseph Kerr had left me. Why had he done that? Surely in the two years he'd been gone, he — or his twin Josephine — could have sent a letter, a note, even passed a word of his being alive.

Unless they really were dead.

But Roy talked about them as if they still lived. Mr. Hart asked me to find them.

Where could they be?

The Concern

Soon the storm passed, and I lay with my head upon the desk, just staring at the wall.

If any of the Kerrs were still alive, they needed to know that the Spadros Patriarch planned them harm. I couldn't think of a more dangerous enemy anywhere.

Perhaps this was why Mr. Hart felt so desperate to find Joe.

From his reaction to Joseph Kerr, when Tony and I went to the racetrack for our anniversary two years earlier, they'd obviously had some bitter disagreement. Joe told me then that Mr. Hart was jealous about our love for one another.

But Mr. Hart had sponsored Mr. Polansky Kerr IV into the Hart quadrant from the Spadros Pot, something which was unheard of. He'd allowed Mr. Kerr to sponsor Joe and his twin Josie — as well as their housekeeper Marja — in from the Pot. Mr. Hart had even given Mr. Kerr one of his own horses!

I couldn't recall Mr. Hart ever speaking once about the man, but from Joe's account, they couldn't be closer. Could Mr. Hart's real concern be for the grandfather?

That made more sense.

I wished I would have asked more questions of Mr. Hart when I was with him. The man always put me off balance: something about him wasn't right.

I vowed to **think** when I next had these kind of opportunities arise, not let my feelings distract me so.

Why would Roy choose **me** to approach Cesare Diamond, rather than one of his own men? Or even Sawbuck! As Tony's right-hand man, Sawbuck was the natural choice for Tony to send to inquire about his son's safety. But Roy hadn't mentioned him at all.

Perhaps Roy hated Sawbuck as much as Sawbuck hated him.

So why not send his **own** right-hand man?

Who **was** Roy's right-hand man, anyway?

I'd only heard of him. And no one knew his name.

The Knife Man, some called him, a name to frighten children: "be silent, or the Knife Man'll cut your tongue."

But no one had ever seen him. Or at least, no one admitted to it.

A Patriarch had to have someone they could talk to. An elder, or a friend, who tempered their worse instincts, or pushed them when they didn't want to do something they needed to.

Sawbuck had become a public face for the quadrant because his only concern seemed to be taking care of Tony.

But I suppose it wasn't particularly odd that I didn't know Roy's man — I didn't know who Charles Hart, or Julius Diamond, or Alexander Clubb consulted with, either.

Perhaps Mr. Polansky Kerr was Mr. Hart's adviser.

But that couldn't be true. If so, why didn't the Kerrs go to Mr. Hart for protection when Tony put out the search for them?

I felt as though I was missing something.

Roy's mystery adviser obviously didn't want to go to Diamond quadrant, and none of Roy's main men were thought suitable. So the task fell ... to **me**?

I thought I'd be the last person for Roy to give such an assignment. A Pot rag woman who'd publicly betrayed his son ... in formal talks with the Diamond Heir?

The Diamonds might consider that an insult.

What was Roy trying to do? Start a war?

Or did Roy think I left Tony because I felt useless, and that giving me some role would entice me to return?

I recalled Tony's question to me two years past: *Do you want the Family, Jacqui? Is that what this is about?*

At the time, it made no sense. How could a **woman** lead the Family? No quadrant-man would follow!

But somehow, sending me to speak with Cesare Diamond made sense to Roy. Which meant he knew something I didn't.

Tony's footman Skip Honor had vowed to bring me news of anything inside Spadros Manor which risked my safety. Yet he hadn't said a word.

So either he didn't know this would happen, or he didn't realize how much danger Roy's request put me in.

The Knife Man sounded too uncomfortably close to my old enemy Jack Diamond. By all reports, Jack loved knives, and had publicly threatened to use them on me more than once. I shivered.

The bell on the side door to the alley rang, far off in the kitchen. The clocks outside chimed the half hour. And I laughed at myself: sitting around thinking all day was equally absurd.

I wiped my face and looked through my mail. Two letters appeared to have been opened, then resealed. "Mary!"

Blitz came in. "The second housekeeper candidate just arrived. Something I can help with?"

"My letters." I held them up, backs facing him, then set them down. "Did she say anything about opening them?"

"Not sure why she would." He picked up one, and without turning it over, examined the back. "Then reseal them like that?" Blitz shook his head and set the letter down. "Who are they from?"

"Friends." Well, informants. But Blitz didn't need to know that.

"Well, that's strange. Why go through your personal mail?"

I shrugged. Then I recalled my friends from the Pot who'd stolen my mail. Stolen it, not opened and resealed it. "Anyone who was seriously looking for something would be clever enough to reseal these without being noticed."

Blitz grinned. "A message of its own, then."

I let out a short laugh. "Indeed."

"You need anything else?"

"No, that's all."

Blitz nodded, closing the door behind him.

Now, I thought, let's see what this messenger knows.

In these particular letters, I couldn't find anything unusual: replies telling me they'd found nothing about "your inquiry." Or rather, the elusive former Detective Constable Albert Sheinwold.

I sat back, tapping my chin with my letter opener. It was good to have a friend out there. But someone had been opening my mail and successfully fooling me about it for long enough that this secret friend felt compelled to tell me so.

First stealing my letters, then forging them, then opening them. What was this obsession with my mail? Why wouldn't these people leave me alone?

It seemed best to assume all my mail was being opened. Which made getting information ever the more difficult.

Perhaps I could entrust all my messages to a Memory Boy?

Memory Boys remembered all that they heard or saw, and were called to send messages too secret to be written.

Which sounded good until you remembered that this was Bridges. Everyone reported to someone. The big problem was: who did Memory Boys report to?

To learn the answer to that question, I'd kept any real messages to a particular Memory Boy named Werner Lead, giving false information — or coded messages easy to misinterpret — to others. I'd gotten the idea from Jonathan and Gardena a year prior.

Who asked questions later, what made its way back to me — it told me much.

It didn't take long until when I called for a Memory Boy, only Werner arrived. Try as I might, though, I'd not been able to learn who little Werner reported to.

But sending messages through Werner was expensive. My only other option was sending messages through others. After what had happened to Morton's informants, though, the list of those who I trusted with mine was thin.

I opened the last letter, feeling a certain anxiety. Were my informants safe? I dared not make any obvious move to warn them; each time I'd done so in the past, that person had ended up dead.

In the envelope was an invitation to tea from Tenni Mitchell.

Tenni was Madame Biltcliffe's shop maid until Madame moved her shop to Clubb quadrant. After Madame's murder last year, Tenni took over the shop as its manager and moved her five younger sisters there. It'd been some time since I'd seen her, so the invitation pleased me greatly.

I sent a letter of reply, had Blitz send for my plain carriage, and told him to notify Mary (who was still interviewing housekeepers) that I wouldn't be home for tea.

Then I returned to my desk. Under my mail lay several of the pamphlets and tabloids which had sprung up with the decline of the *Golden Bridges*. One was called *Bring Bridges Back*, and upon it a note was affixed:

    Something odd about this one.

The note was from one of my newer informants, a rather cynical man who worked in the taxi-carriage office. I peered over it:

    The Apple Trees of Bridges

    12th Street Girl Wins Knitting Award

    Treasures of the Kerr Dynasty

    Interviews Of Our Elders: The Days Of Old

    Top Ten Shoreline Parks

I could find nothing odd about this pamphlet, other than it catered to the low-card elderly. That sort always wanted to muse about times past. Which in itself was odd, because for the past hundred years, this was the most peaceful time we'd had. Well, up until Cesare Diamond began his little quadrant purge.

I resolved to have one of my other informants learn more about this paper.

We'd taken to eating breakfast fairly early, and never needed much in the way of show. No morning prayers, no large morning meeting, no lengthy breakfast buffet. Even with Roy's visit — likely timed to upset us — it wasn't yet ten.

Amelia wasn't here yet to dress me for my luncheon with Jonathan. So I wrapped my long elderberry-colored shawl around my house dress like any other woman on my street might do, and went for a walk.

This time, I decided to go right instead of left outside my front door. The day was still cool. The sun above the buildings as the narrow street wound along shone far ahead but brightly slanted, sparkling the dew upon the banisters as I passed. To my left and above, a man sang somewhat off-tune to the sound of water and dishes clinking.

Several of the buildings had entryways rising steeply to a door as ours did, but also an open-air balcony upon the second floor. To my right, a beautiful young woman with dark eyes and straight brown hair loose about her shoulders sat rocking a baby. She smiled when she saw me.

Would Nina Clubb have looked like her if she'd lived?

Suddenly melancholy, I lost interest in walking. An alleyway appeared to my right; I went down it.

The alley was much like ours: narrow, grimy. Empty, but for a few trash cans beside a kitchen door.

I was almost to the other end when a pale-skinned man stepped into view, blocking my way.

The Debt

The man was tall, thin, and in his fifties, with sandy hair and green eyes. Though he seemed familiar, he didn't look happy to see me. "You owe my father money."

I took a step back. "Who's your father?"

"Doyle Pike."

That was why he looked familiar. "Perhaps there's been some misunderstanding. I just spoke with him the other day."

The man put his hands on his hips; a gun hung in its holster from his right side. "The only misunderstanding is what'll happen if you don't pay him."

Footsteps came running up from behind, and the man's eyes widened. I turned to see a dark-skinned man hastening forward, gun in his outstretched hand.

I moved to one side in alarm. Yet the gun seemed to be trained upon Mr. Pike's son rather than me. I glanced behind: the sandy-haired man was gone. I knew the day would come when Mr. Pike sent men after me. I just didn't think it would come so soon.

The dark-skinned man came to a halt some six feet off, panting, and holstered his gun. "Did he hurt you?"

This man was of an average height, perhaps forty, dressed in gray tweed and cotton. I shook my head. "Are you one of Master Diamond's men?"

He gave me a wry smile and tipped his cap. "Mr. Theodore Sutherfield at your service, mum. Blitz is my youngest brother."

Blitz did mention in the past that his family had many fathers. "Well, sir, I'm glad to see you."

"You shouldn't walk the alleyways here. I'll escort you home."

When we emerged from the alley, the street was quiet.

Mr. Sutherfield said, "I hope my brother's tending to your home better than he's safeguarding you."

"He's not to blame: I completely forgot to tell him I was leaving for a walk."

We turned right, then right again, and the men outside the Backdoor Saloon tipped their hats, grinning as we passed.

When we approached my front porch, Blitz came rushing out, eyes wide, then visibly relaxed when he saw us. "If you're with her," Blitz said to his brother, "then she came to mischief."

"One of Pike's men," I said. "Apparently he's sincere about wanting his money."

Blitz shook his head. "Your maid's here." From the tone of his voice, Amelia was more than a bit upset.

"Then I shall see to her at once." I turned to Mr. Sutherfield. "Thank you for your kindness, sir. It was a pleasure meeting you."

He tipped his hat, nodding. "Good day, Mrs. Spadros."

I went to my room; Amelia sat mending the one of my dresses.

Amelia looked as if she'd been crying, then did what she could to cover it. But she smiled and curtsied when I came in. "Oh, very good, mum. You're back. I hope your morning's gone well?"

I shrugged. "Well enough."

"Luncheon with Master Diamond today?"

"Yes, and tea with Miss Tenni Mitchell."

Amelia's face soured. She didn't like a shop maid becoming an owner: it violated her idea of how the world should be. She believed in working your way up to a position that she felt Tenni had been merely given. "As you wish, mum."

"You're welcome to stay here when I go to tea, if you'd prefer."

Amelia relaxed. "I may just do that, mum — I have a great deal of washing."

We had no house-maid, and with it becoming harder and harder for Mary to get up and down, many of those chores had fallen to Amelia — another item she'd been unhappy with.

But Roy Spadros had demanded she be here, and Tony agreed, so here she was.

I'm sure she felt it beneath a lady's maid to wash sheets and scrub floors. But even if I had the income for a house-girl, we had nowhere for her to sleep. "Would you rather I get a day maid?"

Amelia considered this. "I don't wish to burden you, mum. Only if the finances can bear it."

"I'll speak with Mary."

Amelia thought Mary and Blitz being given their positions another case of "leniency and over-generosity," but today she only said, "Very good, mum."

Perhaps Pearson — Mary's father — had a talk with (or to) Amelia. She was beginning to sound like him.

I knew why Amelia had been crying. To have Roy appear here, of all places, must have been a blow after what had happened between them. She must have felt nowhere was safe.

I still felt a bit unsteady after encountering him, then Mr. Pike's threatening son, so close by. I draped my shawl upon the bed and went into the hall.

I meant to return to my study, but Blitz stopped me. "May I speak plainly, Mrs. Spadros?"

"As you always do."

"You can't just leave without telling anyone, not even to go for a walk. What if my brother hadn't been there?"

I felt abashed. "Point taken, sir. I apologize."

"You scared us half to death. It wouldn't go well if you should be harmed when we could have stopped it."

I pictured Tony's reaction, and it must have showed, because Blitz said, "And I don't mean your husband, either."

"Why would Roy Spadros care about what happened to me?"

"Do you really not understand?"

"Understand what?"

Blitz crossed his arms, turning away for a few paces, then faced me. "They say that once you're in the Family, you never go out. That card has two sides."

"Because I'm still married to Mr. Anthony."

"Because you're the Lady of Spadros. You pledged to the Family. You'd be avenged should you die at a scoundrel's hand. And that would include punishment for the rest of us."

"Why?"

"Because we left you unprotected!"

Protected. Of course. Tony might not be present, but he still tried to control my life. "So I can never escape."

"Don't be under any illusion, Mrs. Spadros. They own you." He gave a wry grin, and at once I saw the resemblance to his brother. "But they owe you as well."

"Because I pledged to them." I remembered the day. It wasn't how others had described it, burning one of the Holy Cards, or killing someone, or shedding your own blood. I was little more than a child. But in a moment of weakness, tired of fighting, I signed a paper.

I can't to this day say that they forced me to: I did it of my own free will. I never imagined what it all would mean, though.

"It's something you can use," Blitz said, "if you need to. An Ace up your sleeve, if you will. Use it, and the entire might of the Spadros Family lies behind you." He turned away. "The whole city knows it's there. Just use it wisely. You may only get one chance."

The Match

I returned to my study, pondering all that had happened in the past few days.

The trains failing. Mr. Pike suddenly extorting me. Roy asking me to be his emissary to, of all people, Cesare Diamond. The Four Families' lie to the city about the Bridges Strangler being dead. Mr. Bower's evident distress. And whatever Katie was involved with.

Why, after a year's peace, was all this happening now?

* * *

This day, Jonathan and I met at the same restaurant Mr. Hart had taken me to. The room was full, so we were at a table in the back corner away from the kitchen door.

As we sipped tea and perused the menu, Jon said, "Mr. Hart said you liked the food here."

I smiled, amused. "True. Yet I ate here just yesterday."

"Then choose something different today — it shall be my treat."

"Jon — you don't have to do this."

"I'm Keeper of the Court," he said softly, leaning towards me. "I don't have to do anything. But I wish to."

When in this mood, he wouldn't be deterred. "Thank you."

He leaned back, obviously pleased with himself. "I learned what's troubling Mr. Pike."

"Do tell."

Jon sobered. "It's his wife. She's quite ill, and he's taking her to Azimoff." He shook his head slightly. "It's all she knew."

"Hmm?"

"One of the clerks at the courthouse. A widow. I overheard her talking about him, so I asked what she knew."

"Why would he need money? He's got more than any man should have."

Jon shrugged. "It must be serious, if he's taking her to Azimoff."

"It must." Did treatment there cost much? I had no idea.

"So what will you do? About paying him? Did you talk with Tony about it at all?"

"I thought you'd know everything."

Jon frowned. "How would I?"

"Wasn't it you that's been opening my mail?"

"Of course not! I would never allow it."

I felt bad for not trusting him. "I'm sorry."

"So what's happened?"

I told him about the "message" of my opened and resealed mail. "Someone wants me to know about it ... but who? I assumed it was you, watching out for me."

Jonathan gave his head a tiny shake. "I had no idea." He took a deep breath, let it out. "What will you do?"

I shrugged. "I could send messages with you. Or through Blitz. I'm pretty sure he only reports to Sawbuck."

Jon gave a puzzled frown, then said, "Oh, yes, Tony's man. He seems steady." For a moment, he seemed deep in thought. "Yet I can't imagine your butler opening your mail."

I laughed. "Blitz seems to have entirely cast his lot with me."

Jon's eyes widened. "He's renounced the Family?"

"All but. When he speaks, he sets himself separate. It's quite encouraging."

Jon nodded slowly. "It could come in handy one day."

The waiter came then, and took our order. And I thought about how much fascinating information Jon must hear at the courthouse. Which reminded me, strangely enough, of Mr. Jake Bower.

Amelia and I stood waiting for him to collect a file for a case he was giving us. A partially-completed certificate lay upon the oval wooden table filling his front room. The writing looked familiar. "What's this?"

Mr. Bower came in, file in hand. "What's what?"

I pointed at the document.

He laughed merrily. "That's my main employment. I trained as a scribe, like my father before me. All those lovely documents you see at the courthouse? I've done many of them." He gave me a broad grin. "It's the only thing I've ever been really good at."

"Do you know a Mr. Jake Bower?"

"No. Should I?"

"He does scribe work for the courthouse. He's also Doyle Pike's main investigator."

Jonathan shrugged. "Never heard of him."

"He reminds me some of your father, but more lively, and with much better humor."

"My father's a hard man. Yet I suppose the troubles of an entire quadrant would drain the humor from any man's soul."

I hadn't considered that. It also explained some of Roy's demeanor. And the way Mr. Hart had turned to drink. "At times, Mr. Bower gives me cases. And he worked for me once." It happened to involve an investigation into Jon's twin brother, Jack. But Jon didn't need to know about that. "I went to see him the other day and he seemed to be in some sort of trouble too."

"That's strange."

"It was. He said something like 'I should never have helped any of you.'"

Jonathan shook his head. "I wouldn't trouble yourself about it."

I pondered this for a moment. "You're entirely correct." Though I did have concern for the man, Mr. Bower would likely not appreciate the Keeper of the Court — or the Lady of Spadros, for that matter — making inquiries into his personal affairs. In fact, he seemed not to want anyone to know about them at all. "I'll not trouble myself about it any further."

Jon smiled fondly. "There's my girl." He gazed at me a long moment. "I'm glad you're feeling more cheerful."

"I am!" Yet thinking about Jonathan's brother compelled me to ask. "Has anyone heard from Jack?"

The night that Cesare Diamond banished his brother Jonathan to Market Center, Jack Diamond disappeared. I had my own informants watching for him: he'd been seen several times at the Prison, which made sense, as he was indeed Keeper of the Prison. Yet it had been eight months since his last sighting.

Jon's eyes widened for an instant, then he glanced away, shaking his head. "He's recently sent a message that he's well." He hesitated, then said, "As well as he ever is."

Everyone knew that Jonathan's twin Jack was mad: both violent and erratic. It'd been the talk of Bridges for years. But Jon seldom spoke of it, and I believe that it hurt him deeply to speak ill of his brother. "Never-mind, Jon. I know the situation grieves you."

Jon nodded, eyes downcast, seeming far away. "I wish **everything** had gone differently."

Our luncheon came, and we ate, and my food tasted just as delicious as the last time.

I wished things had gone differently, too.

Jack Diamond hated me fiercely, and it was most disturbing that the man roamed freely, even if presumably bound to his quadrant. I believed he needed to be put in a ward, for his own sake, if not mine. But the last time I'd said so, it upset Jon tremendously. So I stayed silent.

"Would a loan help, Jacqui?"

At first, I didn't understand what Jonathan meant. "No. Not really. I owe Doyle Pike a **lot** of money." I leaned forward, whispered. "Over nine thousand."

Jonathan gasped, drawing back, his face horrified. "For gods' sake, Jacqui! How -? No, I won't ask."

I was grateful he didn't, because I felt just as horrified at how it all happened. The man had bullied and blackmailed me into signing the agreement in the first place, and the long string of mistakes on my part which led me to this awful result seemed too humiliating to relate.

"So what will you do?"

"I have no idea what I **can** do."

"Well ..." Jonathan seemed hesitant to speak.

"What?"

"I know you don't want to. But you could return to Tony."

I scoffed. "He wants nothing to do with me."

Jon said nothing.

"I can't go back, Jon. I won't go back, even if Tony wanted me to." Which I wouldn't blame him one bit if he didn't.

"If you begged for mercy, your Family would surely help you," Jon said. "And being in Spadros Manor would keep you safe from Pike." He tapped the tablecloth with his butter knife, then shrugged. "I suppose they could just kill the man."

The Spadros Family couldn't kill Mr. Pike: after being my lawyer, he knew too much about the Family. Sawbuck suspected Mr. Pike had some mechanism for releasing his knowledge to the papers should he die unnaturally. And Mr. Pike had no compunction about using what he knew for his own benefit.

Tony warned me. Even Mr. Pike's grandson Thrace warned me.

The man was dangerous. The Family could protect me for a time. But if Mr. Pike let it slip that I'd lied about Ma — or worse yet, found her himself ...

It could start an uproar.

People widely believed the Family had manipulated my trial. Roy's bloody beating of Mr. Freezout — now our Mayor — whilst the police stood watching made people fear Roy, true. But it made them trust the not-guilty verdict even less.

As Blitz said, my position was precarious. Which Doyle Pike knew, which was why he dared defy the Family.

Jonathan watched me. "He's got something on you."

I nodded, wishing I hadn't eaten so much.

"It doesn't matter." Jon leaned forward. "The rest of the world can go to the Fire. But I will **never** let anything happen to you." He reached across the table and took my hand. "Be at peace, my love. We'll figure something out."

Our eyes met, and I got a fluttery flustered feeling deep in my soul. I smiled at him, squeezed his hand, and eyes stinging, returned to picking at my food.

Jonathan meant well. But until we found whatever information Mr. Pike had hidden, what could he — or Tony — actually **do**?

* * *

Later that day, I took my plain carriage to Clubb quadrant to visit Tenni for tea.

I loved the way the pale gray cobbles became golden sandstone as we crossed into Clubb. Tourists were more plentiful here, closer to the zeppelin station and the Aperture beyond. They hinted at the world outside, that I longed to explore.

I'd be glad to see Tenni. But I wanted to visit for another reason.

Tenni and her sisters had lived with us for a time after the Red Dog Gang broke into their home and drove them to me in fear. They'd stayed in the room Morton now had, an odd room, where until we'd had it fixed, one might hear all that was said in the house. It was a tense time, and Sawbuck had become so agitated that he'd threatened me.

Unknown to us all, Tenni's youngest sister Emma overheard.

Then after moving to Clubb quadrant, Emma read the news reports about the Bridges Strangler.

Being just eight, so much turmoil unhinged the girl. She'd had nightmares of ghosts in the walls come to strangle her and her sisters in their sleep.

It got so bad that she almost lost her position as a twine-braider for the *Bridges Daily*. I'd had to reassure her that she was safe, Sawbuck was a friend (in another quadrant), and all was well before her fears relented.

I hoped the poor girl had been able to recover.

*　*　*

The name on Tenni's storefront hadn't changed:

> Madame Biltcliffe's Dress Shop

But along the bottom of the window was something new. A message, inscribed in gold:

> In memory of Madame Marie Biltcliffe Sabacc

The vision of Madame lying inside in a pool of her own blood stopped me on the sidewalk.

"Mum?" Honor sounded concerned. "Are you well?"

"I don't rightly know." He'd been with me that night. "How much grief can one hand bear?"

His voice was kind. "There are only four two's in the deck, mum. Your hand will improve in time."

I nodded, encouraged, and pressed forward as Honor opened the door for me.

The shop was large, oak-paneled, and trimmed in brass, as most were here in Clubb quadrant. Mannequins stood displaying their gowns beside round tall racks of gowns already made. Large rolls of fabrics hung upon racks on each wall. In the back, to my right, were bookcases containing large binders full of dress designs for customers to choose a custom order. A closed door read "Storage."

In the center of the back wall were three curtained rooms for dressing and fitting. On the back wall to the left was a door marked "Private." On the left wall, a glass case containing gloves and fine hats sat in front of the open office door.

Tenni Mitchell, a woman of twenty, emerged from her office wearing a fine greenish-gray dress, stepping to one side and turning back. "I'll bring the girls over at eight, then."

A familiar-looking brown-haired woman perhaps ten years older emerged next. She beamed, cheeks coloring, and kissed

Tenni's cheek. "Splendid!" She turned to me and curtsied. "Mrs. Spadros! How nice to meet you."

Tenni used to double for me when I went out on cases. She was taller than me now, but we shared the same light brown skin, the same reddish-brown curls. "Mrs. Spadros, may I present Miss Cheisara Golf."

Miss Golf curtsied. "You know my sister. Karla Bettelmann?"

"Oh! I do indeed!" So that was why she looked familiar. "A pleasure to finally meet you."

Miss Golf glanced at the Clubb carriage which now stood outside. "I must go. Enjoy your tea!"

Tenni followed the woman to the door. Once she'd left, Tenni locked the door, turning the placard on it to "Closed — entry by appointment only." Then she turned to me. "I hope you're well?"

"I am." I pointed to the inscription at the base of the window. "I like that very much."

"Monsieur Sabacc insisted on it."

Monsieur was the chef for Spadros Manor. More to the point, he'd been Madame's husband. Madame had left him to come here, and he'd thought her dead until he learned of her murder by the Red Dog Gang.

Because of me.

Tenni took my arm. "Come." She led me to the door on the back left wall. It opened into a parlor with several doors to the left.

"It's lovely." She'd decorated in a deep rich blue, with a large blue, white, and black woven rug upon the oak floor.

Off to the right, a stand filled with small sandwiches sat on a wrought-iron tea-table, surrounded by oak furniture fit for Spadros Manor. Her youngest sister Emma — now nine — brought in a tea tray, curtsied to me, then set the tray down before us. She poured a cup of tea, handing it to me.

The transformation in their status seemed astonishing. "So your shop does well indeed!"

She smiled to herself, her cheeks coloring. "Monsieur has helped us greatly. But yes, it does well. We've had much support from

Madame's former customers, here and in Spadros." She took her tea from Emma. "You can go play."

Emma beamed, set down the pot, then scampered off to the door at the far left, which she closed behind her.

I turned to Tenni. "How is she?"

Tenni set down her cup and took a small sandwich. "She seems recovered. Cheisara knows a Tinkerer who's made a braiding machine for her! She's able to more than double her work."

"I'm astonished." I took a small sandwich of my own. "And will this Tinkerer provide it to others as well?"

Tenni paled. "I hope not. If the *Bridges Daily* learns of the machine, they'll be able to do their own braiding. Hundreds of young girls will lose their jobs!" Color returned to her face. "For now, he believes it just a toy for Emma, to please Cheisara."

I nodded. "So they fancy each other, then?"

Tenni let out a laugh. "Hardly. Well, he does, but —" She hesitated, just an instant. "— the feelings aren't mutual."

The dinner invitation … the woman's blush … the kiss on the cheek. "She's your paramour."

Tenni chuckled. "We've come to an understanding. It seems amusing, when said that way."

"How long have you been together?"

"Me and Cheisara?" Tenni smiled to herself. "I'd fancied her for some time, but at Madame's funeral she spoke her regard for me."

I took her hand. "I'm grateful you're happy. You're a brave, smart woman, and have been a true friend."

"Thank you, mum." She let go of my hand, took a sip of her tea. "I have some cloth for Mrs. Bryce."

Tenni gathered cloth from the other fabric sellers — bits or ends they were unable to sell and would otherwise throw away. Every few months, she'd send them to Eleanora. "That would be wonderful," I said. "I'll bring them by for you."

Tenni smiled. "I'd appreciate that."

I sipped my tea. I'd bring the cloth next time I —

Wait, I thought. I was suddenly reminded of what Eleanora said a few years back: *I got a good sale the beginning of the month. A pretty young thing, about your age with black hair.*

Tony thought that this black-haired woman might have kidnapped David.

This woman could be Black Maria.

Eleanora could identify her.

But the last time I'd rushed to warn someone who might be able to identify Black Maria, it was Madame. And I'd found her dying. I took a deep breath, heart pounding, trying to make my voice light. "Any news on the investigation?"

Tenni let out a breath, shoulders drooping. "They've closed Madame's case. They're calling it a burglary gone wrong." She shrugged. "They only kept it open as long as they have because of the Detective Constable."

"The one from Spadros?"

She smiled to herself. "Yes. Detective Constable Briscola. I think for a time he fancied me. He visits as his work allows. But I think he's become more interested in my sister Oma."

"And does she share his interest?"

"We've signed betrothal papers."

I hadn't realized the girl was sixteen yet. "So it's that serious?"

"It's hard to say with her, mum. But it's a decent match. She'll have to move back to Spadros quadrant, of course. But your Mr. Howell got me a meeting with the men on his street: she'll be well-protected. We have little dowry to offer, so it's better than we had any right to expect for her."

"Then give her my congratulations!"

She set her teacup down. "May I ask something personal?"

"Certainly."

She hesitated. "I don't wish to offend. But do you know when you wish to move from mourning garb? I'd be happy to make your half-mourning dresses. It's just ... I'm not as fast a seamstress as Madame was." Her cheeks colored. "I'd need some notice."

I'd sold all my gowns except four charcoal ones to wear to the trial — on Doyle Pike's recommendation.

I still had the last dress Madame made me, kept safely in tissue paper and hung in my closet. It was so beautiful. Yet I didn't dare to wear it: if anything were to happen, I had nothing else to remember her by.

But my charcoal dresses wouldn't last forever. I sighed. "Let me think on it."

Tenni nodded, eyes reddening. "I understand."

I did still mourn Madame. Yet it wasn't only that. I wasn't sure I could afford to buy one dress here, much less an entire wardrobe. Tony had always bought my dresses for me, and now, of course, that was out of the question. "I've always wondered something."

"Oh?"

"Madame was remarkably fast at her work. What does she do that others don't?"

Tenni laughed. "How nosy you are!"

My cheeks burned: Roy had said the same. "I don't wish to pry; I only wondered."

"Forgive me. I should never have spoken. You've done more for me than anyone, even Madame herself." She hesitated for a long moment, then rose. "I'll show you."

I followed Tenni into the door furthest to our left, which would put the room directly next to the office. Indeed, there was a door there on the left wall which had to open onto the office itself.

Inside the room was a marvel: a sewing-machine, yet of a sort I'd never seen before. A clear case covered its body. Inside lay gears and wheels, points of glowing light, and along the flanks, letters that moved! A brass plate on the base read:

> The Nitivali Machine Shop 1889

Around the room, of course, were racks of cloth, notions, and various tools. Yet I could see little else but this fantastical device.

Tenni closed the door quickly behind us and locked it. "It runs on electricity!" She sounded excited, and slightly awed. "Madame must have bought it in Paris and had the machine wired to run on Bridges power. She'd had a socket secretly installed here."

I gasped. Illegal tech. Not only that, but used for a profit advantage. The Cultural Correctness Committee would be furious. But what a wonder!

"Want me to show you?"

I nodded, realized my mouth hung open, and closed it.

Tenni sat, drew two random scraps from a basket beside the bench the machine sat upon, and placed them into the sewing area. She pressed upon a small pedal below, and the machine sewed! She held up the seam, and it was perfect. "No real foot motion. It's much quicker and less tiring."

"Am I wrong, or is this louder?"

"It is. That was why Madame only sewed after-hours, when she felt sure no one would need her service."

I nodded. Madame must have had it smuggled in.

"I don't even let the girls in this room. They've never heard any other sewing machine, so they think nothing of it."

"Does Miss Golf know?"

Tenni shook her head. "I can't chance it. One wrong word —"

I nodded. The penalty for cultural contamination was ten years in prison. Not the Bridges Prison, mind you: you'd be taken to Hub to stand trial, never to be seen again.

"Does Monsieur know?"

"He looked over the manifest, that's all. I listed it as 'sewing machine.'" She smiled to herself. "For all his skill as a chef, I don't think he knows one bit about sewing."

"Madame must have trusted you very much."

Tenni laughed softly. "I never knew until I took over the shop."

Dread overtook me. "Then the police have seen it."

Tenni stared at me in horror. "But no one's ever asked for money to keep this quiet."

I nodded. "Your Detective Constable has done you greater service than you know."

* * *

During the drive home, something occurred to me.

Miss Cheisara Golf had been Madame's customer for some time, even when the shop was in Spadros quadrant. So it seemed reasonable that she and Tenni might meet, and sharing the same inclinations, fancy one another.

But I just couldn't help but feel that the timing was curious, especially in light of the police's discovery of the illegal sewing machine at the same time. Why would Alexander Clubb's granddaughter speak of her undying love to a shop maid — at a funeral?

No Spadros Detective Constable could possibly have the means to bribe all the Clubb officers who now knew of the device into silence. Which meant the Clubb Family had declared Tenni off-limits. That one of the Clubb grand-daughters now was in a relationship with the woman became quite the coincidence.

If the Clubbs had simply put Tenni under their protection as a favor to me, I thought that I'd have heard of it by now, given Regina Clubb's penchant for bragging. So why do it?

The only explanation was that the Clubbs wanted something from her.

The Clubbs were no admirers of the Cultural Correctness Committee. If it weren't for the CCC, their daughter Nina might be alive today. So I didn't think Tenni was in any danger.

Did they want the machine? That seemed unlikely. Did they want to know how it got into the city? Surely it was smuggled in, and it was just as certain that Tenni didn't know the specifics.

But then I recalled that Miss Cheisara Golf had been visiting Madame for some time before her death.

Ah, I thought. They want information about **me**.

I was still the Lady of Spadros, the most important customer that shop ever had. And the shop was now owned by Spadros Manor's chef. Any interaction either of us had with Tenni might be passed to her paramour, and who knew what Clubb quadrant might find useful?

I felt pleased to have solved this puzzle, but sad for Tenni. Did she suspect how this woman used her?

She must suspect something, I decided. Otherwise, why not share her most exciting discovery?

Poor Tenni, I thought. She deserved better.

* * *

The rest of the day I wondered how I might contact Eleanora without putting her into even more danger. Yet no answer came.

After dinner, I sat in my study, thinking about Sheinwold, Katie, and how these two mysteries might relate to whatever the Red Dog Gang — and by extension, the High-Low Split — might be doing.

We'd been searching for former Detective Constable Albert Sheinwold for over a year. Surely Zia had the Red Dog Gang searching for him as well. Since his strangled body hadn't appeared, perhaps the man was still alive, as Morton hoped.

But where could he be?

Mr. Hart's idea that the man didn't want to be found made sense, particularly if Sheinwold believed that Morton betrayed him. Zia Cashout was just clever enough to have put the idea in the man's head, which made finding him even more difficult.

Yet Katie's situation bothered me still more.

Why had Katie gone to the **Pot** to fence jewelry? How would the fifteen-year-old daughter of the Spadros Patriarch, living on 192nd Street in Spadros Castle, know anything about fencing jewelry in the first place, not to mention know where to go to do so?

She had to have had help.

Which pointed to one of Roy's men. "Blitz!"

His footsteps approached my study. "Yes?"

"Come in."

Blitz came in, closing the door behind him. "What's going on?"

I beckoned him to approach, and spoke quietly. "One of Roy's men has been compromised. I don't know who. I need you to go to Spadros Castle tonight and tell him so."

Blitz paled, shaking his head. "I can't do that." He took a step back. "I won't do that."

His response confused me. "Why not?"

"Roy Spadros has hundreds of men. Those men are my family. My cousins. My brothers. He'll torture them all to find out which one has betrayed him." He straightened. "You can't send this message until you know who!"

"I'm sorry; I didn't think how this might affect you."

Blitz let out a breath, then a short laugh. "You scared me there." His eyes narrowed. "Where did you get this information?"

"Sit down, Blitz."

After glancing at the curtains, which were shut, he sat across the desk from me.

"How did Katie know to fence the jewels in the Pot?"

Blitz shrugged.

"Katherine Spadros. She's fifteen. How'd she get out of the house unseen? How'd she get to where the jewels were, much less the Pot? She doesn't have her own horse — she's made an unholy commotion about that alone. And none of Roy's drivers would take her to the Pot. You see? One of his men has to be helping her."

"Let me ask around, Mrs. Spadros. No one would care or notice if my brothers came to visit, what with the baby being dealt in any day now."

* * *

Like most nights, after I changed into my nightgown, I turned off the light and sat, window and curtains open, listening to the darkness. That night, the fog came in.

Mary came to my room candle in hand, pale with fear. "A man to see you, mum. He said only you. And he wouldn't come in."

"Did he hurt you?"

"No, mum. But — something about him frightened me. I left him outside, locked the door and called for my husband. He sent me here."

I put on my robe. "Let's see who this man might be."

We went through the back hall and to where Blitz stood beside the closed kitchen door to the alleyway. "It's your friend," he said, then opened the door.

Benji stood in shadow, past the beam cast by the kitchen lamp.

I went outside and closed the door behind me, pulling my robe close against the chill. "What are you doing here?"

Benji grinned. "How might I see you otherwise?"

"You scared my housekeeper."

"I promise I did nothing you quadrant-folk find offensive."

A pit formed in my stomach. *You quadrant-folk*. With two words, Benji put me with the enemy of our people.

I felt weary. "What do you want?"

"You asked who your young miss sold to. From what I can tell, no one in the Pot."

"Then someone claims the Pot and don't belong."

"Who might do that?"

"Whoever the High-Low's recruited."

Benji's eyes narrowed. "You think they'd take in quadrant-folk?"

I shrugged. "They took in Spadros traitors."

"Well said. If they're there, I'll find them."

"Thanks, Benj."

He smiled. "For my small sister, an honor."

"Just be careful. These men are dangerous."

He chuckled. "So am I."

* * *

The next morning, Mary came in with my provisional tray as usual, my morning tea and toast, along with the newspaper and mail. But she looked different somehow.

"What is it, mum?"

"Your baby. It's lower today."

"Is it?"

Excitement flashed through me. "It is! You're sure to have the baby soon."

She rested a hand on her belly. "I'm glad. I'm ready." She looked at me. "The midwife's supposed to visit this afternoon." She turned to go. "Oh!" She spun to face me. "I almost forgot. A Mr. Hambir Dashabatar made an appointment to see you at eleven."

"Me?"

"Yes, mum. It's something about the investigation into Major Blackwood's murder."

"Oh. I thought that was concluded."

"I thought so, too." She shrugged. "But he's not an officer; I believe he's a lawyer. I can have my husband send him away if you don't wish to see him."

"If they need help finding the scoundrel, I'd be happy to oblige."

I didn't know Major Blackwood well, but the times I had seen him, he'd been a kind and friendly old man. Not to mention his work with the *Golden Bridges*. I believed the Red Dog Gang — more to the point, Frank Pagliacci — killed him because he objected to their persecution of me.

These people had no shame: murdering an old man, an Army man at that — in his bed? It was horrendous.

If any of my mail had been opened, I couldn't detect it. One letter was from an informant, a middle-aged woman in the Records Hall, who I'd asked about the *Bring Bridges Back* pamphlet:

> Dear Sir:
> Your document is a copy of H1778. The original is not on file, but it may be found on Hub.
> Please advise.

Hub. So she thought the Feds might be involved with this?

The Feds were known for subtlety. Everyone knew that the Feds wanted the removal of the Four Families. And what better way to do that than to make people long for "better" days?

But I was reminded of a certain Fed — well, former Fed — already in the Red Dog Gang: Zia Cashout.

The letter H clearly meant Hart quadrant. Roy had mentioned Hart quadrant as well. Was Zia hiding there?

But only four numbers were listed: a pair of Sevens, an Ace and an Eight.

Four cards wasn't a full hand. Did this denote a hand after the discards? Were we nearing the end of a play? Or did this mean something else?

And what did the numbers mean?

The former Mayor — the one before Mayor Chase Freezout — was Mr. Siete Badugi. But he was now dead, and his killer still hadn't been found. The only Eight I knew was Roy's man at the Backdoor Saloon, Mr. Eight Howell. Surely he wasn't involved in making pamphlets. And he wasn't in Hart quadrant in any case.

Maybe I took this note too literally. Perhaps the numbers meant nothing at all. If so, why use them?

Unless ...

The H could mean a wild-card was in play.

Not many believed in the wild-card: it was controversial even amongst the Dealers. Not allied with any of the suits, the wild-card could become anyone, anything, and at will. The wild-card was a masterful card, with great and terrible power, and could determine the fate of an entire round.

Not many knew the reason that the wild-card was such a controversy. In days past, those children whose Blessing indicated that they were a wild-card were quietly killed.

A Hart quadrant wild-card.

I got up, still in my robe and nightgown, retrieved the pamphlet from my study, and returned to my bedroom.

I could find nothing to indicate where the pamphlet even came from. But it seemed clear it wasn't as innocent as I first believed.

* * *

When Amelia arrived, I got into my street clothes for the appointment with Mr. Blackwood's lawyer. I wasn't sure how long the meeting would last, and I didn't want to be late for luncheon with Jonathan.

Mr. Hambir Dashabatar arrived right at eleven, and I met with him in the parlor. "Good morning, sir, how may I help you?"

"I'm in charge of Major Blackwood's estate. When looking through his files, I came across something addressed to you."

He was, like Major Blackwood had been, a short round fellow. Yet he wore a suit, not a uniform. The man's skin and eyes were pale and his hair brown, as if he and Major Blackwood had been color-reversed. The thought amused me. "Oh? What sort of thing?"

Mr. Dashabatar handed me a sealed envelope. "I found this along with several others in his safe atop a packet to be opened upon his death." The thought seemed to sadden him. "We were great friends, but hadn't seen each other in many years."

I set the envelope in my lap. "I wasn't well-acquainted with the Major, but he seemed a good man."

He nodded. "He was."

"I suppose you were well-acquainted with his work here, then."

Mr. Dashabatar hesitated. "He oversaw the Army's recruitment center. As an consultant only, of course, being retired and all."

I wondered how he had time for that, with all the parties he attended. "No, the other thing."

Mr. Dashabatar gave me a gentle smile. "And what sort of thing might that be?"

"I know about his work on the paper. Mrs. Pike told me."

"I'm sure I don't know what you're talking about, madam."

Major Blackwood had been one of the members of the *Golden Bridges*. This man knew more than he let on, but I decided to let the matter drop. "What did the police finally decide about his death?"

"Murder. Yet the villain has yet to be found. Some believed it to be the work of that Strangler fellow, you know, the one they executed. But the two crimes are so different that the Detective on the case is convinced it was the work of another."

It did seem so: the same scoundrel who murdered the Bridges Stable-master. Why murder men in their beds? I let out a sigh, taking up the envelope to examine it. To my surprise, it was addressed to me at Spadros Manor. But why send it to Spadros Manor, when everyone knew I lived at my apartments?

Inside, it was dated shortly before his death.

My dear Mrs. Spadros:

I never properly thanked you for your generosity at inviting me to your home for Queen's Night last year. This is one of many items I've neglected to communicate over the short time we've known each other.

But news has come to me that you have allied yourself with the Kerr family. I must beg you to reconsider.

You may not understand the depth of information I have gathered on this topic, but I have just sent a package which will enlighten you.

My dear, do not be dismayed; we all make mistakes in our choice of allies. But for your sake and the sake of your Family, reconsider. For I fear a storm approaches, and I don't wish you and those you love to be caught up in it.

I understand this may mean we can no longer speak as friends. I regret any harm or upset this may cause you. But it's not possible for me to visit, and I can no longer delay.

Your servant,

Wenz Blackwood, Major, MFUA (Ret.)

I felt stunned. Not just that he wrote about the Kerr family. But that this man wrote to me at all. "The letter mentioned a package."

The man stared blankly at me, shaking his head. "The packet in his safe held letters to his family. I found nothing further for you."

"Perhaps the messenger boy lost it, or it got misplaced." Pearson had misplaced a letter once — from the Clubbs, no less — for almost a month. "I'll have my butler inquire at Spadros Manor about it."

Mr. Dashabatar nodded. "I hesitate to ask, my Lady, but the Detective did wonder if anything inside might pertain to the case."

I read over it again. Joe and Josie? Old Mr. Kerr? How could any of them strangle a man in his bed, even if they hated him?

And how would they even come to know him? Mr. Kerr seemed well the last I saw him, almost three years prior. But he was a recluse, and if he still lived, nine and eighty. Joe and his twin sister

Josie had done the party circuit before they disappeared. But Major Blackwood seemed to run with an older set.

And no one had seen any of the Kerrs in over two years.

Yet Major Blackwood had gathered information on them. Why?

He must have thought — at the time of his death last year — that they still were alive. Otherwise, why write this?

"I can't imagine what." I rose, yet felt unsteady. "Thank you for delivering this. I do appreciate it."

"Thank you for seeing me, Mrs. Spadros."

Blitz let the man out.

I went to my study, hands shaking. Major Blackwood thought that the Kerr family was a threat to me.

I don't know why I felt so alarmed, so upset, so uneasy. But looking back, I think it was being confronted with Joe again. Having to remember him. Having yet again to defend him.

I sat behind my desk, read the letter. Could the Kerrs be involved in some scandal? Perhaps Major Blackwood feared that I — or the Family — would be caught up in it.

That night the year prior when Jonathan brought me to see the little boy who looked so much like Joseph Kerr flashed before my eyes. The face of that woman weeping in her window-seat had haunted me ever since. Yet I dared not meet with her for fear of the scandal it might bring — to me, to Tony, to the Family.

I never asked Blitz to look into the package Major Blackwood sent. I didn't want to know any of it.

I thought I'd recovered from the harm Joseph Kerr had done me, but I felt his loss, his betrayal, just as keenly as I had two years past. I loved him. And for an instant, I hated him.

I wiped my eyes, collected my mail. And my eyes fell upon the bartender's note.

Perhaps I'd go have that drink after all.

The Bar

The first time I had a chocolate martini, I was with the most beautiful man in the world.

Wouldn't you know it: the next time I have one, the bastard shows up again.

I sat at the bar smoking when a great commotion came from behind. A body fell with a thud, and looking down, I saw him.

Joseph Kerr lay on his back beside my right boot, his face bloody, his clothes disheveled. I had never seen him in such a state.

And he had the effrontery to glance at my hem, after everything that had happened.

"Master Kerr," I said. "What a surprise."

The men in the room helped him to a chair, and he motioned for me to approach. His lip was split and I supposed speaking would have been painful, so I bent over him.

"I must speak with you alone," he whispered.

I straightened, appalled that he would even consider such a thing. But something about how he said it made me reconsider; I leaned over to speak in his ear. "If you must see me," I hissed, "2917 East Thirty-Three and a Third, the side door, at ten. Ask for Amelia." If he truly was part of the Red Dog Gang, as Roy thought, he'd know that Amelia left before dinner.

But the green eyes gazing into mine never changed.

Oh, gods, those eyes: they were stunning.

But I couldn't have anything to do with him. I turned towards the bar. "Call a surgeon."

The bartender nodded, and the men brought Joe in a back room off to the right.

Joseph Kerr. The sheer and utter gall of this man! Outrage filled me, partially at his boldness in appearing before me after everything he'd done — and partially wrath at whoever had marred that beautiful face.

I sat at the bar, not wanting to consider that for too long. He could no longer have any hold over me.

The front door to the foyer flew open and my husband Tony came in, flanked by his men. "Where is he?"

Anthony Spadros: an ordinary-appearing man who kept his feelings hidden behind a pale, emotionless face. We were the same age, but the change in him over the past year shocked me. He'd visibly lost weight. His face seemed drawn, his deep blue eyes cold and hard.

It both grieved and frightened me. But I was in a predicament, and must use any means I could to protect myself. I stood slowly, drawing myself up into what I imagined to be a most proper form. "Mr. Spadros."

Tony nodded. "Mrs. Spadros." His jaw tightened. "I will ask once more. Where's Joseph Kerr?"

Damn. A whole room of witnesses saw him.

"He arrived quite by surprise." I gave Tony a long sideways look, heart pounding. "Beaten harshly."

His eyes narrowed, but his face flushed in embarrassment.

I don't suppose in his shoes I would have done any differently. "He had the audacity to speak to me. My reply was equally harsh."

Tony gave the first real smile I'd seen from him in years.

In a way, that made me feel sad. "I called for a surgeon. They brought him somewhere —" I waved my hand in the general direction he'd been taken. "— back there. It's what any decent person would've done."

Tony growled at the bartender, "Get him."

I put it at even odds that Joe had left, two to one for if he heard Tony and his men, even if half dead.

We stood rather awkwardly until the bartender returned to say that Joe had indeed gone.

Tony glared at me. Then he yanked me out into the foyer. "Where'd he go?"

I stared at him in shock. "Surely you don't think —"

"What should I think?"

I shook my head. "I haven't seen Master Kerr in years ... and ... I'd be glad to never see him again." It was the truth.

Tony let out a breath. "I'll post more men outside your door —"

Oh, no. I'd asked Joe to meet me there. "Tony ... I'm grateful for your attentions, as undeserved as they are. But surely your men's time could be better spent on other things. I do have my servants, after all."

"I'll have someone escort you home. Notify me if he attempts to contact you again."

Joseph Kerr. What could that scoundrel possibly want to speak with me about? Over two years without a word, and now this.

Tony probably said something as he put me into his carriage, but I remember none of it.

Why was Joe here? Where had he been? How had he avoided capture? The Four Families were after him; he had loan sharks and gambling halls hunting for him. Not to mention all the women he'd used then discarded.

Shame flooded through me: I'd been one of those women.

When I was sixteen, we'd had one night of love, then I'd been brought to Spadros quadrant, never to see my home again.

Yet Joseph Kerr never came to me, never tried to reach me, never even sent one word.

For six years, I'd endured Roy's torments, Tony's attentions, the scorn and hate from quadrant-folk who never accepted me as anything more than a "Pot rag."

Joe claimed his grandfather threatened him into silence. At the time, I believed him.

But yet again, when I needed him most, he'd left me sitting, humiliated, at the zeppelin station.

He knew what would happen if he failed me.

The D.A. had asked for the death penalty. I'd faced an angry city, a hostile courtroom, and an assassin. If it hadn't been for Jonathan Diamond, I'd be dead today.

Whatever Joe's feelings for me, I couldn't count on him. I couldn't trust him.

And I had an idea.

I owed Doyle Pike over nine thousand dollars.

When I left Spadros Manor, Tony put up a ten thousand dollar reward for Joseph Kerr's live capture.

Joe just solved my problem.

The Solution

Tony's carriage pulled in front of my apartments, and the footman came around. He was a slender man close to thirty with pale skin, a sprinkling of freckles, and light brown hair, dressed in black and silver Spadros Family livery. He looked familiar.

He opened the door, then stood aside, one hand out to help me down the steps.

I stepped out to the sidewalk. "You're one of the Pearsons."

He snapped to attention. "Alan Pearson, mum, at your service."

I thought he'd become Tony's night footman. Perhaps the arrangement didn't work as well as he'd hoped. "A pleasure." He didn't reply, so I went up the steps.

He moved past me, knocking on the door, then stood aside, at attention once more.

Blitz opened the door, and he did not look happy. "Mrs. Spadros." As I passed, he said to Alan, "Tell your Ma she's doing fine. Midwife says a week at least."

The men continued speaking together.

I went into my bedroom.

Amelia stood with the ironing board open, setting the iron aside as I entered. "Oh, there you are, mum! Let's get you into something more comfortable."

She'd laid out one of my house dresses on the bed. I turned around to let her undo the buttons on the back of my dress, loosen my corset (a true relief!), undo my petticoats. Release from the sheer weight of clothing made me love coming home. A cool thin house dress sliding over skin felt wonderful.

When I faced her, Amelia said, "Are you well, mum?" Her face turned alarmed, then angry. "I smell drink on your breath! You've gone to another bar!"

I turned to face her. "I suppose I did." I'd gone to over a hundred bars in the past year, searching for one which knew how to make a chocolate martini. All for the longing to have something I'd shared with Joe. But this one had been poorly made: it didn't taste the same at all.

Amelia's eyes reddened. "I won't have you die on my watch, mum, I won't."

Feeling moved, I took hold of her arms. "My poor Amelia. Hush now." On impulse, I hugged her. "I did find my drink, yes." I let go of her, pulling back to take hold of her arms once more. "But now that I've had it, I'm done with going to bars. It wasn't what I thought it would be at all."

Amelia nodded slowly, her eyes never leaving mine.

A carriage went past outside.

Who knew what Roy — or Tony — had done to Amelia after I'd been found almost dead from drink, right here in this room? Another death Jonathan Diamond saved me from.

I should never have searched for that drink in the first place. Maybe if I hadn't, things might have turned out very differently.

A knock, then Mary's voice. "Luncheon's ready, mum."

Luncheon! I rushed to the door and flung it open. "Mary, send word — I won't be able to attend luncheon with Master Diamond."

"Already done," Blitz said. "When you arrived in Mr. Anthony's carriage, and so late, then went into your bedroom, I knew you wouldn't arrive in time. I called for the messenger at once. I was still talking with Mary's brother when your carriage arrived; I sent it on its way."

A huge relief swept over me. "Thank you, Blitz."

I needed to write Jonathan and let him know what was going on. So I went to my study and wrote:

> He's returned. Please visit: I need your counsel more than ever.

But then I stopped. Six months past, Cesare Diamond had named his brother Jonathan a Spadros spy. Since then, Jon hadn't come to visit once, fearing that his people might think it true. Would coming here put him in danger?

I crumpled the note and threw it away. I had to think.

I had to decide, today, without Jonathan's help.

What would he tell me to do?

Mary came in with a tray. "I know you're busy, mum. But you must eat." She came around to my right to set the tray down. Then she put her hand on my shoulder. "I know you'll find another case soon." She winced, her left hand jerking to the side of her belly.

I sat up, heart pounding. "Are you well?"

She chuckled. "Little pains, mum, never fear. The midwife says my womb's practicing for the big day."

"I never considered such a thing!" In the brothel, women would complain of such things, but I never knew what the pains meant.

"I never did either, before she said it. But it makes sense."

I nodded.

"I best get back to work. The floor needs mopping."

"Can't Blitz do that?"

"He's out front digging carrots." Her face grew stern. "I'll not have that new housekeeper find the place a shambles."

I let out a laugh, remembering Roy's words, which seemed an echo of hers. "So you **did** pick someone."

"Yes, mum. A widow. She was in the Dealers long ago, so she's familiar with birthing, and had six of her own. She's been housekeeper to one of the old families on 190th."

"Why would she want to work here?"

"She was let go when her lady died last year. It's hard to find work at her age."

"Will she be able to do the work?"

"She's only hired for the next month, so …" She smiled. "And if we need her longer, the option's open."

"When does she start?"

"The day after tomorrow. I'll show her around and do some canning."

"Only work for as long as you must. I'll not have you take risk for appearance's sake."

"Never fear, mum." She rested her hand on her belly. "I'll do nothing to harm this one."

* * *

There were only three reasons Joseph Kerr might want to see me: apology, threat, or seduction.

With the tremendous price on his head, Joe might believe I'd set the Family against him. I didn't dare meet him alone.

Blitz must be in the next room listening. Not only for protection, but so I had a witness to what transpired. Tony must be made certain that I had no part in any seduction. Though the thought of Joseph Kerr so close by made me yearn for his taut golden body pressed to mine, any hint of impropriety would be suicide.

Tony hadn't forgiven me for my first betrayal; even the idea of another could send him into a rage I didn't think I could stop. His men might stand by — or even participate — as he killed me.

But considering the matter, I realized the truth.

Joseph Kerr wasn't stupid. The only reason for him to visit was to present his apology and throw himself upon my mercy, so I might shield him from the Four Families' wrath.

A thin shield, these days. But he might believe me more powerful than I actually was.

A part of me hoped he'd stay in whatever hiding place he'd found for himself and his family. But another part of me hoped he would visit me, for many reasons.

I could not think of that.

No.

I'd decided.

Joseph Kerr would arrive — or not — at ten. If he arrived, I'd have Mary call for Tony at once and have Blitz listen at the door.

I'd stay well away from Joe and hear his apology. I'd learn why he left, why he returned, where he'd been. Why he never tried to contact me or give me one ounce of help or comfort.

Then when Tony arrived — and he was sure to bring several of his men — I'd announce my proposal.

The play had a decent chance of success. Since I'd "led" Sawbuck and his men to the Spadros traitors — the Ten of Spades, as they'd called themselves — Tony's men seemed to hold me in higher esteem.

And I'd make Joe's safety part of the bargain.

I paced the entire day, worrying, planning. I wrote a list: where he'd been, the women he'd lied to, the children he'd fathered, why he abandoned us all. Were his sister and grandfather safe? Where were they now, and why hadn't his sister Josie tried to contact me?

I could understand him not being able to. Perhaps. But surely Josie could have gotten a message to me.

Blitz, Mary, and Amelia watched me, obviously curious as to the cause of my distress, but perhaps knowing me too well to ask. Amelia left before dinner, as she usually did.

During dinner, I said, "A knock may come at that door," I pointed at the door to the alley, "at ten." I pointed to Blitz. "You answer. No matter who it is, make no cry of surprise, show no alarm. He should ask for Amelia. If he does, let him in, then lock the door so he can't leave. Bring him to the parlor and stay with him until I arrive. Don't let him out of your sight. Mary, you stay hidden, and when he's seated, come notify me." Knowing I had to stay in my room until Mary knocked would give me the strength to wait. "When I enter, you're both to watch, and listen."

Blitz nodded. "Should I be armed?"

I recalled: Joe might be out for blood. "It may be wise."

Blitz said, "Should we let this man in? Who is this, anyway?"

"I don't dare say. If this goes wrong, you must swear on the Holy Cards that you never knew who was to come here."

Mary drew back, the two exchanging a glance. "I'm sure you know best, mum."

After everything that had happened, this moved me. I took her hand. "I'll never do anything to harm you, not ever."

Blitz said, "If we might be called to swear, you're talking about who? Roy Spadros? Mr. Anthony?"

"Most likely the latter."

"Then you're putting us in danger yet again," Blitz said. "And the round's begun without ever consulting us."

"I had but an instant to make a decision. I can't go into more detail, not and protect you." Should I tell them more? "This may solve the problem with Mr. Pike."

"Oh," Mary said, sounding impressed.

But Blitz frowned, eyes narrowing. "I have a bad feeling about this, Mrs. Spadros."

I did too, for what I imagined to be entirely different reasons.

I feared this meeting. Joseph Kerr had better have some damn good reasons for what he'd done.

The Confrontation

As a peace offering, I helped clean the kitchen, then we each retreated, me to my bedroom, Mary and Blitz to theirs. I'm sure they were afraid, but they never showed it.

I loaded my gun and put my calf holster on. Then I turned off my lamp and peered out into the darkness. Not so much as a cat yowled outside. I locked the window, then drew the curtains.

The kitchen bell rang; Blitz and Mary's footsteps hurried through the hall. The kitchen door to the alley opened. Men's voices, then footsteps into the parlor.

A soft knock. "He's here, mum," Mary said.

"Call a messenger, but keep it quiet. Tell my husband to gather every man he has around him and come here at once." Joe might be out for blood. "Then get your shotgun. Don't let him past you."

Her eyes widened. "Yes, mum." She hurried to the front door, turning on the light for the messenger.

I moved across the hall, wrapping a shawl around me, then opened the parlor door.

Joseph Kerr sprang to his feet when he saw me. "Did I wake you? You said to come at ten."

Blitz had dressed in his butler suit, and stood where he might watch both Joe and the door to the hall. His coat was unbuttoned, his holster strapped to his side. "Please stay seated."

Joe gaped at me as if he'd never seen such beauty. He'd cleaned his face, but his clothes still had spattered blood on them.

Blitz glanced at me. "Mrs. Spadros?"

I took a few steps into the room. "Please sit, Joe."

"But, Jacqui —"

Blitz put a hand on his holster. "You speak to the Lady of Spadros, sir. You've been asked to sit twice now. Would you please do so?"

Joe seemed dismayed. "Forgive me. If you insist." He sat on the sofa, face troubled.

I turned to Blitz. "You may go about your business."

Blitz gave me a fake smile. "Good night, then."

I moved to the armchair across from Joe and sat. "You said you had to speak with me. I'm here."

Joe stared at me, mouth open. "Jacqui, what's wrong? Why — I don't understand. I've risked my **life** to find you."

"The whole city has known where I was since you ran off to let me die. I —"

"No, Jacqui. That's not it at all. Why would you say that?" He shook his head, face astonished. "I don't believe this. You really think I — I **abandoned** you?"

"Well ... yes." I leaned back, crossing my legs.

"Talk to me, Jacqui. What's wrong?"

"Where have you been? Why didn't you meet me at the station?"

Joe blinked, face uncertain. "At the station?" He put his hand to his forehead, then looked up at me. "You didn't see my mark? On the windowsill? The night I had to flee. There at Spadros Manor."

I shrugged, heart pounding. "Ten. We were to meet at the zeppelin station. You never arrived." I felt ready to cry. "I was there, Joe, well before ten. Until after midnight. You never came, after you promised me you would."

"I don't know what to say. Could you have possibly forgotten our signal? I wrote 'Oh-one' ..."

I gasped, remembering the mark of his finger in the dust on the windowsill that night. Horror spread through me as I realized what I'd done.

"Oh-one" meant everyone for themselves. Flee now, for if we stop for anyone, we all might die. And there was always a meeting place set beforehand. I stared at him. What had I done? "It was upside down!"

He didn't seem to hear me. "... and I thought for sure you'd know where to meet up." His face fell. "I waited for you all night, Jacqui." He shook his head, downcast, then faced me. "I can't believe you didn't remember our meeting place. I even asked you if you remembered our —"

"Last time together." At the broken statue of Benjamin Kerr, Joe's ancestor, who'd built this city. We'd made love our first — and up to then, only — time there.

He'd waited for me there?

"No one knew about it but us, Jacqui. Why did you tell them?"

"What? No! I told no one —"

"Well, someone knew, because about one in the morning there were Spadros men everywhere. I was shot —" he pulled up his sleeve to show a healed graze scar on his right lower arm, much like Tony had on his face from the shootout at Spadros Manor, "— but I got away." His voice turned bitter. "I would never have waited if I'd known you'd forgotten us. Me and you." He put his face in his hands. "I've been running for two years now, and the only thing that's kept me alive is the hope of this night. And come to find out you'd forgotten?"

Guilt and shame swept over me. "Joe, I'm sorry. I thought —"

"You thought I'd left you. How could you think that? After everything we've been through?" His face turned stricken. "I feared you were dead! That he'd killed you! By the time I heard you were at the Clubb Hotel, I was running for my life. I've been running, hiding, ever since."

Oh, gods, I thought. The numbers were upside down. I never understood. "Why have you never tried to contact me?"

"I've tried, three times I've tried. Each time, I've come close to dying." He gestured to his face, his blood-spattered clothing. "You see what they've done to me this time."

Tony almost caught Joe twice and never told me? "What about all the women?"

Joe's face turned into a confused frown. "What women?"

"The woman at the pool hall in Hart quadrant. The five women who went to the Court about your seduction —"

Joe stared at me blankly, mouth open. "I don't know what you're talking about. Who told you this?"

"Jonathan Diamond told me everything." Then I felt abashed. "Well, technically, I wasn't supposed to know about the women. But Jonathan Diamond is Keeper of the Court and —"

"By the gods, Jacqui! You believe a **Diamond**?" He peered at me, face disgusted. "You believe a Diamond over me. You've known me all your life! How can you think me so deceitful?"

"Joe, I saw your son. Joseph Polansky Kerr?" The Kerr Dynasty had lasted four hundred years, until traitors overthrew the rightful king, Polansky Kerr I, for whom Joe's grandfather was named. For an instant, part of me hoped this boy was part of some plan Joe and his grandfather had to restore the city. Something to make all this make sense.

Joe squeezed his eyes shut, then gave his head several little shakes, frowning. "Who?"

"For gods' sake, Joe, he looks just like you. Why would any woman name a child that if you hadn't pushed her to?"

I watched him, mind racing. Why would he deny it? Was he afraid of people listening?

Joe let out a breath, his shoulders drooping. "These women just want the money they think we have because we're Kerrs. They'll say anything to get hold of our imagined riches." He shook his head. "She likely got herself with child and created this tale to escape the Pot. Maybe she thinks if she names the boy after me, I'll have some affection for him?" He shrugged. "I don't know."

Any rumors of secret Kerr gold hidden in the quadrants came from before the Coup. I'd been to the Kerr's home: they'd barely been surviving even before the Families turned against them. "Speaking of money — where's the money I gave you?"

"I bought the tickets for us." His face turned concerned. "You don't remember?"

"I do remember, Joe." I remembered the shower of blue-edged ticket stubs on the zeppelin station floor the night I escaped. "You showed me years-expired tickets to trick me —"

"What? I just bought them the day before!"

I scoffed. "No, Joe. You showed me old tickets edged in red. False tickets —"

"No, Jacqui, they were real." His head drooped; he fell silent for a time. Then he raised his head. "When you never arrived, and the Clubbs were detaining anyone who looked like us, I sold them so my sister and grandfather might live." His shoulders sagged. "But I couldn't leave you, even if you'd forgotten me."

My heart clenched. But I'd finally caught him in a lie. "The color for that year's tickets was blue. The ones you showed me were edged in red!"

Joe laughed. "What is this? Some kind of joke? The tickets I showed you were edged in blue. Don't you remember? One for you, one for me, and one for —" Joe shook his head, mouth open. "The ones I showed you were edged in blue!" His eyes narrowed. "You really don't remember?" He put his hand on his forehead, then dropped it to his side. "It's not surprising, really — you were so drunk you could barely stand. Then you threw yourself at me and began pulling at my belt." He shook his head sadly. "It's a wonder you remember anything at all."

I stared at him, hurt by his interpretation of what happened, astonished that he would lie so. "They were red!"

"No, Jacqui, they were blue. Maybe you're thinking of the orange tickets from last year?" He smiled at me as one might smile at a child, and his words were kind. "They were blue, just like your eyes. When I saw them, I knew we were meant to leave here. Three tickets in blue: one for me, one for you, and one for Josie."

"Now, wait. Before I gave you the money, you said that Josie wouldn't come with us because she felt her place was with your grandfather —"

"Why would I buy three tickets if only you and I were going?"

I leaned forward and spoke softly. "You remember. You bought one for my Ma. Who'd you tell about her, anyway?"

Joe's face turned astonished. "Your mother's alive? Oh, gods, Jacqui, that's wonderful! All this time, I thought she was on the zeppelin when it exploded!"

I had a terrible thought: now Mary and Blitz knew my mother was alive. I lowered my voice. "Joe, I told you she lived when I asked you to buy a ticket for her. That's why I gave you all my money. I'd saved it my entire life to leave Bridges —" I leaned back, disgusted. "And you threw it away gambling."

"What? Jacqui, no. I never, ever spent that money for anything but my family." He shook his head. "Jacqui, I love you. But you're confused, and you're upset." His face grew concerned. "Have you been drinking?"

I felt outraged. "No!"

His shoulders slumped. "I saw you drink there in the bar." He took a deep breath. "Maybe we should talk about why I'm here."

"Why **are** you here, Joe? It's clearly not to apologize for abandoning me."

His face turned astonished. "Abandoning you? You abandoned **me**! I've been living in ditches, as you lounge here in comfort!"

Remorse stabbed at me, but my anger overcame it. "I've been threatened, Joe. I've been shot at. I've been swindled, and … and **bombs** have gone off near my home. I almost died! If it weren't for Jonathan Diamond I wouldn't even be here today."

"Then you're not going to like what I'm going to tell you."

I crossed my arms. "I'm listening."

"Are you? Because I risked my life to come here, and if you don't want to listen, I'll leave right now." He began to stand.

I pictured the men outside. "No, Joe, wait. I'm sorry. Please tell me." Now I regretted telling Blitz and Mary to call Tony. "Quick, before my staff calls my husband!"

He took a deep breath, let it out. He spoke slowly, hands clasped in front of him. "There are people trying to have your husband killed. It would've been wrong not to tell you." He glanced away. "I felt surprised to learn you lived here: I figured you'd gone back to him."

That hurt. "Who's trying to kill him?"

"There's a fifth group, besides the Families — I don't know its true name, but I've heard it called the Red Dog Gang. I told your husband of it a long time ago. But I just learned more. There's a secret alliance between the Diamond and Hart quadrants to defame and murder the Clubb and Spadros Families then take over the city. They're plotting assassination, and they're using this Red Dog Gang to take the blame for it."

"Joe, who told you these things? How do you know this?"

"Remember the Grand Ball a couple years back, when Jack Diamond tried to attack you? I brought him aside, and he said something that made me suspicious." His eyebrows knit together. "I can't remember what it was offhand. At first I thought nothing of it. But after we had to run, I had more time to think. Once I got my family to safety, I began investigating them. The Diamonds have spies everywhere in Spadros quadrant." He pointed to the window behind him. "Even outside here. You have to believe me, Jacqui."

I recalled the plot against Alexander Clubb and his son Lance by rogue factions of the Clubb Family. And our problem in Spadros quadrant with the men who rebelled against Roy. Could this be some dissident faction in Diamond? "Joe, who exactly is in on it?"

"Those five older Diamond heirs. They want the whole city to themselves. They have spies everywhere. They set that crazy one Jack to tormenting you since Air got killed. They've got Jonathan and his sister pretending to be your friends to spy on you. This whole thing is to get back at the Spadros Family for stuff that happened during the Coup. They're all mad."

"But ... I don't understand. I mean ..." If they wanted me dead, why did Cesare testify for me at my trial? And I couldn't believe Gardena and Jon were against me.

"Jacqui, you have to believe me." His voice dropped to a whisper as his eyes gazed into mine. "I love you more than anything. There's been no other women. There's been no one else but you. I swear by all the gods: I've been with no one but you, ever. Oh, Jacqui ... you're the only thing I live for!"

I felt a thrill go through me. But I had to think. "Are you certain it's the Diamonds? You told me some time back that the Red Dog Gang was started by the Clubbs."

He frowned. "Why would I say that? Aren't the Clubbs allied with Spadros? You must be mistaken." He let out a breath with a slight shake of his head. "You were so drunk all the time, I'm surprised you even remember us talking." He looked me in the eyes. "I'm sorry, Jacqui. But I have to tell you the truth. Jonathan Diamond is at the heart of it."

I felt stabbed in the chest, and the pain of it blurred my sight. "Jonathan Diamond is my best friend, my closest ally. He's saved my life more than once."

"Who better to whisper in your ear? Who better to move to your side, maneuver you closer to theirs? I suppose you're great friends with his sister as well."

A pit formed in my stomach. "Why, yes, but —"

"They want you with them when they strike. Have they offered you sanctuary?"

Mrs. Rachel Diamond and Mr. Charles Hart sat in the place Joe sat now, offering that very thing.

"Your butler's right. You're a powerful woman now, Jacqui. People here like you. But you stand in their way. If they were to lure you to their side, then kill your husband and his father, the Spadros quadrant would fall."

I stared at him, horrified.

He covered his face with his hands. "I can't help it, Jacqui: I still love you." His hands dropped to his lap, and he gazed into my eyes. "I'd do anything for you. But with all the rumors about you and Jonathan Diamond, I couldn't let you stay in the dark about him any longer."

Jonathan would never hurt me. Never. "I've heard of this Red Dog Gang before," I said bitterly. I felt skeptical of his intentions, upset at his lies and slander. "And you say Jonathan's part of this."

"You obviously don't believe me, but it's true. I swear it." Joe let out a sigh, shoulders drooping. "It's getting late. Why don't we —"

The front bell rang. Joe flinched, eyes wide. "What's going on?"

"It's nothing. My butler will send them away."

But many footsteps trod the front hall, and the parlor door opened. Tony said, "So this is your emergency."

The Defeat

Tony strode into the room, followed by Blitz, Honor, Sawbuck, Alan, and many others of Tony's men. "Have you two taken up together again?"

Joe turned to me in horror. "You betrayed me! Good gods, Jacqui — how could you?"

I went to Tony. "I must speak with you alone."

Tony glanced between Joe and I, then nodded. He turned to his men. "Wait here."

Sawbuck came over to stand beside Joe.

Joe looked at the men, then me. "No! Jacqui! For gods' sake, please, don't do this!"

I went with Tony into the kitchen, leaving the door open: we stood in full view of them all.

Tony said, "What's this about?"

"He claims he came back to warn us about someone trying to kill you."

Tony snorted. "He's a couple of years late."

"I know. But that's got to mean something. Don't hurt him."

Tony flinched. "I never wanted to hurt him." He sighed. "Those first few months, maybe. But — oh, Jacqui, I just wanted to know what I did to drive you away."

Gods, it hurt. But I had to be strong. I didn't do this for nothing. "And I want the reward. For his capture. The ten thousand. Or he walks free, and you can start this chase all over again."

Tony began to laugh. "Just when I thought I'd seen everything." He lowered his voice. "You're going to sell me your own lover?"

Joe came to warn me.

But I needed the money.

I raised my voice loud enough for all his men to hear. "I got him for you. Are you going to keep your word or not?"

Tony's shoulders slumped. "It's yours." He took a deep breath. "Jacqui," he said softly, "what's happened to you? You would never have done this before."

The boy's face in the window ... that night when I thought I faced the gallows ... "I don't trust him anymore."

Tony stood silent for a long moment. "It's difficult when you lose trust in someone."

I felt sure he was referring to me.

Joe sat gaping at us.

Tony said loudly enough for everyone to hear, "I'll have the money transferred to your account in the morning." He gestured to his men. "Take Master Kerr to Spadros Manor."

Joe's face grew alarmed, tears in his eyes, and began bucking to get away from the men holding him. "No! Jacqui, please! I beg you, please, don't do this!"

I went to him, clasped his beautiful face in my hands, wiped his tears away. The sight clenched my heart. But I had no other options. "He's not going to hurt you, Joe. He promised. Just go with him. All will be well."

The men left, and Joe with them. But I couldn't sleep. The look on Joe's face ...

Could any of the things he said be true?

Tony promised not to hurt Joe. But what if his cousin Sawbuck or one of Tony's other men took it on themselves to hurt him?

What if Roy seized him?

Blitz sat in the parlor, reading a book beside a small lamp turned low. He glanced up. "Are you well?"

"I must go to Spadros Manor."

Blitz let out a laugh. "At this hour? I can send a messenger —"

"No. I have to go myself."

* * *

Tony's butler Pearson answered the door. "Mum! I wouldn't have believed it!" Then his face turned alarmed. "Is my daughter —?"

"Mary's well. I need to see Mr. Spadros at once."

Pearson hesitated. "Wait here." He closed the door, leaving me to stand on the porch.

Me. The Lady of Spadros. On the porch!

What in the world was going on?

Ten minutes later, Tony appeared, fully dressed for the street. When he saw me his eyes turned cynical. "Well, well, well." He stepped onto the porch, closing the door behind him.

"Tony, why have I been left out here?"

"Because I gave strict instructions to my servants not ever to allow you inside."

"But why?"

"I suspected you might come here. I hoped to all the gods that you would not. But here you are. You're so … very … predictable."

"I don't understand. Can't we go inside? It's cold out."

Tony laughed bitterly. "You vomited at the thought of coming here when it was me you might face. But at the mere thought of a hair being harmed on your beloved Joe's head, you rush here, even after I gave my word — my **word** — that he wouldn't be harmed."

He pointed behind him. "When I was shot in this very house," at this, he faltered, "you didn't come here. You didn't even send a note to inquire after my health. Even after I worked tirelessly for months during the trial to save your life, you didn't give me a word of thanks, though it almost ruined me."

He turned his face aside for a moment. "No, Jacqui, you can't come in. And he's not here in any case. Do you think I'd let that snake anywhere near my servants, after all he's done? And I won't let you anywhere near him, either. It's clear he's got you right back where he wants you."

"But —"

"He's alive, fed, and very well. I put him into a safe room with my own hands. He's guarded by my most trusted men. I get reports from Ten every hour. At last report, he was sleeping. Which is what you should be doing."

He gestured to his cousin Blitz, who stood beside the carriage. "Take her home. And don't bring her here again unless I call."

When we got home, Blitz turned on me. "How much longer will you use us?"

"I don't know what you mean."

He spoke in an angry whisper. "Do you not trust us, after everything we've given up for you? You lied to us about your mother. And sneaking away today yet again, after promising you wouldn't." His face grew fierce. "I won't have my wife and child harmed because of you."

"I don't want that either —"

"You told my wife, nine months with child, to get her shotgun? What would have happened to the babe inside her if she'd fired?" He glanced away. "You're no different than Miss Katherine —"

"Now see here —"

"Reckless, childish —"

"What?"

"Uncaring about anyone besides yourself. We swore to you. Do you mean to kill us for it?"

Oh, gods. "No."

"Then you best decide. Because I won't see them pay for my error in coming here."

* * *

My dreams were particularly horrid that night, and the next morning, I felt weary, drained.

Mary came in as usual with my tray. "Here you are, mum. Master Jonathan must cancel your luncheon."

I felt alarmed. "Oh? Is all well?"

"The message didn't say."

"Did you get a chance to speak with your brother?"

"Oh, Alan? Not really. Just a word or two." Mary smiled to herself. "But it was good to see him."

I suddenly missed Benji. "You're very lucky." I took a deep breath, let it out, my eyes stinging. His constant telling me not to see him hurt. I'd been trapped in the quadrants for eight years. Why had he never sent a message or come to see me before?

"Are you well, mum?"

I nodded, not sure if I was.

"Then I'll see to breakfast." How she was able to curtsy in such a state was beyond me.

How she was even able to look at me was beyond me.

I forced down my tea and tonic, but I couldn't read a thing.

Mary announced breakfast. I sat in the kitchen, staring at my plate, until Blitz came in.

"Mum? What's wrong?" Mary sounded concerned.

I looked up at them, feeling tears on my cheeks. "I've wronged you both. When I came here, I should have told you everything."

Blitz just stood looking at me.

"Oh, mum." Mary sat beside me, putting an arm around my shoulders. "It's been a terrible frightening time for you. We just want to be of service."

Blitz chewed his lip a bit, then nodded.

"Sit down, Blitz. I best tell you everything." And I did. Mary gasped at learning of my morning tea, but they listened without a word. "If anyone asks, the tea is a recipe my mother gave me. But no one must ever know the truth. Roy would kill me."

They stared at me, eyes wide. Mary gripped my hand. "No one will ever hear of it from us, mum."

* * *

Morton arrived mid-morning.

I met him in the hall. "How was your trip?"

"I have something for you." He handed me a portrait: a strong-looking, narrow-faced man in his early forties, skin tanned, close-cropped hair graying, with penetrating pale eyes. "I got this from a policeman who's also looking for him."

"This is Sheinwold, then."

Morton nodded. "Now you have something to show."

I slid it in my pocket. "Thanks." We'd tried approaching the police who might have known him, with little result. Most either would say nothing, or their attitudes were such that I put them on the list of suspects. Apparently the man had not been well-liked.

"Any word on a new case?"

I shook my head. "I've had a personal problem to deal with."

Morton snorted in amusement. Then he shrugged. "I'll see what I can find. But first, I think I'll unpack my things." At that, he grinned. "Not sure why I do, I'll likely just be off again."

Morton was rather the clotheshorse. He seemed particularly fond of his shoes: I'd find him examining or polishing them. The man was quite unattractive, so perhaps this was a compensation.

I put Albert Sheinwold's portrait into a file in my study. If he were alive, as Morton believed, where was he?

The most reasonable answer was that he kept moving, to keep away from Zia — or whoever she had hunting him.

I took luncheon in my study. A few hours later, the doorbell rang, and shortly thereafter, Blitz knocked. "A letter for you."

The letter was from the bank, confirming the deposit of ten thousand dollars, transferred from Tony's account to mine. Though the letter brought me joy and relief, it also brought sadness. I never wanted to hurt Joe or Tony, and it seemed as if I'd hurt them both.

Then I realized a good many men were in the house. By now, the whole Family knew I had the money. They'd expect me to pay my Family fees: ten percent of all money that came into my hands.

A thousand dollars.

But I owed Mr. Doyle Pike over nine thousand.

So I had a dilemma.

But I did have options.

If I paid the Family fees, I'd still owe Doyle Pike. Not much, compared to the whole, but I'd still be under his thumb. And he'd do anything to keep me from getting jobs so he might compound more of his interest fees.

I had more than enough to pay Mr. Pike then buy a zeppelin ticket to anywhere in the world. Which was fortunate, because if I didn't pay the Family, I'd be running the rest of my life.

The thought did cross my mind that I could just take the money and run. But I'd have to betray everyone: Tony, Mr. Pike. I'd have to leave Joe in whatever cell Tony had him in. Blitz and Mary would be tortured until they revealed where I went.

And it wouldn't stop there. Anyone who ever knew me might face Roy's torture room: Eleanora's little family, Tenni and her sisters. Amelia. Pip. Morton. Even Benji and the Cathedral might fall under the Family's anger.

I'd never learn who murdered Madame. Who killed Marja, the woman who helped raise me. Who framed me for the zeppelin bombing which murdered Dame Anastasia. Who took David Bryce, and what they did to him.

I'd be free. But everything I'd gone through these two and a half years would have been for nothing.

I went to Morton's room. He stood there, door open, brushing and hanging his trousers. "Do we need to hire you a manservant?"

He grinned. "Are you offering to pay?" He returned to his brushing. "He'd spend most of his time trying to keep up with me."

"Might I ask your opinion?"

He hung up the pair of trousers he held. "Sure."

I leaned on the door frame. "Say you —" I hesitated, unsure how much to reveal. "You came into money, you said, when your parents died."

Morton nodded.

"What did you do with it?"

"Made a damn fool of myself, drinking and wenching." He peered at me. "I was about your age, come to think of it."

"What do you wish you'd done?"

He shrugged. "Perhaps invested. I'd paid my debts —"

The year before, I told Sawbuck: *Pot rags pay their own debts*.

"— but I wish I'd bought more property, instead of frittering so much of it away."

I nodded, hardly hearing him.

"Heard about what happened last night."

This startled me. "How did you hear about that?"

"From my driver." Morton chuckled. "He won a bet."

If drivers were talking about it, the whole city knew. "What do you think I should do?"

He knew I owed Mr. Pike a lot, and I'd mentioned the interest fees, but I never told him what I owed him so much for. "I don't know, Mrs. Spadros." He let out an ironic laugh. "I wouldn't have gotten myself into **that** mess in the first place."

Well.

"No offense," he quickly said. "As an attorney, Pike's one of the best. But he's not known for his honest dealings."

"As I'm coming to learn."

I went to my study and slumped into my chair. And I recalled what Sawbuck said a year earlier: *I considered leaving, once. I stood in the zeppelin station, ticket in hand. And I found I couldn't go. I couldn't leave him alone in this terrible place, not even if I could never speak.*

I couldn't leave Josie and her grandfather here. I couldn't leave Joe. I didn't trust him. But I still loved him, and I wanted to help him if I could.

I'd pay the Family fees. I'd pay Pike most of what I owed him. And I'd put some into savings, in case the apartments needed some major work done in the future.

I sat with the bank's notice in my hands. Now that I'd decided to pay my Family fees, how might I do it?

I recalled that false taxi-driver of Frank Pagliacci's who assaulted me for the ten dollars in my purse, among other things. I didn't dare withdraw a thousand.

A check, then? The bank had given me a few when the account was opened, but I didn't know how to write one. They lay in my bottom drawer along with a jumble of other things. Perhaps someone at the bank could teach me what to do.

And when I learned how to make one out, who would I give it to? Mr. Eight Howell seemed nice enough, but I wasn't going to hand a thousand dollars to him.

I had to go to the bank to transfer the money to Mr. Pike in any case. So I asked Blitz to call for the plain carriage.

The bank was several stories of sandstone with beautiful golden tile inside. The teller directed me to a stern-looking man. "We'll need Mr. Pike's bank details for the transfer, which you can get from him. But I can show you how to write a check easily enough."

I listened to his explanation. I didn't write anything, nor did I tell him who I wished to write the check to. The fewer who knew about this, the better. "Can you answer something for me?"

The man gave a polite smile. "That depends on the question."

"It concerns the lock-boxes." When I'd first opened the lock-box Dame Anastasia Louis gave me, it only held her necklace. The second time, it also held the deed to my apartments. But someone else opened it to take the photograph Cesare Diamond and I found the day of the zeppelin bombing. "Who has access to them?"

"Anyone with the key."

"So someone could steal the key and still access it?"

"We do inquire about the person's identity. There's a list of those approved to access a particular box."

"Might I see the list of those approved to access mine?"

"Of course, madam. One moment." He returned a few minutes later with a document. "As you see, there are four names. Yours, and of course your husband's. I see that the box first belonged to Dame Anastasia Louis. A Mr. Frank Pagliacci is on the list as well."

So Frank Pagliacci had plenty of time and opportunity to do anything he liked in this matter. "May I see the document?"

All was typed: I gleaned little from it. "Remove Mr. Pagliacci."

"I will, madam."

"Thank you for your help, sir. I appreciate it." We'd made inquiries into Frank Pagliacci in the past: no one was registered in the city by that name. "How did you verify this man's identity?"

"Oh, we have any number of ways. But I can inquire into the matter and contact you later, if you wish."

Then something else occurred to me. "Do you keep record of who accesses a box and when?"

"Of course."

I realized I didn't want to know all of the times Frank Pagliacci had rummaged through my lock-box. It was bad enough that he'd done so in the first place. "Send your findings to my husband."

The man's eyes widened. "Oh. Yes. At once, madam."

"And if he comes in again, my husband — and his father — would be most grateful if you were able to apprehend him."

The manager's jaw dropped. "We — of course, we'd do our best, madam, but this isn't a police station."

"I understand, sir. Yet Mr. Roy Spadros would be most personally grateful if you did."

I smiled at his reaction. By the day's end, every employee in the bank would be looking for the man.

* * *

After treating my staff at a little shop for tea-time, I went to Mr. Pike's office. Amelia and I were sent up at once.

I left Amelia in the hall, unsure of my reception. But Mr. Pike seemed glad to see me. "I hear you've come into some money."

Hmph, I thought. "I need your bank information to transfer it."

Mr. Pike opened a drawer, handing me a slip of paper from a stack there.

So he took in large sums all the time, did he? I almost confronted him, but throwing his wife's illness in his face felt petty. "I hope your grandson's well?"

Mr. Pike shrugged. "I've not seen him."

"Does he no longer work with you? I thought —"

Mr. Pike let out a weary breath. "The little scamp got a job with the DA's office. After everything I've done for him! And I had to find out from one of Freezout's men."

"Wait. He said none of them would see him."

He gave me a surprised glance. "All I know is one day he said he wouldn't ever work for me again. It was a horrendous row, one I now regret. I've not seen him since."

I'd seen Mr. Pike active, confident, bold. For the first time, his demeanor was of a man who'd suffered a sudden, unexpected defeat, one that shook his sense of how the world should be. He raised his eyes to mine. "I suppose we'll stand on opposite sides, as it seems we've always done."

* * *

By the time I brought the information to the bank and returned home, the sun peeked orange between the rooftops. Over her protests, I sent Amelia back to Spadros Manor with the plain carriage. Surely Tony wouldn't begrudge her riding with them.

To my surprise, Sawbuck sat relaxed upon my sofa.

I felt dismayed. "My goodness, Ten! I had no idea you planned to visit. Have you been waiting long?"

Sawbuck grinned. "Haven't you figured it out? Only been here a bit. I knew when you left the bank."

Ah. I sat across from him. "Would you care for some tea?"

"You have something else I want."

I made my face all innocence. "Oh?"

"Something much too valuable to be given to an Associate."

"I did wonder about that."

He smiled, relaxing into the sofa. "So how would you like to handle this?"

I felt very proud that I'd learned to write a check.

An unexpected benefit — and now, looking back, well worth the money — was learning the entire chain of command from my block's runner-man Mr. Eight Howell up to Sawbuck himself. Every one of them, except Sawbuck, came by to thank me.

The Newcomer

After Sawbuck left, I went towards my study.

Blitz met me in the hall with a letter: Lance Clubb — of all people — wanted to meet for luncheon on Market Center. I didn't recognize the address. "Send word I'll be there." I peered at the invitation. "What could this possibly be about?"

Morton came out of his room. "What is what about?"

"Oh, just an invitation to luncheon tomorrow. Is tea ready?"

"I was just going to check," Morton said.

Blitz turned to him from the front door. "See if my wife needs help with anything, will you?"

Morton bowed, a wry grin on his face. "At once, sir."

Blitz and I laughed. Master Blaze Rainbow was a gentleman, well above Blitz in standing. But Morton had a fine sense of humor. And he never seemed to care one bit about formality.

It was almost as if he wasn't from Bridges at all.

* * *

We had dinner together to celebrate the hiring of the new housekeeper. Even if only for a month, this was the last night with just the four of us at the table.

Morton said, "Where will she be staying?"

"Upstairs," Mary said. "It wasn't altogether satisfactory for her, the space being without a door, but my husband moved the bed we bought to the corner and stretched curtains across the angle. And he put another curtain across the entryway. At least she'll have a place to dress without fear of discovery."

We ate for some time in silence.

Then Morton leaned back. "I got another sighting of our man."

He must be referring to Sheinwold. Morton never shared much with Mary or Blitz, and nothing important in front of Amelia. "Will you be gone long?"

"Depends on what I find."

Blitz leaned forward. "When will you be leaving?"

"Not until mid-afternoon. And my carriage has been arranged." He glanced at me. "I should be here when you return from your luncheon. If I learn more in the meantime, I'll let you know."

I nodded. Morton had collected a new network of informants to replace the ones Zia murdered. With her hunting him, though, it didn't surprise me that he stayed here as infrequently as he did.

* * *

The next morning, the housekeeper arrived, a Mrs. Claudete Crawford. To my surprise, the wrinkled brown woman could still curtsy to the floor.

I took her hands to help her rise, although she didn't seem to need it. "You do us great service, Mrs. Crawford."

She blushed. "Thank you for your kindness, mum."

After touring the house, the woman put on her apron and went straight to work. We'd found a great many vegetables on sale. She and Mary began putting them into jars for the winter. I left them chatting about what to expect with childbirth — Mary rather dazed-looking — and had Amelia get me ready for luncheon.

Amelia seemed downcast, subdued, but she got me ready to go. All off, then a fresh chemise, split-crotch bloomers (essential whilst wearing a corset), and a petticoat. Then a thin under-corset, one of my high-necked charcoal dresses (with lots of ruffles in back) then an embroidered black over-corset (all the rage this year). Makeup, jewelry, stockings, boots, and a hat with a veil. It seemed overly much for one woman to bear, but I managed.

Once dressed, I stood watching out of the parlor window for the carriage as Blitz polished the candlesticks. I spoke softly. "What do you know of her?"

"This is the first we've met. Her husband was a Family man."

"Oh?"

"To Mr. Acevedo."

Roy's father, who died when Tony was small. They say Mr. Acevedo was killed by his own men. "Well, that's comforting."

Blitz chuckled. "He died before all that. You need anything?"

"Not at all, thank you. Amelia should be out shortly."

So she was, right as the carriage arrived. "Mum, if you will, I'd better stay and help them finish. Your young housekeeper's becoming fatigued."

Amelia never would call Mary by her name. "That's fine, Amelia. Thank you for your help."

To my surprise, the carriage brought me to the Governmental District at the very center of the island, a few blocks from the Courthouse itself. The sign on the wall outside the wrought-iron gate read:

Keeper of the Court

Two men dressed in the navy and silver livery of the Court stood guard outside the white stone wall, with two more beside the dark wooden front door across the courtyard beyond. The one to my right said, "The Keeper's expecting you."

The same dark wood covered the floor. Portraits framed in white and silver hung on white walls. A man in a black suit glanced up from a podium. "Mrs. Spadros! Right this way."

I followed him down a short hallway to the left to a door.

Jonathan sat at the head of a small rectangular table, his cane beside him. His lips looked a bit pale, but he smiled when he saw us. "I'm grateful you could meet me here." He gestured to the seat at his left. "Sit with me."

"Your home is lovely." I sat, grasping his hand. "I'm so glad to see you, Jon. Are you well?"

Jonathan blushed, smiling to himself. "Never better." He turned to Lance Clubb, who sat beside him. "Be at peace, sir."

Lance Clubb was a year my elder, with heavy straight golden hair and a sprinkling of freckles across his nose. He rose and bowed. "Mrs. Spadros." Then he returned to his chair.

I'd never seen Lance Clubb and Jonathan Diamond sit together before, and it intrigued me.

After the plates were cleared away, I said to Lance, "I'm pleased to be here. Yet I don't understand why you came all this way to meet with me."

Lance always seemed a shy man, looking younger than he truly was. Today, though, he didn't hesitate. "Something's wrong. I fear for Miss Diamond. I've not heard from her, and her last letter gave me concern for her safety. You must help me."

I felt confused. "Me? Why me?"

Lance gestured at Jon with his chin. "Master Diamond tells me you managed to sway his brother once. Perhaps you might again."

This could only mean Jonathan's eldest brother, Cesare. "He's barred you from seeing her too?"

Lance nodded gravely. "He accuses everyone of spying, even the boy's father —"

Roy said Cesare had prevented Tony from visiting. But to accuse Tony of spying?

"— and in this matter we have common cause. I can't bear the thought of her being trapped by that man. He's gone from prudence to paranoia. We fear his hate has turned him mad."

Jonathan nodded, eyes downcast.

Madness ran in the Diamond Family. Jonathan's identical twin Jack certainly appeared mad. Some said their ancestor Caesar Diamond had been mad as well. By Gardena's own tale, her grandfather had lapsed in and out of madness before he died. "Why would Cesare Diamond let me into the quadrant?"

Lance said, "I have permission to enter Diamond quadrant two days from now with a bodyguard —"

I almost laughed, it was so audacious. Me, pose as a bodyguard to the Clubb Heir?

"— yet I choose you because you of all people can speak to Miss Diamond without her brother or his men present. You'll tell me the truth. I must know if he's hurt her —"

Would Cesare hurt his own sister?

"— or her son. Whether she's safe and well. You know her better than anyone save her brother here. Even if Mr. Diamond might allow him into the quadrant, the doctor says Master Jonathan's still not well enough to travel to their Country House."

"Does my husband know you're asking this?"

"Yes," Lance said.

Tony actually agreed? Matters must be worse than I thought. "And what do I get in return?"

Jon gaped at me, horrified. "Jacqui!"

"Lance Clubb's mother tried to seize me once already." I turned to Lance. "Your courtship of Gardena was broken a year ago. You speak of her son — your son, if the marriage commences — as 'the boy.' From what I can tell, you're only interested in an alliance."

Lance seemed dismayed.

"I feel concerned at my husband not being allowed to see — **Roland**, in case you've forgotten. But I don't believe Cesare would harm either his sister or his nephew. If he wants war with Spadros quadrant, though, he has no reason to let me return." Not to mention that Gardena would be at the Diamond Country House. Who knew whether my old enemy, Jonathan's twin Jack Diamond, would be there as well?

"He wouldn't dare," Lance said. "You forget that Clubb is allied with Spadros. And I'm certain Hart would aid us." His face turned grim. "We would crush him."

"Which would do me no good whatsoever. You beg me to put myself into danger and possibly start a war over not receiving letters which might simply be lost?"

"Not lost," Jon said. "I have evidence my brother has been destroying her mail."

This was concerning. But I feared making a mistake. "Let me think on it."

Lance rose. "Then I await your reply." He bowed to Jon. "Thank you for your hospitality, sir."

Once Lance left, Jon turned to me. "Whatever possessed you to speak to him like that? He only wants to help!"

I leaned away, resting my elbow upon the chair's arm. "I had a most enlightening discussion with Joseph Kerr."

"Did you now."

So Jonathan heard of Joe's capture. "He claims you and your Family are out to kill Tony."

Jon's face turned stricken, and I immediately regretted speaking. His eyes reddened, became moist. "I love your husband, Mrs. Spadros, as much as I love you. I would never —" at that, he faltered. "What kind of monster do you **take** me for?"

"Oh, Jon, I never believed him, not for an instant. Please forgive me — I should never have spoken."

Jonathan wiped his eyes and nose with his handkerchief. "**That** man is who you should suspect. After I brought you to see his betrothed, I obtained a photograph of them together. I'll show it to you right now, if that's what it'll take for you to —"

"No, it's not necessary." I didn't want to see it. I didn't want to know. "Please forgive me, Jon. I never meant to upset you."

Jon sat for a moment, then took my hand. "All is forgiven." But he didn't meet my eye.

"How do you know Gardena's mail has been destroyed?"

Jonathan took a deep breath, let it out. "I wrote about something only she would know; she would feel forced to reply. Yet she never addressed it. And her letters are coming at odd intervals. Your husband has said the same. Someone is destroying mail that they don't want the other to receive."

"So Cesare believes Gardena's a spy as well."

Jon shook his head with a disgusted sigh. "Maybe my brother truly **is** mad."

* * *

When I returned from luncheon, Morton's bags sat in the hall. He sat in the kitchen smoking a cigarette. "Ah, there you are. I hope your luncheon went well?"

"Well enough." I sat across from him. "We need to talk."

Morton knew all Four Families. But what interested me was the Diamonds. "How do you see matters in Diamond quadrant?"

Morton shrugged. "It's more difficult to get in — or out, for that matter — but life goes on."

"Wait — you've been there recently?"

"I went to see Mr. Julius a few weeks back."

"Did you happen to see Gardena? Is her son well?"

Morton held up a hand. "Whoa there. What's happened?"

I lowered my voice, aware that the housekeeper was still on the premises. "I just left a meeting with Lance Clubb and Jonathan Diamond. Gardena hasn't been heard from in over a week, and they fear for her safety."

Morton's face twisted in disbelief. "In her own home?"

"Jon claims Gardena's mail is being destroyed. Lance fears Cesare's gone mad."

"And does Master Jonathan agree?"

"Jon hasn't seen his brother in months. Cesare won't allow Jon to visit them. He's all but named Jon spy and traitor!" I blinked back tears. "And Jon's sick. He needs his family more than ever."

"What possible motivation would Cesare Diamond have to harm his sister?"

"None, as far as I know. But —" I stopped myself just in time.

"But what?"

Then I remembered: Morton knew about Roland. "What you told me at Vig's saloon last year. When I dressed up. Think about it. Cesare **hates** the Spadros Family."

Morton sat stock still for several moments, eyes distant. Then his eyes widened. "Wait. What?" He peered at me, frowning slightly, as my heart beat, it seemed, loud enough to be heard in the street. Then his face changed: realization, shock, horror. "Good gods, you don't think he'd **harm** the boy?"

"I have no way of knowing."

Morton leaned back, hand to his chin, considering. "I was only there for dinner; I never saw the boy. But there was definite unhappiness in the house, perhaps even fear. I could feel it in those who served us. Miss Diamond seemed well — if quiet."

Gardena, quiet?

The doorbell rang. "That's my carriage. But as luck would have it, I'm off to Diamond."

"Really?"

"A friend has seen Sheinwold, alive, and just heard I searched for him. I'll be at his home for a few days; with how long it takes to get in, it's hardly worth going for a one-day."

I grinned at him. "Enjoy."

Once he left, I sat pondering what to do.

I didn't tell Morton about Lance's request on purpose. Morton was discreet. But if I did decide to go with Lance, the fewer people who knew of it, the better.

Why would Tony agree to this? It was entirely unlike him.

Amelia came in from the hallway. "Oh, there you are, mum."

"Have you eaten?"

"Just now, upstairs with Mrs. Crawford. Let me get you changed from these clothes."

I followed her into the hallway. Normally, Tony'd be terrified of anything happening to me. To send me into the presence of his enemy seemed unbelievable.

Something must be terribly wrong.

"How was your luncheon?"

I wasn't paying attention, so caught up was I with my own thoughts. "It was lovely."

Amelia draped one of my house dresses upon the bed. "Here, sit, I'll get your boots off."

The way Amelia moved caught my eye. "Is something wrong?"

She remained head down, focused, it seemed, upon untying my boots. "Not at all, mum."

"How's the new housekeeper working out?"

Amelia slipped off my boot. "Perfectly well, mum. She's a bit set in her ways. But very capable."

That amused me. "Old-fashioned, you mean."

"Well, mum, it took her a bit to understand the situation. You living here. And me not living here. Apparently, in her day a lady's maid didn't get married, much less have a 'brood of children.' She lived to serve."

"I'm sure it's hard for the old to understand the new."

Amelia chuckled, then winced.

"What's wrong? Are you hurt?"

"I'm perfectly well, mum. Thank you for asking."

"You're not well." I reached out to touch her shoulder, and she shied away. "Tell me at once: what's happened?"

Amelia froze. "I don't wish to speak of it."

"Was it Mr. Roy?"

She shook her head, gazing at the floor.

"Surely —" Then I recalled something Amelia said many years back: *We would be brought out back and whipped if caught stealing.* "You've been beaten."

"Please don't tell Mr. Anthony I said so, or I'll be beaten again."

"My husband **beat** you?"

"He had Mr. Pearson do it."

"But **why**?"

"He'd forbidden me to ride your carriage, mum, not without you inside it, but —"

My heart dropped. "But I insisted."

"Yes, mum. But you mustn't blame yourself. I was tired. I let myself be persuaded to defy him."

"Has the doctor seen to you?"

"No, mum, but —"

"I'll call for the doctor."

"Please don't." Tears filled her eyes. "My girls need a mother."

She feared Tony would **kill** her? What happened to the man I once knew? "Very well. But when the midwife visits, will you have her look at it?"

Amelia shook her head. "I'm grateful for your concern, mum, but Miz Jane has been tending to me." Jane Pearson was Mary's mother, the housekeeper at Spadros Manor. Amelia pulled off my boot. "I'll manage."

"I want you to tell me if my husband has forbidden something. Do you understand? I want to know so **I** don't defy him."

She nodded, head down. "Yes, mum."

The doorbell rang. "Let's sit here a moment, in case that's someone to see me."

Amelia smiled to herself. "That would be prudent, mum."

Sure enough, a few minutes later, Blitz knocked. "A Miss Finette Pasha to see you."

I didn't recognize the name. But a new case would be most welcome. "Put her in my study. I'll be there momentarily."

Amelia got me changed into a house dress and shawl, then I went to see who this was.

A woman sat hooded and veiled. But when she raised her veil, I did know her after all. To this day, I will never forget that face. Pale skin, golden curls, eyes of clear blue. "Josephine Kerr. What the hell are **you** doing here?"

The Blame

Josie was Joseph Kerr's twin sister. She appeared taken aback. "I thought you'd be glad to see me."

"You gotta lot of nerve coming here, after what you pulled."

"Whatever do you mean?"

"You set me up. You set up times and places for Joe and I to be alone, knowing I was married. Knowing your brother just wanted my money and had no regard for me. Why? I loved you, Josie." I felt close to tears. "And I feel as though you've **used** me."

For a moment, she stared up at me, mouth open. "Jacqui, yes. I set up times and places for you to meet, without your husband knowing. It was what I believed you wanted. You were so unhappy. You were drinking yourself to death! How could I just stand aside and watch?"

She turned aside, eyes shut, handkerchief to her mouth, then faced me. "But you're wrong about Joe. He loves you more than anything, and it's been his downfall. We used your money for tickets on the zeppelin. When you never arrived, I begged him to use your ticket to take our grandfather away from here. But he wouldn't go without you."

I went to my desk and sat. "So you planned to go all along?" This was completely different from what Joe had told me the night Tony caught us together back at Spadros Manor.

Her clear blue gaze never wavered. "Of course, Jacqui. You, me, and Joe. That was the plan all along. My grandfather refused to go until it became clear your men hunted him." She waved a hand dismissively. "There's nothing for us here."

Her hand fell to her side, and her eyes turned sad. "But now we're utterly ruined. We couldn't get out, just like our ancestors before us." She raised her eyes to mine. "Joe didn't want to sell the tickets, Jacqui. But he had to. I can't tell you how many times I've had to take my grandfather and flee somewhere we thought safe. The nights we spent cold and wretched outdoors. In a cave, or a ruined basement."

She gazed aside, shaking her head. "I'm astonished Grandpa survived it. It was terrifying. We all feared you were dead. We never knew what happened until we could get hold of a paper."

This was different from what Joe had just told me a few days earlier. But perhaps he never told Josie I was being held by the Clubbs. "You were under Mr. Hart's protection! Why didn't your grandfather flee to him?"

"We did!"

Did Tony know Mr. Hart had Joe in his grasp and let him go?

She sounded bitter. "When we needed him most, Charles Hart turned us away. He raged at my grandfather, forced him to leave. After everything my grandfather's done for him!" Josie shook her head. "I don't think he'll ever recover."

Grief stabbed me. It sounded too close to what Sawbuck said about Tony after I betrayed him.

Josie sighed. "I don't know what else we could have done." Her face turned sad. "I've always loved you, Jacqui —"

With a shock, I realized I'd never heard her say anything which felt so true.

Tears lay in her eyes. "— I hoped we might leave this city together. You never arrived —"

Shame stabbed at me: how could I have forgotten our place? Our gang's sign?

"— but I don't blame you. It's been so long since you were home — anyone would have forgotten."

"I'm so sorry, Josie. I truly am. I should have been there."

If I'd known.

If I'd remembered.

We could have gotten out of there.

We could have been free.

Josie's voice broke in: "But Jacqui, where's my brother?"

I stared at her in horror.

"I begged Joe not to take the risk. My grandfather commanded him not to go. But Joe insisted you must be told. Someone plans you great harm, Jacqui, and Joe couldn't rest until he'd found you. Did he find you? Where is he?"

Joe mentioned the plot against Tony but never said anything about **me** being in danger. "He came to me and my husband captured him. But my husband assures me he won't be harmed."

I expected Josie to cry out, flinch, or turn pale. Instead, she went very still. "Do you trust him to keep his word?"

It came to me with certainty. "I do." In spite of his scorn of my actions, the things he'd had to do, Tony was at his core an honest man. Perhaps too honest for his own good.

The thought humbled me. "Be careful. I spoke with Roy Spadros the other day, and he believes your family means ours harm."

"What harm could **we** do to him?"

I had no idea. The whole matter angered me still.

"What do you think of the Diamonds?"

I shrugged. "My husband seems ready, should they attack. But I don't believe they will."

A frown marred Josie's perfect face. "Did Joe tell you of the plot against you?"

"He did."

"Yet you don't believe him."

"I'm not sure what to believe." I certainly didn't believe — if there was a plot against the Spadros Family — that Jonathan would have any part in it. Jonathan had said more than once that he considered Tony as a brother. Hopefully he'd never said that in Cesare's presence.

Or perhaps he had, which was why he sat in exile now. "Just be careful. The Families know of this plot. They're looking for someone to blame."

Josie seemed not to have heard me. Then she stirred. "So you don't think there'll be war between Spadros and Diamond?"

I remembered the first Spadros-Diamond war. The fighting outside the Cathedral, huddling in back rooms as men took what they wanted from the women there.

The ones who slept afterward were easy to deal with, but at least according to Ma, every one was found and killed.

And I recalled Benji and little Tim. His building had been smashed in that war. If there were another war, everything Benji rebuilt would be destroyed.

At once, the answer came to me. To this problem, at least.

Josie said, "What is it?"

I smiled, but I didn't feel it. "I know how to free your brother."

The Negotiation

I refused to go into any details. Once she'd left, I had Blitz call a Memory Boy.

When I saw him standing at the bottom of our steps in his bright red jacket, I smiled. "Good afternoon, Werner."

"Hi, Mrs. Spadros."

Werner Lead was a boy of eleven with white-blond hair. His two brothers, just approaching puberty, stood as his armed guard. A dismal and tiresome life, to be sure, but better than most: their family wanted for nothing.

I spoke to them all. "Do you like your work?"

The two older boys never glanced my way: their job was to watch for any threat. "Sure," one said. The other nodded.

"Of course, Mrs. Spadros," Werner said. "How may I help?"

Werner would never so much as lay foot upon my steps. I sat so our heads were of equal height. "My message is to Spadros Manor. But it's to go to Mr. Anthony himself. His ear only. Is that clear?"

"Yes, of course."

"If he won't come out, then wait there until he does."

Werner nodded, face serious.

"Here's the message: You have a deadline. I can help."

Werner repeated it back to me. I put his fee into his hand.

"Very good, mum. Do you wish a reply?"

"As a matter of fact, I do. I'll give you what I just gave you if you return today."

He beamed. "Yippee!" He bounced down the street, his brothers hurrying after.

Could Roy have been right? Did Josie set me up?

I felt dirty for even considering it. She'd just been trying to help. She wanted her brother to be happy.

Four hours later, Werner returned, looking tired. "He says be ready to leave at eight."

* * *

The carriage stopped in front of Sawbuck's home on 190th. Perhaps Tony thought I might see that as neutral ground.

Eight in the evening was dinner-time, yet no smell of food greeted me. Tony sat at the bare wooden table, not rising when I entered. Sawbuck stood off to one side, hands clasped in front of him, eyes straight ahead.

So that's how they wanted to play this. "I'm here, as you asked."

"Sit down, Jacqui," Tony said.

I couldn't tell what he was feeling. I used to be able to.

I sat across from him, folded my arms, leaned back, and waited.

Tony sounded annoyed. "You said we needed to talk. I'm here. What do you want?"

"Isn't this more about what you want? You want me to see Gardena and make sure Roland's well. Am I right?"

A flash of hesitation-surprise-fear went through his eyes. "You're correct."

"You want me to go into a heavily guarded quadrant, led by a man who hates me, to the home of another man who's publicly threatened to kill me, and see to the well-being of your mistress and her bastard son."

I watched as Tony's face passed through fear to anger and back again. He hesitated, then nodded.

"So you're asking a great deal. What reason do I have to help?"

Tony leaned forward. "Do you care nothing for Gardena —?"

I snorted, and he realized his error. Yes, I did care for Gardena, but he had no right to bring her up, not now. And it showed he still thought about her a great deal. For all his honesty in other matters, he would never be honest about this.

He said, "For Roland, then?"

I felt abashed. "Of course I care. But I won't be ordered to my death without gaining something in return."

Tony blinked, his face surprised. "What is it you want, then?"

"First, I want Joe released —"

"Why am I not surprised?"

"Don't be ridiculous. I want to see what he does next."

"Well, there's a whole line of people — some not as gentle — who'd like to see him too. Mr. Charles Hart has sent men every day demanding Master Kerr be released into his custody." Tony's face turned amused. "To be a fly on the wall for **that** meeting!"

"What does Mr. Hart have against Joe, anyway?"

Tony's face turned guarded. "It's not a matter for me to tell."

"Very well. What happens to Joseph Kerr is up to Joseph Kerr, I suppose. But would you try to see that he doesn't come to too much harm?" For an instant, I felt afraid. Was I doing the right thing? "I need to know why he's here."

"You really don't trust him."

I shrugged. "I won't lie." I gazed into his eyes. "I still love him."

Tony flinched, his face turning paler than usual.

I realized Mary was right. *He still cares.*

"But something's not right. And Josie came to me today. Their stories don't match." I shook my head. "I'm not sure I trust her either." I glanced at Sawbuck, who hadn't moved the entire time. "She claims Mr. Hart had the Kerrs in front of him and let them go. After he knew you wanted them."

Tony looked weary. "What else do you want?"

Did he not hear me? Or did he already know this? "I'd like to know why you destroyed the Old Plaza. You had no right!"

Tony and Sawbuck shared a glance.

"It was my doing," Sawbuck said. "He said it would upset you, but I persuaded him it would cause the least danger to our men."

"You?" I had no words. Why would Sawbuck want to destroy his own homeland?

But I remembered his conversation with Benji the night the rogue Spadros men were slaughtered. Sawbuck didn't even recall living there.

Tony said, "What else do you want?"

"Why did Roy have an innocent man killed, claiming he was the Bridges Strangler?"

Tony looked confused. "What?"

"He's started killing again. I believe this man and Frank Pagliacci to be one and the same. We can't go after scapegoats if we want to catch him!"

Tony's face didn't change. "I'll speak to him about it."

"He knows. I confronted him on it." I shrugged, looking away. "When he asked me before."

"What else do you want?"

I let out a breath. "Mrs. Eleanora Bryce. The merchant whose son was taken. I believe she can identify the woman leading the High-Low Split. The group working with the Red Dog Gang, who suborned your men."

"What about her?"

"I fear for her life. Would you have men guard her? We need to get a portrait, and —"

"Well ahead of you, Jacqui. I put her under guard when you first told me of the situation."

"Oh." Why didn't he tell me? "We need to get a portrait of the woman who visited her. The one who bought all the cloth."

"Anything else?"

"Why didn't you protect Madame Biltcliffe?"

Tony's jaw tightened. "She left our protection when she renounced her allegiance and swore to Clubb quadrant."

The table had seen a lot of use. "I understand." But did she?

"Is there anything else?"

I wasn't sure how to say this. "Have your men found Joe before? And you didn't tell me?"

Tony snorted. "Is that what he's saying now?"

Joe lied about that too? Why would he lie about **that**?

"Jacqui." Tony sounded irritated, or as if he were in a hurry. "Is there anything else?"

Should I say? "I wish to speak in someone's defense. You must promise not to retaliate: I forced the truth from them. They don't know I'm making this request, and I'll not have harm come to anyone else on my account."

His eyes narrowed. "It depends on who you speak of."

I crossed my arms. "Then you can get someone else."

"Good gods, you want me to sign a blank check for some miscreant's behavior?"

Tony was insufferable. "If you want me to do your bidding."

He ran his hands through his hair. Then he faced me. "I won't so much as frown at them."

"Why do you make Amelia Dewey's life miserable? Has the woman not suffered enough?"

Tony's face turned confused. He didn't know what Roy had done to her?

"Why force her to take a taxi to serve me? Why beat her for wanting a ride home?"

Tony let out a weary breath. "Why do you care so much about **servants**? If it weren't for the fact that her husband's our stablemaster, I'd have let her go long since. She's conspired for years to hide your business from me, she's defied me numerous times, and I don't see that she's suffered much at all for it. Her punishments were dispensed by my butler, the same as anyone else in my household would get for such action. If you believe he's been overly harsh, take the matter up with him." He leaned back. "I'll have Joseph Kerr released in the morning. Will that be sufficient?"

Sawbuck watched me.

Dismayed, I nodded.

Tony rose. "Then we're done here."

I stared after Tony as he stalked out.

Amelia helped raise him, she defended him, she loved him. And he'd allowed her to be beaten like a — in the Pot, we didn't even beat our dogs. People weren't beaten in the Cathedral, even for defying the Eldest, although I'd never seen anyone dare to do so.

These quadrant-folk were so different it was like living in another city.

Sawbuck hadn't moved from his spot. "I got your information."

"What information?"

"About the lock-box. Good thinking."

"Did you find out about Mr. Pike?"

He chuckled. "The Clubbs keep increasing the amount before they'll let him leave the city."

"There are a lot of Clubbs. Who exactly is extorting him?"

Sawbuck gave a slight shrug.

Those people! "Thanks for letting me know." I rose. "May I borrow the carriage? I need to go into Clubb quadrant."

"At this hour?"

"It'll help with the meeting tomorrow."

Sawbuck nodded. "Come on, then."

Before he got to the door, I said, "One more thing. Where's the Diamond Country House?"

He didn't turn. "Best intel we have is mid-countryside, twenty miles from the West River."

* * *

By the time we reached Tenni's shop, it was half past nine, and it took her some time to come to the door. She held a pistol, peering through beveled glass before opening up. "Just a precaution, mum, after everything that's happened."

"I understand."

Tenni locked the door behind us. "How may I help?"

I raised my dress, taking my gun from its calf holster. "Tomorrow, I'm going to be searched. How can I hide this?"

Everyone knew I carried weapons: I said so at my trial. They'd be suspicious if I had none on me. So I'd leave my boot-knife on. But it'd snow in Hell before I faced Cesare Diamond unarmed.

Tenni examined the little revolver. "It's small and not too heavy. Let me make you a holster. She reached behind me, took hold of my dress. "If you were to pin it to the ruffles," she shook them a bit, "no one would ever know."

I followed her then watched as she measured the gun onto some tissue paper. Then she cut and sewed the holster, double thick, sliding the gun into it. "There!"

"Thank you so much." Filled with gratitude, I kissed her cheek. "You have a treasure here. Keep it secret from everyone. And I mean everyone."

"Believe me, mum, I will."

* * *

I was supposed to meet Lance Clubb at noon near the Market Center bridge to Diamond quadrant. To my surprise, Amelia appeared at my bedroom door at seven. "A plain carriage with outriders will arrive at eleven. You must be ready to leave at once."

At least a half hour to Market Center. It wasn't far to the Diamond bridge, but there might be traffic along the Promenade.

She then turned to my bed. "I'll get this straightened —"

"I'm sorry, I didn't expect you to be here so early."

"Never you fret; I'll be here at seven from now on."

Did my talk with Tony the night before had anything to do with this? "Have you done the tally I asked for?"

Amelia plumped a pillow. "Yes, mum."

"Have Blitz pay you when he's up."

"Thank you, mum."

This actually might work out for the best. "When you've done that, I have something for you to work on." I ate my toast, drank my morning tea and tonic, and considered how Tenni's idea might be accomplished.

Amelia straightened the room and draped my clothing upon the bed then left, bringing back a "quick tray" as she called it:

scrambled eggs, regular tea, and more toast. "Eat up, now. You don't know what those Diamonds will have for you."

I smiled to myself as she bustled off to draw my bath.

Before getting into the bath, I showed her the holster and told her how I wanted it arranged inside the ruffles.

"That's going to have to be attached to the waist or it'll pull the back of the dress down. Do we have some black cloth ...?"

I'd forgotten to bring the cloth to Mrs. Bryce! "Oh! Yes! We do." By this time, I was already in the water. "Would you get it? It's in the bag in my study."

Amelia returned with the bag. "This should work. It's not near the same quality as the dress, but no one will notice. I'll just make a ribbon of cloth for the harness to attach to, open up the waistband, and thread it through!"

"You should have been a dressmaker, Amelia."

Amelia chuckled. "Me? Make clothes for fine ladies? I'm perfectly content with yours, mum."

I washed out my hair. She never could see anything for herself other than toiling for me then going home to toil for her family. I emerged from the tub and dried off, wrapping up in my robe to put on my makeup and comb out my wet curls.

Amelia was quick with a needle. She had everything done by the time I put on my bloomers and chemise and fixed my hair.

"The bow should tie here in the front," she said, "double tight. The gun hangs inside the dress, under the back ruffle. I added an additional panel to the inside, here in front of the gun, so no one can see it from underneath. And I sewed the panel around the back opening, so when you unhook the back, no one's the wiser. They'd have to goose your behind to find that!"

I laughed at the idea.

"Just undo the bow, and it'll slide right out!"

The doorbell rang.

Amelia frowned. "Now who might that be?"

I put on a house dress and some slippers just in case.

Blitz knocked on the door. "Master Joseph Kerr to see you. I put him in the parlor. Shall I stand guard?"

"No." I expected Joe, just not so soon. "This won't take long."

Blitz opened the parlor door. "Mrs. Jacqueline Spadros." He sounded so formal that I almost laughed.

Joe stood when I came in.

"Good morning." I sat across from him. "I must leave at eleven, so I can't offer you breakfast. But if you'd like some tea —"

"I can't stay long." He gave the clock a quick glance. "Oh, Jacqui, I'm so proud of you. Selling me to your husband for the reward then getting him to release me was a really great play!"

He had a beautiful smile. In it was the free abandon of childhood, the joy of summer. His eyes caressed mine, intimate as a kiss, his gaze reaching into my very soul.

It took a moment to recover. Taking a deep breath, I said, "It was of no consequence."

"And now we have the money, we can go! But it has to be soon."

"What?" A laugh burst from me. "You've got to be joking."

"No, Jacqui, truly, I'm not. I don't have much time before I'm caught again. I have to leave town. Men pursue me even now —"

"Yes, the loan sharks. And the gambling halls. I heard."

"— and I have to do something. Let's go. We can go together, now, and be on the zeppelin before noon. Or if you must have your meeting, give me the money and let me buy them."

I sat back. "You are beyond belief. I gave you my entire life's savings for the promise of tickets. Do you think me a fool?"

"I had to sell the tickets to survive!"

"Those tickets were fake, Joe. You took my money —"

"No! You saw them! They were real!"

"— and you spent it on whores and gambling —"

"Good gods, Jacqui, none of that is true."

"So the red-haired woman with you when you were almost caught at the pool hall in Hart quadrant **wasn't** a whore?"

"Who told you about that?"

"Jonathan Diamond."

"He's a gods-damned liar! He's using you, Jacqui. You have to believe me. I helped you. I came back for you. I risked my life for you. Surely you owe me something. I need to pay these men before they kill me! Can't you help me, after all we've meant to each other? Can't you just give me a little?"

I wanted to, indeed I did. Instead, I rose. "Go to the women you've had all those children with if you want money. I have bills of my own."

Joe gaped at me. "Jacqui, what women? I don't understand —"

"Now, if you'll excuse me, I have a meeting to attend." I turned and left. Heart pounding, I went in my room and locked the door, leaning upon it, eyes closed, until Joe left.

How could he possibly think I would give him more money?

How could I possibly have not?

Had I just condemned him to death?

* * *

Amelia had my dress ready. I didn't bother with an over-corset this time: we were going to negotiate, not promenade. It took some fiddling, but we were able to suspend the little revolver below my waist inside my dress.

Blitz wouldn't go with us. "Mary's too close to her time. Besides, I doubt they'd let me cross the bridge with you."

I chuckled. "True."

Then I approached my front door. With this gun situated as it was, would I be able to sit believably? Would I get past the search at the Diamond bridge? Were Gardena and Roland safe? Were they even alive? Would I be able to persuade Cesare to speak with Tony, or to stop the war? Would Cesare let me out of Diamond quadrant?

Would Joseph Kerr be outside my front door, waiting for me?

Blitz opened the door, and a glance told me at least I wouldn't be confronted with the latter. I feared if he were to beg, I might promise him things I must not.

The gun bounced a bit when I moved too quickly, but I kept my face still as Amelia and I approached the plain carriage. At least Honor was there to open the door. "Good morning, mum."

I smiled at him, feeling weak, frightened. "Good morning. I trust you know our destination?"

"Yes, mum. Market Center, Diamond bridge."

"Right. You should see a Clubb carriage there."

Honor held out his hand, and I climbed into the carriage, Amelia sitting across from me.

It wasn't as difficult as I thought to sweep the gun into all my ruffles and flounces, which gave me a great relief. If I were caught with this, I'd not have anyone able to say they even suspected it to be there.

Except Amelia. "You mustn't go into Diamond quadrant."

Amelia seemed confused. "Why?"

I leaned far forward, waiting until she joined me, the coldness of the gun hard on my tail-bone. "You dressed me. If what I carry is found, they'll know you had part in it." Remembering what her husband once said, I felt moved. "I'm supposed to shield you from harm, not put you in it."

"Mr. Anthony said I wasn't to leave your side for any reason."

They'd beat her if I left her at the bridge. Cesare would have her killed if he found the gun, surely in violation of whatever pact he'd made with Lance. I put my face in my hands. What was I to do?

"You'll ruin your makeup, mum."

I sat up, dismayed. Why did I bring the gun with me?

But I had good reason. Cesare thought me insignificant, worthy of nothing but disdain. If Jack Diamond seized me, or Cesare planned betrayal, the surprise of me having a gun might be our only chance of escape.

Sawbuck said the Diamond Country House was twenty miles from the West River. If this went wrong, Lance and I might be able to flee into Hart quadrant.

Falling into Mr. Charles Hart's hands — or worse, his wife's — would be unfortunate, but there at least I had more room to maneuver. Roy might consider me expendable. But so far as I knew, I was still under Clubb protection. If the Hart Family refused to release us, it would provide the perfect pretext for our two quadrants to destroy them.

Yet I couldn't bring Amelia. I pictured her in the midst of a gun fight, having to run twenty miles through a forest, or swim the mile-wide river.

This wouldn't do. I had to keep her out of harm's way.

I considered the matter all the way to Market Center. By the time we arrived behind Lance Clubb's brass-trimmed oak carriage, I had my answer.

Honor opened the door, and I took his hand to exit the carriage. Amelia began fussing with my train.

I spoke in Honor's ear. "Do you serve me with your life?"

Honor drew back. "Of course, mum."

"Then don't let Mrs. Dewey out." I gripped his hand, hard. "Mr. Anthony will be wroth. Furiously so. He'll want someone to punish, perhaps kill. Do what you must, but don't let it be her."

Honor swallowed. Last time Tony was angry, he'd put his revolver in Honor's face.

Then Honor let out a breath. "I understand."

I sighed with relief. "Thank you, sir. May the gods bless you."

The door slammed behind me, Amelia's screams muffled by the closed windows.

Heart pounding, I moved ahead. Two men in brown and gold Clubb livery holding gold champagne horses stood beside Lance's carriage. When I reached the carriage door, a brown-haired footman in Clubb livery took my hand, and I stepped inside.

Lance Clubb sat there. "Good morning, Mrs. Spadros."

The clock on Market Center struck noon. I drew my dress in, sitting across from him on deep brown glossy leather. "Good day, Master Clubb."

Lance took up the brass speaking tube. "Drive on."

The curtains had been drawn on all sides. After perhaps thirty feet, we stopped this side of the river at the first guard station. The driver spoke, his voice muffled. "Lance Clubb and his guard to see Cesare Diamond." We started off again.

I felt amused. "I'm seriously to be your guard?"

Lance gave a small smile. "They never asked nor specified the person's identity." He peeked through the curtain to his right. "This deception will get us across the river. What happens next ..." Doubt crossed his face, and a hint of fear.

Yet he was venturing into the camp of — for now — an enemy. "You love her."

He smiled to himself. "Yes, Mrs. Spadros, I do love her. And the boy, although that's caused me difficulty more than once."

I didn't know what the driver knew, but he — and the footman behind me — had to be listening. "Because of his father."

"Yes."

So Spadros and Clubb quadrants weren't such fast friends after all. "I'm grateful."

His lips twitched into a small fond smile. "I don't expect you to be my actual bodyguard, you know."

"I'm sure you're quite capable." His father Alexander Clubb was said to be formidable, accomplished, and deadly, even with his mechanical left arm.

Lance gave a small shrug. "If faced with overwhelming force, as I expect we will be, it won't matter. It was for your wits I chose you, and your connections, not your fighting ability. Although I hear that's not as small a thing as one might expect."

"For a woman."

He chuckled. "If you wish to say so."

I pushed open the curtain to my right, peering at the gray water beyond the bridge, the approaching skyline of Diamond quadrant. Jonathan Diamond had taken me this way shortly after one of Tony's own men, suborned by the Red Dog Gang, had tried to kill me outside the Courthouse.

What Joseph Kerr said about Jonathan Diamond had to be a lie. Jon had saved my life numerous times. He'd carried me from a room where I lay dying, risking his life and freedom to bring me to safety. He nursed me back to health for weeks in defiance of his duties to the Court. He killed an assassin sent to murder me, barely escaping death in the process.

Though all others might be false, I'd never believe it of Jonathan. Why would he risk himself so many times if he meant me dead?

Men dressed in Diamond livery — white trimmed in silver — rode ahead of and behind the carriage. Startled, I closed the curtain, hoping none had glimpsed me.

On the far side of the river, a stout, dark-skinned man in a navy and brass uniform with the Diamond Symbol on his shoulders opened the door. "This way."

Lance let me go first. A large crowd of high-card children near Katie's age wearing green and black school uniforms stood across the street, shouting and waving signs. We were led past the guard box to a building which hadn't been there the last time I'd visited Diamond quadrant. The size of a small house, it was painted black, with the door labeled, "Search."

That made its purpose plain, to be sure.

This door opened into a small, rather warm room with a desk. A wizened dark-skinned woman with gray-coiled hair sat at a typewriter, never once glancing up. "Name and purpose."

Well, I thought. "Not even so much as an introduction, I see."

She pointed to a placard before her which read:

I am not here to converse.

Please answer the question.

"Very well," I said. "Mrs. Jacqueline Spadros, here with Master Lance Clubb to see Mr. Cesare Diamond at his request."

Unruffled, she began typing upon a sheet of paper, then pulled it out and handed it to the stout man.

Then she put another sheet into the typewriter. "Next."

Lance stepped forward. "Lancelot Clubb for Cesare Diamond."

The woman handed this new sheet to the stout man.

He gestured for us to follow. Several doors lay upon the wall to our left. "Mrs. Spadros, please, this way." He handed one of the papers to a woman holding a clipboard. She wore an outfit remarkably similar to the man's, except of course with a skirt.

The door was marked "Women," so I presumed it to be the Ladies' Room. Behind the door, however, stood an unsmiling woman of a middle age, as dark-skinned as the rest, in a room the size of my dressing room at Madame's old shop. Another woman, somewhat younger, stood with her back to the wall, a pistol hanging from her right side.

The woman holding the clipboard followed me in, shutting the door behind her. "We know you carry weapons," this woman said. "You will surrender them."

Anticipating this, I raised the left side of my skirt, surrendering the boot-knife I kept there to the older woman.

The older woman's face didn't change. "Turn around. You're ordered to undress."

"Is Mr. Cesare so afraid of me?"

"I've never met him. You will turn round so I might undo your buttons. Or can you do this yourself?"

This was resistance enough. "I suppose not." I let her unfasten my buttons, holding my dress so my gun didn't clank to the floor.

The woman passed her hands along my bloomers, my petticoats. Then she inspected every inch of my under-corset.

"Oooo," I said, when she inspected the top portion. "What interest might **this** hold?"

The woman snorted. "You're leading with the wrong suit."

I rather thought so, yet my distractions seemed to have worked: in all this time, she'd paid no attention to my dress.

"I'll get you dressed, mum," she said.

I bent to pick the dress up, slid my arms in, and let her do up the buttons, heart pounding. Would she see anything unusual?

She shook out the ruffles. "This way, mum."

"When do I get my knife back?"

Her face turned severe. "Young lady, you should be ashamed of yourself! Cavorting round with weapons like a man instead of home with your husband. But if you must have it, you can find your knife here when you return." She wheeled, marching to the door, then opened it. "Out."

Head high, I strolled past her and the line which had formed at the desk as if she'd not said a thing.

Lance stood waiting outside the door. "They sent my carriage back. Come, this way."

I followed him to a Diamond carriage: white, trimmed in silver. Lance's outriders flanked it.

Inside sat a man a bit older than Jonathan. Like Jon, he had very dark skin and black tight-coiled hair. Yet this man had a thin face and large, mournful eyes. "I'm Mr. Beloty Diamond. I'm here to escort you."

"A pleasure to meet you at last." We'd never actually been introduced. But I'd seen Beloty with his older brothers the day I accompanied Gardena to meet with her blackmailer. "Your brother Jonathan has told me much about you."

Beloty snorted. "I'm sure." Then he sat forward. "How is he?"

"Unwell, last we saw him," Lance said.

Beloty glanced away. "It's as I feared. We need to get him home where he can be cared for."

"His butler seems to be doing a fine job," I said, "and Jon's meticulous about his tonics."

"Yes, well, that's a problem," said Beloty. "Cesare's not allowing anything out of the quadrant."

I stared at him, incredulous. "Not even Jon's medications?"

"No, and instead of being sent to him from Azimoff as usual, they were shipped to the Country House. He only has a few days left before he runs out. Last month, they were shipped to the Manor, which was all that allowed me to smuggle them to him. I'm afraid I'm in Cesare's discard pile for that one."

I blurted, "This is horrendous! Would Cesare kill his youngest brother to keep his quadrant controlled?"

"Well," Beloty said, "he hasn't killed me yet, and I'm right in front of him." He chuckled, then his face turned sad. "Although he may have wished to. But I have men of my own, and he can't afford to lose any more of them."

Lance said, "So it's come to that."

This was bad. If Diamond quadrant descended into civil war, one Family member's faction fighting another, only the Red Dog Gang could benefit. For people who'd gotten used to peace, even the threat of war might be enough to make them abandon their Family. "We have to stop this."

"That's why we're here, Mrs. Spadros." Lance reached into the breast pocket of his jacket and took out two envelopes. "Letters of introduction from our Patriarchs."

I gaped at him. "Roy sent you to recruit me?"

Beloty said to me, "Why did you come here, then, if not to negotiate cease-fire?"

I turned to stare out of the window. "They told me Gardena and Roland were in danger."

"I don't think they are," Beloty said, "but I can see how you might think so. I've been sending my sister's letters to Jon, who's sent on the ones to your husband. But when Cesare learned I'd been doing so —"

Lance said, "He cut you off."

Beloty nodded. "I'm not allowed to send anything to anyone anymore, and I can't go to the Country House. So though I can't tell you how she's faring today, I received a letter from her yesterday. She thinks you're getting her letters and wonders when she might hear from you in return." His jaw tightened. "Damn my brother! At times I wish he'd never been born."

I shook my head. "Don't say that. We must help him see reason. This can't continue if the Families wish to retain hold of Bridges."

Beloty blinked, frowning. "What do you mean?"

My gun was poking into my back. "There is a saboteur, yet his play is more subtle than Cesare knows. This man doesn't plan us direct harm yet, rather he wishes to divide us. But he can't see all the cards." I shifted on the black velvet seat. "I don't think he could have anticipated the group which emerged from his mischief."

Lance and Beloty peered at me, intent on my words.

"My husband and his father in agreement on anything is powerful enough. Yet my husband and the Clubb Heir now have common cause."

Lance nodded slowly, face thoughtful.

"And how could they have anticipated that Mr. Beloty Diamond would slip word to the outside against his brother's command?"

Beloty grinned. "I am rather well-known for my lack of action, sad to say. I hope to change that." But then he sobered. "You think Cesare's being played."

"I do. And that, more than Jon's life or anything else, is why we must help." Maria Athena Spade's pale frightened face flashed before my eyes. "The last person I saw on the other side of their play ended up used and murdered. No matter what Cesare thinks, I won't have his face haunting me, not without a fight."

The Brothers

Crowds roared as we passed, their voices angry. "Why have you not told Jonathan? He thought Gardena wrote to him directly."

Lance and Beloty exchanged a glance. "I didn't want him to know what Cesare's done," Beloty said. "That his own brother would withhold his medication …" He gave me a quick glance, then shook his head. "Hasn't he been hurt enough?"

I didn't open the curtains. I already knew what lay outside: streets of white stone; clear crystals atop wrought-iron lamp-posts; dark-skinned people in bright-colored clothing. Although the guards at the search-house had surely sent word to Cesare, I didn't want anyone to see me yet.

Roy had played me. And worse, he'd used Tony and Jonathan to do it. The thought was infuriating.

Yet I felt glad to see Gardena. It'd been unkind and untrue to call Gardena Tony's mistress, as if they'd had anything other than a few moments of pleasure in their youth.

I think back then I enjoyed upsetting Tony with accusations. I felt he'd abandoned me even before we were married. He certainly hadn't trusted me about Roland, and that was what hurt the most.

"If it makes any difference," Lance said, "I advised against deceiving you in this matter."

The person whose opinion I least cared about wanted me told the truth. Yes, he claimed he loved Gardena. But for all I knew, Lance was his mother's mouthpiece, this outing part of yet another ploy on her part to gain my trust so I might reveal what I knew about the Cathedral to the Clubb Inventor.

I knew nothing about Beloty, save grumblings on Jon's part about work undone. Yet he had men, lands, and an heir. He had influence in Diamond quadrant. And he seemed to want to help.

"Cesare will be at luncheon," Beloty said. "I can't promise he'll let you go to them."

We arrived at Diamond Manor: a beautiful white mansion set off a bit from wrought-iron fencing. Daffodils massed around the wide white stone porch. White roses climbed delicate wooden trellises up the face of the building, parting beside the windows on the second floor to billow under the eaves.

Beloty had disappeared into the house. Lance stood waiting.

A dark-skinned, white-haired man wearing a suit like Pearson's ushered us into a parlor. It reminded me of the parlor at Spadros Manor: white, with gray tile. The furniture was silver-wood, though, and the upholstery, black velvet.

Lance and I were directed to the sofa; I sat, mindful of the gun behind me. A green-eyed maid brought in tea. I ignored it.

An angry commotion of words came from far off, approaching. Then the door burst open and Cesare Diamond walked in.

The tallest of his brothers, with the darkest skin, he usually had a commanding presence, a stately confidence. Today, though, he simply seemed angry. "Why did you bring this creature here?"

I felt sure Cesare would have the upholstery cleaned after a "Pot rag" sat upon it.

Lance and I rose. I said, "Why, Mr. Diamond, how lovely to see you too."

Lance said, "This seems an odd way to greet Family emissaries. Would you care to retreat, sir, and enter again?"

Cesare seemed taken aback, and I'll have to admit I was as well. His eyes narrowed. "You said nothing about bringing her here."

Lance gave a small smile. "You specified nothing about the guard I might bring."

Cesare burst into laughter. "You hide behind a woman's skirt, then claim to represent your Family." He shook his head. "Very well, **boy**. Bring us the message your mother sent."

This was rude even for Cesare. "Now look here, Mr. Diamond, you need us."

"I most certainly do not!"

"Actually, sir," Lance said, "you do. Mobs riot at your train stations. Your men battle your father's. Some of your brothers have been forced to defy you to save the life of another, who you at this moment are allowing to die. Whether out of spite, hate, or," Lance shuddered, "some other emotion, all this turmoil is on you."

Cesare frowned at him. "How can you say this?"

Did he really not see? "You chose to seize your father —"

"He was driving us into ruin!"

"— and you chose to expel your brother from his home —"

"He was sending everything I told him to your beast of a husband, a man who attacked my sister and now wants to take her son from his home."

I'd heard enough. "Are you mad? Really. Are you?"

For once, Cesare Diamond had nothing to say.

"Because if you knew anything about my husband, you'd know his fault is that he's too forbearing by half. If I were a man, and a woman I loved seduced me —"

Lance flinched.

"— then I was not only accused of rape but then prevented from seeing my child, **as is my right**, I'd have torn this quadrant apart long since."

Cesare's eyebrows rose.

"You have sons. Would you not have done the same?"

"I would never have been so dishonorable as to lie with her in the first place!"

I just stood there, arms crossed.

His eyes narrowed. "Perhaps."

I snorted. "I'm glad you might consider it, for your sons' sake."

Cesare frowned. "What am I to do with you?" His face contorted in distaste, and he spoke to Lance. "How can you expect me to sit a Pot rag at table in Diamond quadrant?"

"For better or worse," Lance said calmly, "this is the Lady of Spadros. If you can't receive her as such, we'll go. But the wrath of the Families will be upon you."

The Families? It sounded as if Lance meant the Hart Family as well. Why? Was Mr. Hart's fascination with me so great that he would send his quadrant into war against a sworn ally over a slight to my honor?

Lance had not moved. "I am deadly serious," he said. "I wish I were not."

I studied Cesare's face as it went from irritation to consideration to doubt. He gave me a quick glance. "Very well. Follow me."

"Good job, that," I whispered to Lance, who gave a small snort in reply.

In some ways, Lance Clubb was like Tony: soft-spoken, always in control of himself. Yet his control seemed to come from a poised confidence, rather than the mask Tony placed over his anxieties.

Cesare led us to a long dining room, narrower than that at Spadros Manor and with the only doors at either end. Beloty and three of his other brothers — not Jack, to my great relief — were seated there, standing when we entered.

Cesare gestured to them. "Mr. Vienna Diamond, Mr. Moretti Diamond, Mr. Hector Diamond II —"

"Please," Mr. Hector said quickly, "My friends call me Quadri."

Cesare glared at him. "May I present Master Lancelot Clubb and," he hesitated, "Mrs. Jacqueline Spadros."

The others bowed, murmuring greetings. We were seated halfway down the table, Lance across from me.

This was the place of the guest; family sat at either end. Those nearest the head were the eldest, the closest family, the most trusted of his main men, or highly honored guests.

As Family emissaries, we should have been seated next to Cesare; that we weren't said much.

The foot of the table was empty.

"My wife has taken luncheon in her rooms," Cesare said.

I nodded, well aware I was the only woman in the room. Not even maids served us.

The food was good, if a bit dry. We'd arrived late, then been forced to delay whilst enduring Cesare's rants, so I didn't blame the cooks for it.

Footmen took the plates away. After a quick glance at Cesare, Vienna said to me, "How is Jon?"

"Concerned for his people. And when I last saw him, unwell."

Vienna glanced away, jaw set, then crossed his arms.

"That's why we're here," Lance said. Then he glanced at the butler. "But perhaps we might discuss this in private?"

Cesare stood. "Let's pass through to the drawing room, and let the servants do their work."

Cesare led us to a smaller room with a grand piano in one corner. Six straight-backed armchairs were set three feet apart in an oval around the low coffee table in front of the unlit fireplace. Seven of us stood there.

No one was going shut me out of this game. "How kind of you, sir." I immediately went to the fireplace and sat, a twinge of pain as the muzzle of my hidden gun hit my tail-bone.

Cesare turned to Lance, chagrined. "We didn't expect your 'guard' to sit with us. I'll —"

"I'll get another chair," Beloty said quickly. He returned with one in a slightly different style, then the men sat, Lance beside me.

Cesare sat directly across from me, leaned back, and crossed one ankle over his knee. "You claimed we have need of you. Why?"

"Don't be obtuse," I said. "You've gotten yourself in a fix. Or were the crowds on the way here clamoring in love of your rule?"

Lance fixed his attention upon Cesare. "That's neither here nor there. I signed intent to courtship in good faith. Now I'm neither allowed to see your sister nor receive her letters. And Anthony Spadros has similar complaint in the matter of his son."

That last was a tricky matter. Tony did have legal right to see Roland, but that came at a price. Gardena's father Julius had marked on Roland's birth certificate that Tony had violated Gardena. The charge had been suppressed by the Spadros Family, but it put her into some difficulty. Her only other two legal choices were birth due to marriage or whoredom.

Since Gardena was as yet unmarried, if Tony were to contest the charge that he'd violated her, she and Roland could technically be sent to the Pot.

Not that she'd actually go there, but she'd have to leave Bridges, and in the midst of huge scandal. No one involved wanted that.

Unless Tony married her, Lance's offer of marriage was her only means of a decent life, and Cesare had fouled that up with his grasp for power.

I leaned forward, if only to take the pressure off my tail-bone. "We're not here to harm you. All I care about is —" What did I care about in this? "This war has been mild in comparison to the last one. But I lived in the Pot, sir, and I won't have another child go through the terror I did when your father brought men to attack the Cathedral and drag its women away."

Cesare blinked, his face shocked. "My father would never —"

"Oh, I'm sure he didn't order it. But that's what happens in war. And I'll be damned if I see my homeland invaded just because you hate your father."

Cesare drew back. "I don't hate my father!"

His brothers began to speak all at once.

"She's right!"

"I've seen the way you talk about him —"

"You hit that on the head!"

Beloty only sat there, arms crossed, gazing downward. "Then why seize him in the dead of night whilst he slept? I never thought you capable of this —"

Cesare was livid. "How dare you?"

Lance held up a hand. "Let the man speak."

"— but since we're finally speaking our minds, I'll say it. This was cowardly, Cesare. It was dishonorable. I expected more."

Cesare leaned forward, pointing at his brother. "He would not listen to reason! We had spies in Diamond quadrant, spies which could have ruined us —" He turned to Lance and I. "Ruined both of your households as well. It was your quadrant's intrigue, Clubb, that made me know I could never let my sister go there."

Lance said, "So you're defying my agreement with your father?"

"Until you prove she'll be safe."

Lance crossed his arms. "Those involved in the intrigue have been disposed of."

Cesare's eyes narrowed. "I'll be the judge of that." Then he continued, "And when I learned of my mother's lies, which I'm sure you know all about now —"

But from Lance's face, I wasn't sure the Clubb Family — the "spy-masters of Bridges" — even knew.

After her accident eight years earlier, Rachel Diamond made everyone believe she was mentally incapable. She was physically incapable, and as a former Inventor's Apprentice held both the secrets of the Apprentices and of the Diamond Family. So she hid the truth, even from her own children. "She did what she thought best. I only regret her desire to help me put her into danger."

"She lied to us," Cesare snapped. "And now her lies have been exposed, I had to protect this Family. No one else would do it."

Lance said, "I want to see Gardena. Mrs. Spadros must verify Master Roland's safety." His tone turned stern. "Will we be allowed to do that?"

Cesare considered this, hand to his lips. "I've had my integrity questioned, asked if I were mad, then called a coward and a fool. If I'm deemed so unworthy of your trust, my word that my sister and her bastard are unharmed would hardly convince you."

Just the fact that he'd call his own nephew a "bastard" made me doubt his intentions. "You make no pretense that you hate the entire Spadros Family. According to you, Anthony Spadros is a beast who violated your sister. Why would you care what happened to his son? When you prevent my husband from seeing the boy, we can only imagine the worst. Does he still live? Is he well? Is he even being kept with his mother? We don't know unless we see him."

Cesare rose. "We will go. Now, us three, without your men."

Lance blinked. "Without my men? For what reason?"

"No one must know where they are," Cesare said. "I'll prove to you I'm not imagining things."

"But I swore to the Spadros Heir his Lady would be protected by my men!"

I just imagined how Tony would react. "My husband will become alarmed! I can't be held accountable for what he — or Roy Spadros, for that matter — may do."

"Those are my terms," Cesare said. "Take them, or leave."

A knock on the door, and the butler entered. "There's a problem, sir. You're needed at once."

Lance and I looked at each other. I felt unsure what to do, so I watched Cesare leave, closing the door behind him.

"You've spoken exactly right," Quadri said. "Thank you for making him see reason. We agreed to help him. But we never imagined it would come to this."

"It's not over yet," I said. If Gardena and Roland were indeed well, we still had a war to stop. And that might take more doing.

"Tell them we miss them," Moretti said.

"Yes," Vienna said. "Tell Rollie we love him, and hope to see him soon."

Moved, I said, "I will."

Cesare opened the door. Leaning upon Cesare's arm, bruised and bleeding, was Morton.

The Quandry

"Give him a chair," Vienna said. Beloty went to fetch another; Morton sagged into his.

I said, "I see you've again lost your hat."

Morton let out a bitter laugh, then winced. "It was a trap. And my friend is dead." Then he turned to Cesare. "Sorry to barge in like this. I had nowhere else to turn."

"Think nothing of it," Cesare said.

The butler came in, followed by a maid with a tray-table and another with a washbasin and cloth. These she set before Morton.

I peered at Lance Clubb, who'd gone pale, eyes wide. "Are you two acquainted?"

Lance hesitated. "I don't believe we've been introduced."

Morton's face turned amused. "Master Blaze Rainbow, sir, at your service."

If Lance felt squeamish about a little blood, he had much to learn. "Master Rainbow and I are currently business partners." I turned to Morton. "But it looks like you've had a rough day."

Cesare had been watching the exchange. He said to me, "So your husband knows this man."

Before I might answer, Morton said, "Indeed he does."

Lance said, "As does my father. If he were allowed to accompany us, this might allay the fears of my men."

Cesare's eyes narrowed. "That would be acceptable."

Morton glanced at the three of us. "Where are we going?"

I shrugged. "To visit Miss Gardena. That's all I know."

Morton smiled. "Ah, to be regaled about the wonders of the newest bonnet!" He turned to Lance. "And the details of your courtship, when last we conversed at length."

Lance blushed, glancing away. "I hope she's found it pleasant."

"Forgive me," Morton said lightly. "When you've just escaped death, you tend to joke on matters quite serious to others."

"Think nothing of it," Lance said. "Are you badly hurt?"

Morton shrugged. "I've suffered worse." He grasped the washcloth. "Let me clean up, then I should be ready to go."

Even with Morton's help, it took some time for Lance to persuade his men to return to the quadrant without us. Cesare sent men to ensure they did.

Once Lance's men were out of sight, Lance, Morton, and I boarded a Diamond carriage, hooded in its entirety with a thick black cloth. Air could get in, yet it made for a hot and stuffy ride.

Cesare rode in his own carriage. Although he'd accompanied Jonathan and I once during my trial, perhaps that day, riding in a carriage with a Pot rag went beyond what even he might endure.

We rode for at least an hour, perhaps two, in the hot, humid air under the cloak. Lance spoke little, and Morton not at all.

I woke when the carriage stopped. The cloak was removed, and there we sat under the portico of what I presumed to be the Diamond Country House.

To my left, past the white columns standing upon thick stone, lay a wide grassy area in bright afternoon sun ringed by a driveway. Black sheep with curled horns grazed nearby; apple trees lay past the field beyond.

"Mrs. Spadros?"

A pale-skinned footman dressed in Diamond livery held the carriage door open.

So I let him help me out of the carriage and onto the white stone walkway, carpeted in deep gray.

Lance, Morton, and I followed Cesare through a set of stout white doors into a wide stone courtyard. Tall, thin openings appeared at intervals, like narrow windows without glass. Archways sat to our right, left, and ahead, with hallways beyond.

Armed guards stood round its walls. Mounds of flowering plants grew beside them. A silver-gray stone fountain stood in the middle, surrounded by black and white tile. "This is lovely."

Cesare's voice held a smirk. "So glad you enjoy it. Now, if you'll come this way?"

Turning to the right, we moved across the courtyard to the foot-thick archway there, then to the left. More tall, narrow openings showed a grassy area, where dark-skinned children played.

"My young cousins," Cesare said. "Perhaps to bring you here shows my madness. Or perhaps, my goodwill. No outsider has been inside this place since before the Coup."

"So how does my husband see his son?"

"We have several smaller areas," Cesare said, "much like this. One is near enough to Spadros quadrant that it makes a convenient meeting-place."

This was ingenious. If one were to spread the word that each was indeed the secure Country House, then an attacker would have to investigate more thoroughly before attacking, and might possibly reveal themselves. I glanced through a narrow window: it was a foot deep. I felt impressed. "This place is well-defensible."

Cesare gave a thin smile. "I hope it'll never need to be defended." We approached another archway opening onto another grassy courtyard, and Cesare gestured to his right. "This way."

Cesare brought us down one corridor, then another. Three levels of courtyards, some with families relaxing in the sun, others with children playing, then a sturdy door flanked by the same thin windows opened onto a wall sporting a row of hooks. "You may leave your hats here," Cesare said. A few coats hung there already. The men and I hung our hats upon the hooks, Morton having borrowed one of Quadri's before we left.

We moved to the left around what seemed to be a wall, but was indeed a huge rectangular pillar. The floor was of pale gray tile, and led down a flight of steps to the main entryway. Inside, it was much like Diamond Manor; if I hadn't gone past all those courtyards I might believe myself to be there.

Doors stood all round, and a grand staircase ahead. Taking hold of its black banister, Cesare led us up to the second floor and to the right, then knocked at a door to his left. "They're here."

"Oh," Gardena said, "come in."

Gardena Diamond most resembled her brothers Jonathan and Jack, who other than Jack's affectation of shaving his head, were identical in appearance. That is to say, she was beautiful. Dark-skinned with a fine figure, she wore a deep purple house dress, her raven curls down around her shoulders. A deep blue headband pulled her hair off her face. She beamed when she saw me; when she saw Lance, I thought she might faint. "You came for me."

Lance gave her a fond smile. "I did."

Cesare seemed taken aback by her reaction. "I'll allow you to speak in private, then."

When Cesare closed the door, Gardena burst into tears.

I rushed to embrace her.

"I'm s-so glad t-to see you." Gardena sobbed into my ear. "You have n-no idea."

Lance handed her a handkerchief.

I drew back to survey her. "Are you being treated well? Is Roland safe?"

She nodded, wiping her eyes and nose. "But I know nothing of what's happened. Something's wrong: I can feel it."

Lance said, "Beloty has smuggled your letters out — and theirs in — for some time."

I thought it better not to mention Jon's predicament. "Cesare caught him."

Gardena said, "What's **wrong** with him? Why is he doing this?"

"He's afraid," I said quietly, aware he might be behind the door listening. "This began with protecting you and your mother from real threat. But now he's trapped. It's something Jonathan said, oh, a year back, maybe more. Cesare doesn't want to bring shame to your Family like he feels your father did when he backed down in the Diamond-Spadros war."

Gardena slowly nodded. "You're here to help him? After how he's treated you?"

I let out a breath. "Dena, he saved my life. Surely that's worth something." I blinked back sudden tears. "He spoke for me when no one else would. I have to hope I can reach him before he destroys himself."

Morton still stood by the door. "How do you plan to do that?"

The far door to my left opened. "Mommy?" Roland Anthony Spadros, a boy of six, held a tan stuffed bear and a patterned pastel quilt with one hand, rubbing his eyes with the other. "I heard someone cry." Brown skin and eyes, black ringlet curls. He was taller, and his hair had been cut recently, but he looked well.

Roland looked so much like Tony, save his coloration, that no one could mistake who his father was. Perhaps the Diamonds were right to keep the boy hidden.

Gardena rushed over to put her arm around his shoulders. "All's well, my love. Look who came to see us."

His face lit up. "Master Lance!" Dropping the bear and quilt, he ran to hug Lance's legs. Then he looked at up me, confused.

I knelt before him. "I'm Jacqui. Remember? You visited me when I was sick."

He beamed at me. "You were at the cottage with the cows. I saw my Daddy there."

"Yes, you did." I felt impressed that a child might remember something two years past.

"And this is Master Rainbow," Gardena said. "He's our friend. And your Daddy's friend, too."

Roland approached Morton, his hand out.

Morton bent over to shake it. "A pleasure to meet you, sir."

Roland ran to his mother to hide his face in her skirts.

Gardena chuckled, resting a hand on Roland's hair. "We'll have to work on that."

Morton straightened. "A fine boy you have there."

Gardena blushed. "You're very kind."

I turned to Gardena. "I'd like to freshen up. Might you assist me?" All quadrant-women wore split-crotch bloomers, so I didn't really need help and Gardena knew it. But the men didn't. This was the perfect opportunity to get her alone.

She glanced at Lance, then smiled at me. "Of course." To Roland, she said, "Perhaps the gentlemen would like to see your new toys!"

Roland beamed proudly. "Sirs, come this way."

After using Gardena's toilet-room, I felt much better. While washing my hands, I said, "Dena, are you and Roland truly well?"

Gardena smiled fondly, yet seemed sad. "Anthony must be flying into pieces to send you here."

He hated being called that. And I didn't want to talk about Tony. "How can we help? Do you want to leave?"

"This is the only home Roland's ever known." She went to the door. "Let me think on it." When she opened the door, everyone stood waiting. She said to Roland, "Would you like to see Nana? It's almost time for tea."

Roland beamed. "Yes, I would." Then he said to Lance, "Do you know my Nana? She got all better from being sick."

Gardena grimaced: apparently this was one of the things Lance wasn't supposed to know about.

Lance and I exchanged a glance. "We've been introduced." Then he smiled at Gardena. "We would have learned of it sooner or later. I'm just grateful she's well."

* * *

Gardena led us to another room down the hall, guarded by two men. Mr. Julius and Mrs. Rachel Diamond sat there. An attractive couple in their later forties, they both rose when we entered, Mrs. Diamond much more slowly than he.

While working on an electrical mechanism, Mrs. Rachel Diamond had suffered electrocution of the brain. Due to this, her body had been considerably weakened.

When Roland saw them, he rushed over, chattering in excitement about our visit.

Julius Diamond crossed his arms. "Why are they here?"

Gardena said, "They've come to help."

He said to Lance. "You wanna help, get me a gun so I can shoot that no-good son of mine."

"Father!" Gardena seemed shocked. "You don't mean that!"

"He's kept us locked up a year! And for what?" He then seemed to notice me. "You again. Now we're all here, you gonna stand around and gloat?"

Now that we're all here? "We came to make sure you were well."

"You mean that your husband's boy was well." Julius let out a bitter laugh, shaking his head. "Someone done that to me, I woulda shot him."

I said, "Perhaps matters are more complex than they seem."

"Well, then," Mrs. Diamond said slowly, "what shall we do?"

"The first thing we'll do," Cesare said from the open doorway, "is go downstairs and have tea."

* * *

Julius glared at Cesare. But since Julius was unarmed and Cesare had several men with him, everyone went quietly.

Roland held my hand as we went down the stairs, the rest trailing behind. "Grandpa says Uncle Chessy's bad," he said quietly. "But Uncle Chessy's nice. He plays with me."

"Sometimes grownups say things they don't mean," I said, just as quietly. "And they stay angry longer than they should. They love you. That's what matters."

Roland smiled to himself, his steps becoming bouncy. "Will I see my Daddy soon?"

"I don't know, sweetie. He wants to see you very much."

"I hope so. I really like my Daddy."

My eyes stung. "He really likes you, too."

We waited at the bottom of the staircase for the rest to descend. Then Cesare led us to the dining room, which was similar to that at Diamond Manor.

Octavia Diamond, a woman near twenty with tawny skin and long blonde curls, waited at the door. "Come, Master Roland, let's go to your play room for tea!"

The rest of us went into the dining room. To my horror, Cesare took the head of the table, and a lovely, very dark-skinned woman I'd not seen before took the foot.

This must be his wife, I thought.

But they'd relegated the King and Queen of Diamonds to the place of children!

Footmen brought platters of sandwiches and small cakes. Maids poured tea.

"May I present my wife, Mrs. Furaha Diamond," Cesare said.

Morton, Lance, and I nodded, murmuring our greetings.

"Just as much a snake as my son," Julius said. "Don't trust either of them."

Cesare's wife folded her hands, lips pursed.

"Now that we're all here," Cesare said, as if his father hadn't just insulted his wife, "this seems an appropriate time to begin. You've seen Gardena and Roland. You've verified they're well. What do Clubb and Spadros quadrants offer in return?"

Lance frowned. "Seeing Gardena was part of the agreement signed by your father as Patriarch of the Diamond Family. I'll not have her turned into some bargaining chip."

I felt glad he'd said this. "Nor I Roland."

Julius and Cesare nodded in unison, then glared at each other.

I said, "What is it you want? And don't pretend all goes well, or that your people are behind you. You should want this over as much as anyone."

Cesare hesitated. "We'll discuss this later."

Hmm, I thought. He doesn't want to talk in front of his father. "Very well. We'll each negotiate for our quadrants."

Roy said to find out what they wanted. He said nothing about signing agreements. But I'd gotten into the quadrant, and he hadn't.

Maybe he'd treat others better in the future.

Julius burst out laughing. "If Roy Spadros deputized a Pot rag woman, then I'm a silk purse." He wiped his eyes with his napkin. "I wish I was there when you tell him."

I looked at him sideways. "Your son has my letter of introduction."

Lance leaned back, a small smile on his lips.

Cesare's eyes narrowed, but he said nothing.

Julius leaned back. "It's clear I'm being dealt out." Then he pointed at me and Lance. "You might settle with Cesare, but when I'm back in the game, you'll have to contend with me."

"That's not our intent," Lance said. "The position of Clubb quadrant is that you're the rightful Patriarch."

Cesare turned to me. "And what does Spadros quadrant say?"

I had no idea what Roy thought. "The same."

Cesare frowned. "So I'm a usurper."

"No," I said. "You did what you felt best for your Family. Now that your father has recovered, he'll lead once more."

Julius roared, "Recovered?"

Lance gave me a quick glance. "It would settle your men, sir. And explain matters to your people."

"It's a bold-faced lie," Julius said. "I like it. And you," he pointed at Cesare, "are to be taken out back and whipped."

Several around the table — myself, Cesare's wife, Gardena — shouted, "No!"

I did notice that Mrs. Rachel Diamond stayed silent. And Morton hadn't spoken the entire time.

"Father," Gardena said softly, "Cesare sees now how difficult your job is." She glanced at her brother. "Doesn't he?"

Cesare's shoulders drooped. "Sad to say, I do." Then he straightened. "I would take the whip if I thought you'd be man enough to give it, rather than palm it off to some servant."

Julius Diamond had his own child ... **whipped**?

Julius frowned. "This is about what happened to you as a **boy**?"

No wonder Cesare hated his father!

Cesare leaned forward, pointing at his father. "You shamed us all! Giving in to Roy Spadros over a threat to," his tone turned disgusted, "a **girl** —"

"Your sister," I said.

"— when you could have sent her away, pressed the attack, and won! Why else would he make such a low threat, if not in fear?"

I scoffed. "You don't understand anything. Roy Spadros lives to make others afraid." I leaned back, gaining a sudden insight. "Probably why he sent me here."

Cesare stared at me. "He was winning!"

"Yeah," Julius said, "he was. He reminded me he's got most of the ray cannon —"

Morton froze.

What Tony said at the Queen's Night dinner flashed through my mind, and the abject terror with which he'd said it: *we're not anywhere near ready*.

And I recalled the hulking machine the Apprentice was working on when I visited the Magma Steam Generator. The huge sheet-covered shapes in the storage room by Tony's bedroom.

Something was wrong with our ray cannon.

But no one else knew that.

The audacity!

"— and it wasn't even up to me in any case. Your Grandpa Hector was Patriarch." Julius let out a breath. "We have the cannon Caesar Diamond seized the night of the Coup. But Roy's got the rest. Why do you think the other Families haven't stopped him? In one day, he could turn Bridges into a smoking ruin."

Lance stared at Julius in horror.

Cesare lowered his head, and when he raised it, his eyes were red. "I owe you an apology."

Julius tilted his head to the side with a faint smile, giving his son a slow nod.

Lance turned to me. "So why **does** Spadros want peace with Diamond? What's in it for him?"

Heart pounding, I considered this. Roy had a problem: Tony had no heir. I was all that stood in the way of Tony gaining a legitimate heir, and Tony refused to divorce me.

If Cesare had me killed, it would solve Roy's problem. Yet I kept recalling the things Roy had said, the changes in him towards me.

Tony said he'd wept when told about Roland. Wept!

Something's wrong, I thought. Could Roy be sick? "He mentioned the casino was losing money. And he didn't want more violence in our quadrant. To which I heartily agree." Particularly since they'd do most of their fighting in the Pot. "But I think he's worried about Roland. And he seemed to have genuine concern for Cesare's situation."

Cesare's eyes narrowed. "Since when does that monster care about anyone but himself?"

"Sometimes things change when you get older," Rachel Diamond said slowly, her words slurring just a bit. "You see things differently. You regret things that you've done."

This was certainly true in my case.

"Cesare, my love," his wife said, in her voice a hint of an accent I'd not heard before, "we have a chance to retreat with honor. Is that not what you hoped for?"

Cesare seemed to seriously consider this.

Someone banged on the door.

Cesare snapped, "What is it?"

A man rushed into the room. "We're under attack!"

The Battle

The men rushed to the door.

I followed them down the stairs, across the front hall, and up the steps, then through the maze of corridors to the entrance, armed men joining us as we ran. We hugged the walls beside the main door as one of Cesare's men quickly opened it.

And the fortress was indeed under attack.

The terrible rat-ta-tat-tat of the Tommy gun faced us, with only the columns and a foot-thick four foot high barrier protecting the portico. The men guarding the portico were down, bleeding. And the men against us were advancing.

We crouched down, hurrying through the doorway then scattering to each side, chips of concrete, tile, and wood flying as the bullets hit. I hid beside a bush near the thick, heavy door, pulling it shut behind me with some effort while the others moved beside the men already positioned there.

One of Cesare's men handed him a revolver, and after an instant's hesitation, Cesare handed it to Lance, then took another.

Morton drew his weapon. Julius grabbed a gun from the hand of one of the fallen men.

I undid the bow in front of my dress which held my loaded gun in place and let Tenni's holster sag to the ground behind me. Then I moved aside, took up the pouch, removed my little revolver, and chambered a round.

Cesare stared back across the driveway at me in horror. Then he scrambled to my side. "What are you doing here? How did you get that gun?"

I cocked the hammer. "Jonathan gave it to me long ago."

A pale-skinned man had crept behind the barricade line and taken aim at Cesare's back. I shot the man in the head.

Cesare's hands flew to his ears. He glanced behind him, then at me, face astonished. But he quickly recovered. "Stay here. Cover our flanks. We can't let anyone else get through."

I nodded at his back as he rejoined the other men. I only had six bullets — well, now five — so the plan made sense.

The door behind me was set over two feet into the wall. A thick column stood directly in front of me. From where I was, anyone approaching from either side wouldn't be able to see me, but I could see them once they cleared the barricade. The death of the man who'd taken aim at Cesare, though, seemed to dissuade them from such tactics.

Men fell on both sides. I heard shots from high above me. In the distance, dark-skinned men in Diamond livery approached us along the white walls, shooting as they went.

The gunfire towards us stopped, and a round gray ball came flying up. Without thinking, I stood, took a step back, let it ease into my hand, as I would a stick-ball rock. But then, I felt a sudden burst of anger: *how dare you throw rocks at me?*

So I side-arm threw it as hard as I could between the columns and far back beyond. Halfway in flight, it burst in the air with a terrible loud noise which startled and surprised me.

I huddled down in alarm, unsure what was happening. Screams came from those prone upon the field.

People have asked me since how or why I did it. At the time, it was just like throwing a ball.

Several of the men on our side of the barricade turned to gape at me. Morton had a look somewhere between disbelief and terror. Lance's face was white.

Sounding close to panic, Cesare shouted, "Lower the shield!"

Down came a metal grid in front of the columns somewhat similar to the mesh screen in front of the windows back home, only this was made of what looked to be the same wrought iron as inside the Hedge: black, the thickness of a man's thumb, with spaces between well large enough for the muzzle of a gun.

Bullets rang upon the shield. I felt impressed by this: they'd have no further explosions back here.

From the road to our right, carriages flanked with horsemen came into view, and the attackers began to shout in horror. Some moved towards the new threat, Tommy-guns blazing. Others turned to our left and ran. A few of those were hit by the men on horseback, and fell.

Cesare shouted to Morton, "I want them alive!"

Morton ran with Cesare's men towards the retreating attackers.

Dark-skinned men holding guns poured out from the carriages. But it seemed the remaining attackers had spent too much of their firepower upon us. We watched as the invaders, relatively few in number, threw their guns aside and surrendered.

Cesare came up to me. "Are you mad? What possessed you to lay hands upon a live grenade?"

"Is that what that was?" I never even considered doing anything else. I brandished my gun. "Would you rather be dead?" I snorted, remembering what Tony had said once. "Because I can oblige."

Cesare grabbed the gun from my hand. "Give me that thing." He touched the muzzle gingerly, then cleared the chamber and stuck it in the back of his waistband. "Those guard women have much to account for."

"Don't blame them," I said. "I'd hidden it well."

Cesare drew back, shaking his head a bit, eyes wide. "I don't want to know any of this."

I laughed, surprised by the conclusion he'd come to.

Julius Diamond held a pistol to his son's head. "Not so fast."

Clicks came from Cesare's men all round, pointed at Mr. Julius.

Julius glanced around, then waved the gun at Cesare's men. "Every one of you here are dead."

Cesare said, "You should have shot us when you had the chance." He took his father's gun, handing it to one of his men. "Bring him to his room."

A man at each arm and two behind him, Patriarch Julius Diamond was taken away, shouting insults the entire time.

This won't end well, I thought. Then I noticed a dark stain on the outside of Cesare's left upper arm. "You've been shot."

He scowled, cheeks reddening, then grabbed my arm roughly. "Come along, you."

I could have protested, I suppose, yet in the surprise at his daring to lay hands upon me, I never did. I was more concerned about his injury and curious as to where he might be taking me.

Back along the corridors we went, Lance shouting angrily from behind. I wasn't afraid. Cesare didn't seem angry. If anything, I'd say he was embarrassed.

A "Pot rag" had saved his life, and not once but twice.

As we went, though, what I'd done began to fall upon me. The suddenness of the firefight. The terrible explosion in the field. How close I'd come to dying. My hands began to shake, my heart to pound. My vision faded in and out, and I felt glad Cesare had hold of my arm, for at times, I might have fallen.

After swiftly navigating the maze of corridors, we went to a new door facing a tile courtyard. This door opened onto a rectangular-shaped windowless sitting room lit by a bare bulb overhead.

It reminded me very much of Sawbuck's parlor: nothing on the walls, a few unfinished chairs around a matching round table, a sofa along one side. There was no fireplace, though, nor mantle, and the far wall lay completely bare, its stone chipped and marred with dark splatters poorly cleansed.

A chill came over me. They question people here, I thought. And some, they kill.

Cesare launched me towards the table. "Sit down."

I collapsed into one of the chairs, trying not to let my voice shake. "You must admit I aided you."

"Quiet!"

"I want my gun back."

Lance burst into the room, followed by Cesare's men. "How dare you lay hands upon her?"

"She brought a weapon into my home," Cesare said, "then threatened my life."

"She saved your life! You had no right —"

Weary, I raised a hand; they both turned toward me. "If I wanted you dead, Mr. Diamond, you'd be dead. Stop playing the boy and sit down."

Cesare pointed at his men. "Out." Once they'd left, he leaned his fists upon the table. "A plague upon you and your house and Family!" He glanced at Lance, who still stood there, fists clenched. "For gods' sake, sit down. The Pot rag's unharmed, although I don't know why you care so much."

Lance glared at him. "You're just as much a scoundrel as your father."

Cesare smiled, but it was unpleasant. "Compare me to him again, and I may just kill you."

"Well, unless you intend to kill us now," I said, feeling shaky, "might we sit somewhere that doesn't smell like blood?"

It didn't, really, but it amused me the way Cesare jumped a bit, sniffing the air as we left. I felt pleased that I'd guessed correctly.

I don't know why I'd been so afraid earlier: for all his bold talk, Cesare couldn't kill us. The guards at the Diamond bridge knew who we were, which meant by now much of Diamond quadrant also knew. And of course, our people knew as well.

But it went beyond that. We'd arrived as emissaries of the Families. And his people already didn't trust him. If we were harmed, Cesare's fragile hold on the quadrant would shatter.

Here's why. The people of Diamond might object to an alliance with Spadros quadrant. But what they really feared was Roy Spadros rampaging through their quadrant unchecked, snatching people off the streets to feed his lust for torture.

And although my status amongst the high-cards of Spadros quadrant was in question, to the low-cards, I was the Lady of

Spadros, who'd come down from on high to live amongst them out of love and sympathy for my people's suffering. Or whatever Roy's current propaganda rag said. If I were killed, Roy would be forced to react or see most of his quadrant in riot.

Besides, Lance had been right: if three Families joined in attack, no one quadrant could stand. Anyone with half a deck knew it.

Cesare brought me and Lance to a much nicer sitting-room, with proper furniture and a rug pattered in green, gray, and white. "Jonathan likes this room," Cesare said, almost as if to himself. The door closed behind us. "Perhaps you will too."

Cesare hadn't asked after his brother the entire time. "Why do you threaten Jon's life? Keep him from his family and home?"

Lance took a step back, mouth open, as if he'd forgotten Jonathan entirely.

Cesare snapped, "That's none of your concern."

"Jon's my dearest friend. If I'd have known his life was in danger, I'd have been here long before this. That his eldest brother would do this to him," for a moment, I faltered, "it sickens me. Do you really believe he's a spy, and a Spadros one at that?"

"To my face he's named the Spadros Heir his brother," Cesare said. "That's enough to convince me. He may be Diamond-born, but he's sworn to our enemy." He shook his head angrily. "I'll be damned if I have him here."

"So you would kill your brother for having a loyal friend. Don't you see what you're doing? Instead of punishing him for reaching across the river in friendship, you should use his regard for my husband as a way to prosper your people."

"Ally with Roy Spadros? Are you mad? Right now, my people march under the banner 'Better Die Than Ally.' They were in riot at even the thought of such a thing."

He grasped the other side of the frame with his free hand, head bowed. The dark stain on his left upper arm had grown. His words were quiet, yet he sounded furious. "You come here to whisper poison to my face whilst holding a knife to my back." Then his head raised. "Well, I won't have it."

"You don't have to ally with Roy." I recalled the white in Roy's hair, the weariness upon his face. His words to me in my parlor a few days earlier. "Roy's not going to be here forever. Think of your quadrant's future."

He didn't respond.

How might I sway him? "Roland is Spadros as much as he is Diamond. Through Roland, our Families have a bond. Even a secret alliance with my husband could aid you much. The boy might become heir to Spadros, Diamond, **and** Clubb. Sooner or later, he'll have to step forward."

Lance's face turned thoughtful.

Hadn't Lance considered this long before he asked to court Gardena? To me it seemed obvious.

Cesare looked skeptical. "Not if I have anything to say about it."

"Why? It's true: Roland's young." A small laugh burst from me. "Much too young **now**. But he has a good mind and a kind heart. One day he could lead this city as Mayor, should he wish to. Perhaps in time he could even unite the Families, improve the city. But he'll need help. He'll need training. Who better to guide him than his beloved Uncle Chessy?"

Cesare flinched at the name.

I sighed inwardly, wondering if my mission was hopeless. Then I tried another tack. "Our Patriarchs have too much history between them to bring a real settlement. But look at the boy's face! His father's identity is plain for anyone to see. What has happened will come to light sooner or later; you and my husband must be ready. Make plans as to how to present him. Together."

His face didn't change. What would make him see reason? "Peace between our quadrants is the only way to keep Roland safe! If you were already allied with my husband when the news came out, you'd be seen as the man who brought forth that peace."

Cesare turned to me. "Is that what this is all about? To coerce me to join with you?"

"No," I said, feeling at sea. "Don't you understand? We mean you no harm. We want peace with your quadrant. My husband is not his father. Your brother sees it. Why can't you?"

Cesare said nothing.

I leaned upon a side table which stood next to the wall, feeling weak, shaky. "I was asked not to speak of it. But I'll tell you what this is about."

Lance looked at me, alarmed. "Mrs. Spadros —"

I held up my hand. Nothing more than the truth would work here. "Why Roy said he wanted me here, at any rate. He wants the Inventors — all the Inventors — to meet, in hope that we can restart the trains."

Cesare said, "Are you mad? I'm not letting my young cousin anywhere near that scoundrel."

"Roy doesn't have to be there," I said. "He said nothing about wishing to attend."

Lance said quickly, "You can be there yourself, if it would ease your mind."

Cesare hesitated.

Lance hesitated as well, which surprised me.

Cesare frowned at him. "What else is there I don't know?"

Lance paled. "The Feds know about the trains —"

I gasped, stunned.

"— and my father fears that if we wait much longer, the Feds may put a Motion of Seizure against the city."

This was bad.

Bridges was an independent city-state chartered from the Merca Federal Union. But by the charter, if we couldn't show a working government or the ability to control the dome's mechanisms, the Feds had a waiting list of those more capable.

Cities had been seized before, the entire population scattered and exiled, their lands taken. Not only taken, bulldozed to create the city others envisioned for their culture, the one they thought more enlightened than ours.

Bridges had barely escaped seizure after the Coup. It'd only been the traitor Xavier Alcatraz seizing power with the backing of the Spadros Family that had persuaded the Feds not to act.

Cesare hadn't reacted to Lance's news. I said, "What do you plan to do?"

"Let me think on it," Cesare said.

I held out my hand. "While you're deciding, I want my gun back. Jonathan gave that to me, and I won't have it lost."

Cesare reached behind his waistband and pulled out my gun. After removing the bullets and putting them in his pocket, he handed it over.

I decided to ignore the unspoken insult: he clearly didn't trust me, even after I saved his life. But I had a hundred bucks in the bank! I could buy bullets any time.

Tenni's holster had been lost in all the commotion, so I wiped the gun off with my dress, checked to make sure the chamber was clear, and put it in my pocket. "Thank you."

Cesare's eyes narrowed. "What's going on between you and my brother, anyway?"

"Going on?" I shrugged, a tinge of sadness drifting deep. "I've known him since I was eleven. We enjoy each other's company." I looked up at him. "Why? Do you quadrant-folk have no friends?"

This seemed the exact wrong thing to say. His jaw tightened, as did his fists, his eyes reddened and locked on mine. Yet when he spoke, it was at a whisper, emphasizing every word. "If you **ever** speak about my friends again, I **will** kill you."

I took a step back, for the first time, truly afraid.

The Intruder

Morton burst in, followed by a couple of Cesare's men, who left the door open behind them. "Four of your brothers are here."

I took a step towards Morton, heart pounding. Was Jack with them? "**Which** four of his brothers?"

Cesare appeared astonished. "What?"

Morton nodded. "Good timing: they were able to capture our attackers as they fled."

Cesare didn't seem pleased with the news.

"I'm pretty sure we got everyone, but —" Morton eyes moved to Cesare's left upper arm, now awash in blood. "Good gods, man — you're hurt! Let us call in a surgeon to see to that."

I felt amused at the way a bit of his parents' homeland of Dickens snuck into his speech. But then I felt humbled: Morton truly cared what happened to the man.

Perhaps that was how he, a son of outsiders, had gotten all four Families to trust him.

Another man hurried in. He went to Cesare, speaking in his ear.

Cesare nodded slowly, eyes narrowed, as if he'd suspected whatever the man had said. He stood, hand to his chin, for several seconds, then gave orders in return.

Once this man left, Cesare turned to one of the men who'd come in with Morton. "Bring my brothers and their men to their rooms and keep them under guard."

Cesare's two men moved to the door, but Morton just stood there, frowning, until the men left. Finally, Morton said, "Why under guard? They helped us."

Cesare snapped, "That's none of your concern. Stay here." Cesare left, and the lock clicked behind him.

"Well," Morton said. "This is unexpected." He glanced at me, then at Lance. "What just happened?"

Lance stood there, mouth open, face pale. He shook his head.

"Mr. Cesare is angry with me," I said, "but I'm not sure why."

"Where's Mr. Julius?"

I pictured him being taken away. "Back in his rooms, I suppose. Did they happen to say how Jonathan was?"

"No," Morton said. "Didn't you just see him yesterday?"

I nodded. I couldn't think. What was going on?

"To answer your question," Morton said, "it was the four we just had luncheon with. How'd they know to come here?"

"They knew where we were going," I said.

"No," Morton said, "I mean, why'd they come here now?"

"I don't understand what's happening," Lance said. "There must be something else in play."

I turned away, still shaken by the suddenness of the attack, how close I came to death from that grenade thing, the way Cesare turned on me and threatened my life. That last seemed completely unlike him. I turned to face Lance. "Why does Clubb quadrant extort my attorney?"

Lance stood blinking, mouth open, face pale.

"Answer me."

"I'm sorry," Lance finally said. "I don't have the answer."

I felt astonished. This could be construed, if Roy wished to do so, as an attack on the Spadros Family. "You're the Clubb **Heir**! Why **don't** you have the answer?"

He swallowed, eyes wide. "I can find out, if you wish."

Something in the way he said it made me laugh. "Oh, aren't we a fine crew. What a tale this would make!" I put my hand to my forehead, trying to recall where I'd left my hat.

Morton chuckled. "Well, until someone decides what's happening, I'm going to sit down." He winced. "I've had about as much excitement as I can stand today already."

I felt chagrined: it sounded as though the man had been in his second firefight of the day.

Lance went to Morton's side. "Let me help you."

"We all should sit," I said. "It might do us good."

A door to one side of the parlor was locked. There was nothing to eat or drink in the room, so we simply sat, waiting.

Lance said, "Who's extorting your attorney?"

I shrugged. "They won't let him take his wife to Azimoff."

"That bastard," Lance said under his breath. "He's going to be the death of us."

I'd never heard him use such language. "Who?"

"Mikhail Bettelmann. My niece Karla's husband. He's in charge of the station." His jaw tightened. "I'll speak with him about it."

Well, I thought, at least something good would come of this.

Morton looked rather pale, his lips parched. I went to the door and banged on it with my fist. "I know someone's out there."

"What do you want?"

"Some refreshment? Master Rainbow is injured."

"Oh," the man said. He sounded chagrined. "One moment."

Perhaps ten minutes later, a maid came in with tea, then unlocked the side door, which opened onto a spacious toilet-room with a mirrored dressing-table. After she left, we again sat waiting.

Lance sat close to Morton, seemingly concerned with Morton's health. The two whispered, glancing at me from time to time.

Whispering seemed quite rude, so I smiled at them prettily, enjoying the way their cheeks colored.

The afternoon *Bridges Daily* sat folded beside me. The front page was startling:

TRAINS: MAYOR PROPOSES OUTSIDE HELP

Today, Mayor Chase Freezout made a rare speech outside City Hall, proposing the City Board vote on a recommendation to bring in experts from outside the dome to deal with the train crisis.

Mayor Freezout looked remarkably thin and pale in comparison to prior speeches. "Since the powers that be appear unable to fix the trains, we must look elsewhere for aid. Our City's leadership has brought an end to the villain stalking our steps, and it can do so here as well."

Wait, I thought. If Freezout — who I knew to be allied with the Red Dog Gang — had anything to do with the capture of the false Bridges Strangler ...

Of course. Frank Pagliacci had likely coached the man with the details of the murders. Perhaps the man agreed to this pretense in exchange for his family's sponsorship into the quadrant.

Would these scoundrels stop at nothing?

But when I considered what Lance had said, Mayor Freezout's proposal seemed alarming. Surely the Red Dog Gang didn't want the Feds involved? Or was this a way for Freezout to make jabs at both the Red Dog Gang and the Four Families?

It seemed a dangerous play, assuming Freezout wanted to live.

Lance poured Morton's tea. "What could possibly be going on?"

I shrugged. Cesare wanting to control everything, most likely. It was only after Morton drank his tea without any ill effect that I took some, remembering my Ma's instruction once more.

I set the paper aside. Where **was** Ma, anyway? But for the briefest of return messages, I'd not seen nor heard from her since I was sixteen.

I knew she still lived as of my disastrous meeting with the Eldest the year prior: Ma was in hiding, and the Cathedral blamed me for it.

It seemed clear what had happened. I trusted Joseph Kerr with the fact that Ma was alive, and he told someone, perhaps innocently, who he should not have.

Before this, only two people other than Mrs. Rachel Diamond and my mother-in-law Molly knew for certain that Ma was alive: Joe and Mr. Pike. Mr. Pike wouldn't try to blackmail me about something he thought remained hidden. So it had to have been Joe.

Why did I trust him with that? Perhaps Joe was right: maybe I had been too drunk back then. It'd been terrible judgment to speak of Ma in Spadros Manor, where anyone might have been listening.

I remembered Pearson out in the hall, the vents in the floor. Could someone have possibly overheard what I said that day?

The dark-skinned elderly physician who'd seen to me after I'd been attacked outside the Courthouse came in. He began questioning Morton, and asked him to take off his shirt.

I rose and turned away to give Morton some privacy. How could Joe have possibly not remembered our conversation?

Joe never seemed to remember anything correctly. This business with the tickets — surely he didn't expect me to mistake blue tickets for red?

Joe had never been trustworthy with money, either. I should have kept my money safe, and gone to our meeting spot instead of the zeppelin station. Why did I not see the mark Joe left, remember the clues he'd given? I could have gotten Ma from the Cathedral, gone to the zeppelin station to buy our tickets, and be gone from Bridges long ago.

The physician left. I sat, drank some of my tea. The entire situation with Joseph Kerr had been a disaster.

Yet I survived. I had my apartments, and my business, and a hundred dollars. It was a good start. If all went well, I might in time pay Mr. Pike and save enough to leave Bridges forever.

But could I bear to leave Joe?

Should I dare trust him again?

All those women who'd accused Joseph Kerr of seduction …

Yet he denied every one. *I swear by all the gods: I've been with no one but you, ever.*

Could what he said possibly be true? Could the boy I saw in Hart quadrant just be a boy, his mother spreading tales to keep herself out of the Pot?

If so, why did she have a portrait of them together, as Jonathan claimed? And why search for Joe when he disappeared? It only drew attention to her and her son.

And I realized: Mr. Charles Hart must have brought her and her family in for questioning long ago. I wondered what he might have learned. I wondered what he wanted from Joe, why he demanded Tony release Joe to him, and why Mr. Hart thought I might know where Joe was, even before Joe appeared in that bar.

There were too many questions around what happened to Joe, Josie, and their grandfather the night I escaped Spadros Manor. And then there was Major Blackwood's letter.

Gertie Pike, the wife of my attorney Doyle Pike's grandson Thrace, implied Major Blackwood had stood up against Frank Pagliacci's attacks on me in the *Golden Bridges*, and was murdered for it. Now to find out he'd been investigating the Kerrs, too …

For an instant, I felt curious as to what might have been in that package he'd sent. But I also was afraid it'd tell me things I didn't want to know.

"Something's bothering me," Morton said.

Lance, still sitting beside him, said, "Are you in pain?"

Morton let out an amused snort. "Not really." Then he said to me, "That grenade should have killed you the instant it hit."

I wasn't sure what to think. "Oh."

"I suppose it could have had a fuse trigger. But it should have been much shorter. Five-second triggers are more usual. So either whoever sent these men went cheap on the munitions —"

The rogue Spadros men being gunned down by the High-Low Split flashed before me. "Or they sent them to their deaths."

Morton grinned. "Well, I was going to say that whoever bought them got cheated." Then his smile faded. "But yes. It would fit."

So he recalled that night as well. "Do you have a cigarette?"

"I do," Morton said, "but I wouldn't smoke here, not if you value your freedom. The Diamonds have forbidden smoking in the quadrant for the past thirty years."

"Really? I never knew."

"It was Mr. Hector. The old Inventor, of course: the younger's not yet thirty himself. They say old Mr. Hector claimed the practice shortened life, so he forbade his people from indulging in it. Of course, many do, but you won't see anyone here say so."

Interesting. I'd never seen Jonathan smoke, but I never gave it a second thought.

I glanced over at Lance, who sat pretending to read a book. "Master Clubb, if you wish to pretend not to listen, you must relax your shoulders."

Lance twitched. "I'm sure I don't know what you speak of."

I chuckled. "You don't always lie well, either."

Lance bristled. "Madam, I —"

"I only wish to help. I'm surprised at your parents not teaching you these things."

Lance recoiled, color high upon his pale cheeks.

And it occurred to me: Lance's parents might be sheltering him as much as Tony's had done.

Alexander and Regina Clubb were elderly, and Lance wasn't ready. Taking over his mother's network of spies would be impossible when he himself hadn't the faintest notion of how to proceed. No wonder his brothers-in-law had risen against the idea of him ruling them in the future.

Lance looked between me and Morton. "Would you teach me?"

I stared at him, so astonished that for a moment I couldn't speak. "Master Rainbow might be best, sir. People would wonder if I made too many trips to Clubb Manor." Besides, that was the last place I wanted to go: it'd be way too easy for his mother to claim I never arrived and make sure I never left.

Morton nodded.

Lance leaned forward, elbows on his knees, hands clasped in front of him. His head drooped, and he sat silent for a full minute.

"I've allowed myself not to see what's in front of me for far too long. I let others tell me I was too young, that I didn't need to know, that it would be safer this way." He raised his head to look at me. "But it's almost cost me everything I hold dear."

He took a deep breath, let it out. "I love Gardena, Mrs. Spadros, more than anything. And I love her little son. I want to marry her." He rubbed his face with his hands. "I want to be the father that fate has made it impossible for your husband to be. But I want none of it unless I can keep her safe and make my men accept Roland as their heir." He glanced away. "It's getting harder and harder each day to know how any of this will happen."

I leaned forward. "Have you told your men this?"

Lance scoffed. "To them, I'm a child under their protection."

Morton chuckled. "Sounds like you need new men."

Lance smiled to himself. "Perhaps I do." He turned to me. "I have obligation to your husband. If somehow this ... nightmare of a courtship ends, and I can marry Gardena at last, I vow your husband will see his son as much as he wishes."

My mind screamed: *But I don't want Gardena to marry you!*

Tony loved Gardena. He loved their son. The fact that he sent me here in the first place showed me who he valued more. And I'd never been in love with Tony. I'd been coerced to marry him.

I just wanted Tony to finally be happy.

But his refusing to marry Gardena those many years past out of fear of his father hurt her too badly. And when my plans to disappear ended in disaster, Tony refused to let me go.

Roland was the key. He loved his Daddy, and given time, Gardena would come to see reason. But it needed time. I had to stop this courtship in any way possible.

"You need to be firm." I remembered then how much I valued Tony's ultimatum to Roy. "Your parents must teach you everything, train you on every aspect of the operations. You must run the quadrant, even before anyone believes you can. Then they must step aside." I thought of how completely Tony's parents had done that, even before they truly seemed to believe in him.

But I knew Regina Clubb: she'd never let go of the leash she had on her son. "You must have them move to their own home and hand the reins to you entirely. And if they can't do so, then you must be ready to take Gardena and leave Bridges. It's the only way you'll ever be truly free."

At the uncertainty on Lance's face, I folded my arms and leaned back, pleased with myself. Lance Clubb didn't have it in him.

Even if he did, Tony would never let her leave Bridges with Roland. And Gardena would never leave Bridges without him.

This courtship would be over in a fortnight.

* * *

An hour later, Cesare returned, along with several of his men. He'd changed his clothes, and from the extra padding upon his upper arm, evidently had someone see to his wound. But although it must have hurt quite a lot, and he seemed a bit unsteady, he acted as though he didn't feel a thing. "Follow me."

We followed him through the many layers of the mansion and outside. Several of his men accompanied us.

The dead Diamond men had been removed from the portico and the white stone cleansed. The men lay off to my left under sheets on the drive. Several men in various stages of injury sat or reclined on the grass beside the driveway near them. The old physician and several maids holding tea-trays tended to these men.

The carriages were parked to the right, the white horses unhitched and being fed by their drivers. One of the horses had a large bandage upon its left flank.

After the road cleared the circular drive, it went diagonally and to the right towards the city. Straight before us, a large number of men congregated far off near the treeline; we moved towards them, past the circular driveway and into the field beyond. We passed a few sheep riddled with bullets. The rest must have fled when the shooting began: they were nowhere to be seen.

As we approached, I recognized some of Cesare's men who we'd seen during the day.

Lance, Morton, and I were directed to stand in the shade of an apple tree as Cesare's men finished collecting the bodies of the attackers. They laid the bodies out in several long rows perhaps twenty feet away, leaving enough room to walk between them.

Morton took an apple from the grass and began munching it.

The entire time, Cesare paced, ranting.

"How did they get into the quadrant?"

"How did they find this place?"

"This is unbelievable!"

As we waited, I turned to view the mansion, which was just as lovely outside as in. The roof's shape reminded me of the bottom of a cut gem, sharply pointed and tiled in gray. The front of the wide fortress was white, with carvings in it which I couldn't make out in the distance.

I hoped the firefight hadn't damaged it too much.

Once his men finished moving the bodies, Cesare brought us over to view them.

The dead invaders were dressed alike: black shirts, trousers, knitted caps, and boots, their faces darkened with what looked like soot. Morton went to one of the men and took something from a breast pocket, slipping it into his own.

Cesare snapped, "What's that you've got there?"

Morton straightened, handed something over. I could tell from the way he moved that he felt uneasy with Cesare's behavior.

Cesare glanced at whatever Morton had handed him, then shoved it into the pocket of his trousers.

One of the men lying there looked familiar. I went over to Morton. "Master Rainbow," I said quietly, "isn't that one of the men from the factory?"

Cesare snapped, "What are you two whispering about?"

Morton pointed. "That man, and that one. They attacked Mrs. Spadros and I two years past. Well, closer to three." He appeared abashed. "A case we did together."

Cesare frowned. "So you knew her. And that she was defying her husband. Even then?"

"I didn't think of it that way, but yes," Morton said.

Cesare rolled his eyes and kept walking.

I chuckled. "I don't think he approves of me at all."

Morton smiled to himself.

"Mr. Diamond," I said. "When do I get my bullets back? Despite what Master Rainbow said, I don't believe we've captured them all. If any of those men return, I could help you."

Cesare only shook his head and moved away. But he did begin scanning the area around him.

I doubted very much that his brothers caught everyone. They wouldn't have even known the Country House was under attack until they were in sight of the building.

And I didn't like being out here. We stood in a clearing, with trees on two sides — easy targets.

A rustle in the trees: Cesare's men moved their guns to face it.

Mr. Hector Diamond II emerged with his men.

Sighs of relief filled the air.

I said to Cesare, "I thought your brothers were in their rooms."

Morton said, "That's what I wanted to tell you: Mr. Hector went after those who fled." He turned to Quadri. "Did you get them?"

Quadri shook his head. "They had a boat ready, and escaped into Hart quadrant. We had no way to pursue them."

"Ugh!" Cesare stomped the ground. "This was too well-planned. They knew we'd be here! How?"

I considered this. "You have a fourth spy yet uncaught."

Cesare turned to face me. "Oh?"

I pointed to the mansion beyond. "You said you have many such buildings like that one there. And I presume many know where each lies. Escape could have been already prepared for each location. All someone had to do was report when you left Diamond Manor. Men could be stationed along each route to report back. When they saw you take the road here, the rest was simple."

It would take a lot of men, with horses ready to send the message along. But it could be done.

It had been done. I don't know why I didn't think of it before.

Cesare put his hands on his face.

Quadri took out his handkerchief, removed his hat, and mopped his face, which was damp with sweat. Then he replaced his hat. "Where's everyone else? Our brothers. Are they well?"

Cesare dropped his hands to his side and turned to his men. "Please escort our guests to join the rest."

Lance took my arm, and before I might speak, shook his head.

Quadri looked between us, then put his handkerchief in his pocket. "Very well." He and his men followed some of Cesare's across the field to the mansion.

The shadows fell long across the dead men's faces as they lay there on the meadow. I turned to Cesare. "You'd have to check with my husband, or with Mr. Roy. But as far as I know, none of these are their men."

Cesare scowled. "Oh, really? None are of Spadros? **None**?" His tone was biting, sarcastic. "Well, I have something which might change your mind." He turned to one of his men. "Get them."

The man jogged off towards the mansion. The others grabbed our arms, dragging us away from the rows of bodies, perhaps a hundred yards off, to a wide spot in the center of the grassy field. The sun shone orange through the treetops, blindingly bright.

And I got a horrible feeling: this area, far from either house or men, was the perfect place to kill us.

But of course, Cesare couldn't do that. He wouldn't, if he wanted his quadrant to survive.

Or would he?

"It was a good play, Mrs. Spadros — a very good play."

I felt confused. "What do you mean?"

"You asked what I want. I want these attacks to stop."

"Spadros quadrant has never attacked yours, so far as I know. Which is only from the newspapers, of course: if I ever was privy to any real news, I'm not anymore. But from what I understand, all we've done is repel your invasions."

Cesare let out a bitter laugh. "Come on, Mrs. Spadros. I learned this game before you were even born. Do you really think me that stupid?" He surveyed me. "Or is it you who's being used?"

"Truly, sir, I have no idea what you're talking about."

Cesare took several steps towards me, then pointed back towards the mansion. "You come here under truce, then have your men mark our position."

He dropped his hand to his side then pointed to the bodies with his other hand, wincing as he did so. "These men attack, and oh, look, you're armed. And my brothers, who have sent information to the Spadros before, just happen to show up in time to save us. Quadri put on a great show." He scoffed. "You must think I'm a complete fool: you even brag about your plan!"

I felt astonished. "I had nothing to do with this attack! Why would you ever think so?"

"You try to earn my trust through deception and dishonor, as you Spadros invariably do." He shook his head, face incredulous. "What kind of woman **are** you? What kind of man did you marry? To send his own family to be murdered by his wife as he tries to kidnap his bastard?"

"Wait," I said, now confused in an entirely different direction. "What are you saying?"

Cesare glanced towards the mansion.

Two men dragged a black-hooded figure with hands tied behind bucking and squealing across the field. This figure was entirely dressed in black: shirt, trousers, and shoes. The men forced whoever this might be to kneel before us.

Several more of Cesare's men stationed themselves around our small group, and close by. I didn't like having men so close behind me, but there was little I might do about it.

Cesare pulled off the hood. "You see?"

Black-haired, gagged, blue eyes full of frightened tears. But although also smeared with soot, I recognized this face at once.

"**Katie?**" I felt appalled. "What the hell are **you** doing here?"

The Terror

"Ungag her," Cesare said. As the men did so, he said to me, "You want your bullets?"

I didn't know what he meant, so I said nothing.

In a lazy, relaxed motion which reminded me of the night Tony shot his own man, Cesare took his revolver from its holster, loading bullets from his pocket into it one by one. Then he cocked the hammer of his revolver and pointed it at Katie's head.

Terror struck. "**No!**" I lunged forward, only to be held by the men around me.

Cesare said, "I will ask once: did your brother send you?"

Katie scoffed. "If only he would do anything so competent."

Cesare raised his eyebrows, drawing back a bit, his gun hand dropping to his side.

"Katie," I said, heart pounding, "then why are you here?"

"I only just now learned of the boy," she said, "and that through listening at doors. No one was doing anything to help him!" Her face turned angry. "It's not right. A child belongs with their daddy! I confronted my brother about it to his face. Tony, as usual, just started whining about how the boy might be harmed if he should dare act. His own son! Well, fuck that —"

I felt appalled. But also, more than a bit astonished at her courage. "Katie!"

She scowled at me. "Don't you start — I get enough talking-to from my mother."

"Your mother should tan your hide," I said, and to this day, I don't know why. In the Pot, we never beat our children: it was punishable by death. But I was beginning to see why they did so here. I would never have even considered such reckless defiance. "We almost had an agreement! You're going to ruin everything." It was as if she had no idea at all of which game she was playing, or how very dangerous it was.

Then I stopped and thought. How did she get here? "What do you know about the Red Dog Gang?"

Lance's head jerked towards me, his face surprised.

Katie glanced between us. "I've never heard of them."

Morton said, "Where did you get the men, then? Who gave you the idea?"

"Like I couldn't think of anything by myself?" She scowled back at him, pulling at her arms as if she would have crossed them, had she not been tied. "You grownups always say that."

"You didn't get here by yourself," I said. "So who helped you?"

She glared at me, and I at her, then finally, she said, "One of Tony's men. He's out on the side gate once in a while talking with my father's men. Sometimes he gives me cigarettes."

I said, "Does this man have a name?"

She shrugged. "He said to call him Frank."

The Scoundrel

Morton shook his head. "Frank Pagliacci. I should have known."

"Good gods," I said, at almost the same time.

Lance said, "We must search the bodies. We can only hope we've finally killed the scoundrel."

"No!" Katie seemed appalled. "I don't want him to be dead!"

Cesare stood peering at us. "So you know this man."

"Yes," I said, "but not in the way you think."

Cesare said, "Untie the girl and bring her with us."

As we returned to the line of bodies, I walked beside Katie. "How close were you with these men?"

"I don't know what you're talking about."

"Did your mother ever tell you about blood tea?"

"Ugh," Katie said. "That sounds disgusting."

I let out a laugh in spite of myself. "It's not made of blood — it brings your monthly bleeding. You do get that, don't you?"

Katie scowled. "I'm not a baby."

"Well, the tea will make it return. After you've been intimate with a man."

I lowered my voice, rested my hand on her arm. "None of those are Tony's men. Did any of them take your clothes off? Lay themselves upon you?"

Katie flung my hand off. "No! Eww!" Then she scowled. "Is **that** what you think of me?"

"I just want to help." I lowered my voice still further. "You're becoming a woman. You need to know this. Your mother knows all about it." I glanced around. "If we get you home, you can ask her."

She gaped at me, face pale. "What do you mean, **if**?"

"Before starting this play, you should have thought about what might happen. Master Rainbow had a good point. Who suggested you do this? More to the point, who didn't speak up to stop you?"

She didn't answer.

"Frank is **not** Tony's man. Neither Tony's nor your father's men would go along with such a plan without your father's direct order. So who benefits by you being here?" I grabbed her arm, pointed at the line of dead in front of us. "Those men were trying to get you to start a war. You've led a force to invade Diamond quadrant. You've killed their men! The Diamonds have every right to hold you hostage or even kill you, and there's not much your father, Tony, or anyone else can do about it."

Katie seemed less sure of herself. "I don't want them to kill me."

I put my arm round her. "All's not yet lost. You're still breathing. Let's just see how this plays out."

***

Katie cried when she saw the dead men. "You fiends!"

I said, "Did you really expect this to go without bloodshed? You're more foolish than I thought." I gestured to the rows of bodies. "Which one's Frank?"

She rushed along, peering at them, then sighed in relief, clasping her hands together. "Thank the gods. He's not here."

At this point, I trusted Katie as far as I might throw her. I peered at Morton and to my dismay, he nodded.

"So he escapes yet again," I said. "The man has nine lives!"

Lance snorted, shaking his head.

"Take their portraits and their belongings, then dispose of them," Cesare said to some of his men. Then to the ones holding Katie, he said, "Bring our guests back where they were."

As we returned to the apple trees, I pondered Cesare's words. Was I being used? I didn't think so.

I recalled the men in fake Spadros livery who beat Madame Biltcliffe. At the time, it seemed that the Red Dog Gang simply meant to ruin our name, making our own people distrust us.

Then I remembered the man who impersonated Jack Diamond two years back, harassing our merchants. Now this.

Why did these people want war between Diamond and Spadros so badly?

I turned to Katie. "How did you come to be here?"

Her face darkened. "I'm no snitch!"

"I never said you were, dear. I was only curious."

She hesitated. "We went in rowboats. Across the South river."

Cesare put his hand on his forehead.

"Taxi-carriages were there waiting. Real ones, with Hackneys."

I smiled to myself. Katherine did so love horses. "Tell me about Frank. What does he look like?"

Katie shrugged. "A guy."

"Yes, dear, I gathered," I said. "Was he tall?"

She nodded.

"Taller than Tony?"

She frowned a bit, then shrugged. "I guess."

"What color was his hair?"

"Brown."

"And his eyes?"

She seemed irritated. "I don't know — blue? Green? What do I care about some man's eyes?"

"Was his skin light like Master Lance, or dark, like Mr. Cesare?"

She looked at me. "A little darker than yours."

Cesare said. "This is getting nowhere."

Lance turned away, taking a few steps towards the trees.

"Maybe I can help," Morton said. "I've seen the man. I'm no artist, but perhaps I can sit with one, get you a portrait of him. Don't know why I didn't think of it before this."

Cesare nodded. "Thank you, my friend." He put his arm over Morton's shoulders and spoke with him quietly.

I leaned forward to speak to the girl. "This Frank of yours has been attacking the Spadros Family for almost three years now —"

"That can't be true!"

"It is. He had his men beat Tony badly. He kidnapped two of his men and forced them to spy on us. Dozens of Tony's men are dead because of him. He stole those Tommy-guns you were using —"

Katie pouted. "They wouldn't let me use one —"

"He captured me and Master Rainbow once —"

Cesare looked over at me and Katie, took his arm off from around Morton's shoulders.

"— and we only barely escaped with our lives. He's almost killed me more than once, and now he's used you to try it again!"

Katherine stared at me in shock, then scowled. "I won't believe this. He's a good man. He just wanted to help me get Roland back!"

So the Red Dog Gang knew about Roland.

Yet even though Frank Pagliacci had contacts in the *Bridges Daily* and the *Golden Bridges*, the Red Dog Gang hadn't exposed this — surely the scandal of the decade — to either.

This was a secret which could damage both the Diamond and Spadros Families, the perfect distraction for anything they wished to do. If they wanted to undermine the Spadros Family (or the Diamond Family, for that matter), revealing this one fact would be the ideal way to do so.

So why hadn't they exposed it?

Cesare had been following this last with a slight frown. "Wait. We need to have a serious talk. Who **exactly** is this man Frank?"

The Murder

"Katie," I said, "would you like to meet Roland?"

Cesare said, "You can't be serious."

I rose. "Whether you like it or not, he's her kin."

I met his gaze for a long moment, then he nodded. "Let's go to the house," he said to his men. "Have a man bring Miss Gardena and Master Roland to the parlor."

One of the men jogged away. We followed more sedately, Katie gaping at the halls, the gardens, the flowers, in awe, as if she'd never seen anything like them.

Gardena and Roland were already in the parlor when we arrived. The parlor was white trimmed in black velvet and silver, with a sofa and several silver-wood armchairs around a silver-and-glass coffee table.

Gardena smiled warmly when she saw us. "Hello, Miss Katherine." She held out a white-gloved hand. "I'm Miss Gardena. I recognized you from your portrait. My, how you've grown!"

Katie sneered. "I never pictured **you** for my brother's whore."

Gardena recoiled, her eyes reddening.

"That was cruel and unnecessary," I said. "You will apologize."

Katie looked away, and gave a one shoulder shrug. "Sorry."

Roland stood there, eyes wide.

Gardena said, "You wish for my son to know this woman?"

"She's fifteen. And your son's aunt. So yes, if the boy's willing."

Attention turned to Roland, who clutched his mother's skirt with one hand, and taking a step back, stared up at Katie.

"Master Rainbow," Cesare said, "please escort them to the north courtyard. Have someone fetch Octavia."

The boy's nanny seemed sensible enough, and could intercede if things got too heated. "Go with them, Katie. You wanted to help; this is how you can do it."

Katie scowled, but went along quietly.

Once the door shut behind them, I let out a sigh of relief. "That could have gone better."

Cesare said, "What else would you expect from a Spadros?"

I snorted, amused. "I'm not certain how to respond to that."

Cesare twitched. "No offense, madam."

So now he decides to behave like a gentleman. "None taken."

"Please sit," Cesare said.

I sat on one end of the sofa. Lance took the other end to my right, leaving several feet between us. Cesare took a silver-wood and black velvet armchair, moving it over to sit beside Lance.

"I have files on this Frank Pagliacci," Lance said. "But it sounds, Mrs. Spadros, as if you've had more direct experience with him."

Cesare leaned forward.

I rested my elbow on the arm of the sofa. Dirt lay upon my dress, and I brushed it off. "Indeed I have."

I told them much of the tale: the abduction of a boy named David Bryce whose mother was known to me, the attacks on Tony, the theft of our Party Time shipments — and of the Tommy guns.

"So that's where they got them," Cesare said. "I've not heard that sound in a long time."

I nodded. "They call themselves the Red Dog Gang. The name itself belongs to a children's street gang in Spadros, but those boys had nothing to do with this. At least one of them is dead." I shook my head ruefully. "No, as you've seen, these are men full-grown, and vicious scoundrels at that. They tried to raise a rebellion amongst our men and took over the major Pot gang in Spadros."

Lance raised his eyebrows.

"We took care of the matter." I kept my face and voice steady, but I felt surprised at Lance's reaction. How could the Clubb Heir — of all people — **not** know about this? "Yet the problem is greater still. I believe they framed me for the zeppelin bombing."

Cesare's jaw dropped.

"As District Attorney, our now-Mayor Freezout had a direct hand in it." I suspected Mr. Charles Hart's wife Judith to be involved with the plot. Perhaps she even paid for my framing. Mayor Freezout all but came out and said so.

But when I inquired about the matter when Mrs. Rachel Diamond and Mr. Charles Hart visited my home the year prior, Mr. Hart seemed to deny it. Which had made me reconsider. As Roy Spadros stood beating him on the courthouse steps as the police watched, might Mayor Freezout have implicated anyone nearby to keep from being killed?

Lance nodded. "The men my father captured — the ones who plotted against us — said much the same."

That Lance could say this so calmly astonished me. Those men were his uncles, his cousins. Lance had known these men since he was a boy, and they plotted to kill him, all because they didn't want Roland to one day become the Clubb Heir.

Cesare said, "This is incredible. My father told me none of this."

After today's events, I doubted Cesare's father would tell him anything ever again. "This is their strategy. Divide, using whispers, maneuvering one group against the other. The fact that they make few direct assaults speaks of a small number, yet that they were able to suborn a sitting District Attorney is alarming."

"To say the least," said Lance.

"They even set a listening bell into the wall of my home," I said to Cesare, "so they might spy upon me. We discovered it the night of the Celebration. Your mother and Mr. Hart visited me just two days before. That was why I felt compelled to tell her that her secret was no longer safe." I still didn't understand why they felt forced to come to my home in the first place.

Cesare sounded troubled. "But how did you know, when her own children didn't?"

What should I say? "She helped me when she didn't have to. I don't think she meant me to know."

Cesare shook his head. I could only imagine how it must feel, your own mother keeping something of that magnitude from you.

"This reminds me," Lance said to Cesare. "The Clubb Family is concerned about your father's alliance with Hart quadrant. We have evidence that elements in the Hart Family participated in both the framing of Mrs. Spadros and the plot against me." For an instant, he hesitated. "And we've found no evidence of Mr. Charles Hart taking steps to remedy this matter."

I'd thought so for some time. Yet for the Clubb Heir to say it was interesting, if more than a bit alarming. Had he been sanctioned to do so? "The bottom line, Mr. Diamond, is that you're being played. Who suggested you seize your parents? Who suggested this purge in the first place?"

Cesare stared at me blankly. "It was entirely my idea! The more I heard of this plot against Master Clubb and my sister, the more uneasy I'd grown. But the moment my mother came to us with her revelation, I knew I must act. My father's plan was to do nothing!" He leaned forward, elbows on his knees. "It seemed clear there were spies in Diamond. Even Jonathan thought so. And with the danger to my mother, I had to get my family to safety."

I nodded. "This man is very good."

Lance frowned slightly. "Frank?"

"No, Frank Pagliacci's a two-bit lackey. An amateur. From all accounts, a good-looking, smooth-talking, charismatic amateur, but an amateur just the same. No, I mean whoever leads these men. He's good." I considered the matter. "A real player, one who's been around a long time."

Then I said to Cesare, "But I believe you're missing the point, sir. What if your brothers hadn't defied your orders? What if they'd never arrived? What if those men had killed you?"

Cesare drew back a bit.

"What if you now lay dead? Today, in this attack." I pointed to his arm. "Ten inches to the right would have done it. Or that grenade thing might have killed us all. What then? Let's just assume your father survived. His authority has been undermined. Your men have battled his. He'd have to work weeks, if not months, to recover just from that alone. As it is, he might never regain the respect of his men. But what if he'd been killed as well?"

Cesare shrugged. "I suppose Vienna would take over."

"Is he ready? Will your men follow him? In the meantime, what would happen to Jonathan, who depends on your word to get his medicine? Does your father — or your staff for that matter — know where the shipment is? Does your father even know he's not been getting his shipments?"

Cesare's jaw dropped. He stared at me in shock. "No."

"So even if your brothers had the presence of mind to alert your people that very day, by the time your staff found his medication, Jonathan might be dead as well. Your Patriarch and two Heirs lost in as many weeks? Your quadrant would be in chaos. Your people wouldn't know what to do. The Court would have lost its Keeper without anyone to appoint another. Not to mention the utter scandal of the Clubb Heir and the Lady of Spadros being found dead after coming to Diamond quadrant under your protection. Don't you see the effects of what you're doing?"

Cesare put his face in his hands, not speaking for some time. "My brothers came here to bring Jonathan his medication."

Lance turned pale. "They came in force, prepared for battle."

They meant to get Jon his medicine even if it meant war with their brother! "This can't continue. You must make peace with your father and brothers and get your quadrant under control, or —"

Cesare's head shot up. "Don't you dare tell me what I must do, Pot rag! Your quadrant has betrayed us time and time again. You want to talk about my friends? My friends **died** in the first Diamond-Spadros war, and no one has so much as apologized for the murder which began it in the first place."

Cesare pointed at me. "Your father sits comfortable in Spadros quadrant this very moment after murdering a Diamond-sworn. Instead of being handed over, he's been rewarded! Put up in his own shop, where he snorts Party Time all he —"

"He quit, actually," I said.

"Whatever," said Cesare. "My point is, your man murdered one of ours, and to this day has only benefited from it."

He did have a point. But I couldn't say that.

"Not to mention that Roy Spadros threatened my sister —"

"Who was the same age as Katie is now. Did he hold a gun to her head?"

"No, but he would have, if he'd had the chance." Cesare swallowed, and when he spoke next, his voice shook. "Then he sent your husband to violate her!"

Gardena walked in, resting her hands upon the back of the armchair directly across from me. She'd taken off her gloves. "Nonsense. If Anthony Spadros had forced himself upon me, I would have shot him myself."

I realized my mouth was open, and shut it. "I didn't know you could shoot."

She shrugged. "Jonathan taught me."

It was now Cesare's turn to stare at his sister.

"I'm taking the children to dinner," she said. "Do you wish to join us, or shall I have some sent here?"

"Sent here." Cesare folded his jacket and draped it upon the arm of his chair. Sweat lay upon his brow.

I said to Gardena, "Is she behaving?"

Her face turned amused. "Barely. But I think Roland has charmed her." She winked at me. "Carry on." She closed the door behind her as she left.

We sat there in silence. I don't think Lance knew that Gardena could shoot either.

I glanced at the clock: our tea-time had been interrupted, yet even with all the commotion it wasn't late enough to dress for dinner, assuming we'd brought anything to change into.

But apparently Gardena had been prepared for Cesare's answer. A maid and waiter came in right after she left with all the trappings of a High Tea: meaty finger sandwiches of all sorts, pastries both sweet and savory, tea, milk, lemon, sugar. The maid poured us tea, which Cesare drank at once, leaving the cup half-full.

No ill effects seen on him, I took a sip. Then I said to Cesare, "You may do as you wish, sir. But if you recall, we believed your brother Jack had been blackmailing and intimidating merchants in Spadros quadrant. We caught him in our quadrant —"

"He didn't attack your Country House!"

Ah. He let that slip. "How many times do I have to tell you that this wasn't our doing? At the time, we caught Jack at the home of my friend, the same one whose son had been taken. We believed Jack to be allied with Frank Pagliacci, the man my husband and I believed sent thugs to attack him and his men. The one who we believed stole our Party Time. The one who took the boy and left him ruined. Yet your brother was returned safe and whole, sir. And no guns were pointed at the heads of children."

Cesare's head drooped, and he looked abashed.

"I'm not your enemy. My husband isn't your enemy. Of all people in this, he perhaps wants peace more than anyone. The real enemy is whoever set this up. The one who set Lance's men to plot against him and his father —"

Lance's head jerked up.

"— the one who set our men to rebel against Roy Spadros." The puzzle was becoming clearer. "The one who persuaded your mother to reveal herself to me at my home, where they knew I'd find evidence of their listening, which —"

"Which would force her to reveal herself to me," Cesare said. "Which would force me to act. You believe Charles **Hart** to be behind all this?"

"His quadrant lies serene," I said. "He's been well-prepared for this latest setback. For all his protestations of friendship, he does nothing about those who framed me. His colors lie upon the cards left upon the scene of their atrocities."

Cesare twitched, then glanced at Morton, who nodded. Reaching into his pocket, Cesare pulled out a business card and displayed it. Upon the white card was the stamp of a red dog. "This was upon one of the bodies."

I nodded. "As I've found at each of their attacks."

Lance seemed incredulous. "But why do this?"

The scene at the Old Plaza came to my mind, that moment when the rogue Spadros men were mowed down by the Red Dog Gang. And I thought: were these men today sent deliberately to their deaths? Surely Frank Pagliacci didn't think they'd succeed against a fortress such as this?

I recalled a year past, the horrible rat-ta-tat-tat of the Tommy guns in the darkness, the way the men jerked and fell whilst running to what they thought was safety. "Roy Spadros and Charles Hart have been at war since before any of us in this room were born." Yet I still didn't know why, and now the question bothered me. "Perhaps this is Mr. Hart's plan to remove the Spadros Family on a more permanent level."

At the time, I remembered thinking of my earlier theory — one Roy shared, surprisingly enough — that the leader of the Red Dog Gang was someone much older. Mr. Hart was three and seventy, old enough to have gathered the sort of information the leader of the Red Dog Gang had in his possession.

For years now, I'd wondered why Roy Spadros hated Charles Hart so fiercely. It seemed unreasonable. But could Roy have a legitimate reason to hate him? Could, for example, Mr. Hart know the horrific secret about Roy's treatment by his mother? Could Mr. Hart be blackmailing him? Was Roy so ashamed of what happened that he'd been paying?

Roy would never tell me why he hated Charles Hart. Whatever the reason was, it seemed to pain him almost too much to bear. Yet it seemed obvious to me that Mr. Hart hated Roy in return, enough to want to destroy him. Why?

I recalled the note found in Marja's dead hand:

*I BELIEVE YOU TOO DANGEROUS
TO KEEP ALIVE. BUT I NEED HIM.
SINCE HE WANTS YOU, WE'RE BOUND
TO EACH OTHER A WHILE LONGER.*

Was Mr. Hart the "he" who wanted me alive?

Mr. Hart had tried everything except kidnapping to get me out of Spadros quadrant. Why? What could he possibly want with a Pot woman a third his age who was married to the son of his enemy? Why did he care about me so much?

Charles Hart and Joseph Kerr had an evident disagreement, just as Frank Pagliacci and Major Blackwood did, and both, it seemed, over me. But Joe's assertion that Mr. Hart was jealous because I loved Joe rang false somehow.

Was the disagreement really for some other reason?

Joe tried to tell me of the Harts being involved with the attacks on Tony. And as someone who'd been under Hart protection for years, he'd be in a prime position to know.

But no matter what Joe said, I didn't believe the Diamonds were involved with the Red Dog Gang. They were too fixated on keeping outsiders out of what they already had.

And unless someone were to go on a rampage of mass murder, in any land they took, they'd have to deal with a hostile populace who'd seen others driven from their homes twice in twelve years. Who'd trust the Diamonds not to do so again?

But everyone loved the Harts, with their racetrack and free drinks, their friendly smiles and welcoming atmosphere. Anyone was allowed to live in their quadrant who wished to, no questions asked. If the Hart Family were found to be waging a silent war against the Spadros using the name of a children's street gang — of all things — few would believe it.

Mr. Hart had stood by me through the entire trial. Had he all this time be plotting my downfall? Murdering my friends? I had so many questions, so many things I couldn't yet understand.

The biggest question in my mind, though, was this: Had Mr. Hart been trying all this time to turn me against my own Family?

Cesare snorted. "This is quite an entertaining act, Mrs. Spadros. A fascinating sleight of hand. And you even have Master Lance playing along."

Lance frowned, evidently as confused as I.

"Yet I have a damning bit of evidence," Cesare said, "proving your personal involvement in these attacks against us. What I meant to show you in the first place." He rose, went to the door. "Bring him."

Cesare returned to his seat, relaxing back as if he'd won.

Lance and I shared a confused glance. What possible evidence could Cesare have which was more vital, more damning, than Tony's own sister?

A few minutes later, the door opened. Two men dragged a heavy-set dark-skinned man in. This man's hands hung limply, his hooded face drooped. He made no effort to support himself, his feet dragging behind him. They knelt him upon the gray stone tile, supporting him on each side.

"Assuming I have a spy yet uncaught, Mrs. Spadros, we have five in Diamond quadrant." Cesare spoke lightly, as if speaking about going to the river. "But we just captured this one the other day." His voice turned suddenly cold. "Unmask him."

They did, then pulled the man's head back by his hair, moving his face into view.

I stared at him in horror. His face was bruised and his lip was split, but I recognized him at once.

It was Mr. Jake Bower.

The Shock

Cesare took up his cup, flinging the cold tea into Mr. Bower's face, who sputtered awake.

"This man," Cesare said, "has confessed to consorting with Frank Pagliacci. Yet he has also worked for you, has he not?"

Mr. Bower worked with Frank Pagliacci? He'd been helping the Red Dog Gang? "I — I've gotten cases from him for a year now. And … he — he … I hired him once, yes."

"To do what?"

I'd hired Mr. Bower to gain information on Jack Diamond's whereabouts during David Bryce's abduction and rescue. I didn't think Cesare would appreciate me having done so. "That's confidential, sir. All my cases are."

Mr. Bower gave me a sharp, pleading look.

He'd only ever gotten involved with going into Diamond quadrant because I sent him there — or had he? "How — where — did you catch him?"

"Your idea to trap my sister's blackmailer was a good one."

I couldn't believe what I was hearing. I turned to Mr. Bower. "**You** were the one blackmailing her?"

His face turned angry. "Why shouldn't I? You could have made a fortune — and gotten free of the Family — if you would have brought the evidence I had of your husband's infidelity to the

Court. But no, you had to haggle like the Pot rag you are. So I took what I learned and used it. Anyone would have done the same."

I felt sad. "You understand nothing, Mr. Bower. My husband has confessed everything, and Miss Gardena is my friend. Who suggested doing this? Frank?"

"I'm not stupid enough to tell them! They'd want all the money for themselves!" His expression grew shrewd. "They'd been discussing methods to get you out of the way the day of the bombing. Not to kill you; just to prevent you from speaking with Dame Anastasia." He snorted. "This was months before. Back and forth they went for weeks. Then I found the documents — before you gave me your assignment, Mrs. Spadros, to be honest. I was looking for other information —"

I felt appalled. "What other information?"

His smile turned sly. "Well, that's something we'd have to discuss privately."

"You're in no position to bargain," Cesare said. "Call Master Rainbow —"

Jake Bower froze.

"— and Miss Gardena. They should see the face of the man who's tormented them."

When Morton and Gardena laid eyes on Jake Bower, the three had completely different reactions:

Gardena: confusion. "**This** is the man who blackmailed me?"

Morton: alarm. "It's **him**! The detective at the meeting!"

Mr. Bower stared at Gardena in awe. "How beautiful you are! No wonder Mr. Spadros has been captivated so."

Cesare stalked up to Mr. Bower and backhanded him. "How dare you speak to my sister!" He turned to his men; a spot of blood showed upon the left arm of his white shirt. "Let's send him to the Prison." Then he said quite casually to Mr. Bower, "I believe my brother Jack would like to speak with you."

Mr. Bower's eyes widened in fear. "No! Please! I beg you, don't send me there!"

I gasped, horrified. "You mean to **torture** him?"

Mr. Bower focused upon me. "You said if I needed help, I had only to ask. You know I mean you no harm! You must help me!"

The weight of evidence against Tony and I — even though we were innocent of any malice — was daunting. If I spoke for Mr. Bower, Cesare would surely take it as proof I had a hand in his spying. I shook my head, feeling ill. "I'm sorry. I wish you would have told me all this earlier. Now there's nothing I can do!"

Mr. Bower turned to Cesare. "You don't have to do this! I swear on all that's holy, I'll tell you everything I know."

"Of course you will," Cesare replied. "Then you'll see my brother." He gestured at the guards. "Return him to his cell."

Mr. Bower was taken away, screaming and begging for his life.

I closed my eyes. "This will end in nothing good. It grieves me."

Cesare studied me. "You didn't know. You trusted him."

I had. Mr. Bower had been giving me cases all this time. What a fool the Red Dog Gang must think me!

Morton and Gardena stood by the door in horror, Gardena clutching Morton's arm. Cesare seemed to notice them for the first time. "Come, sit," he said. "Have some tea."

Gardena sat between me and Lance, wiping her eyes with her handkerchief. Morton sat in an armchair next to me.

Cesare sat beside Morton. "My friend, you mentioned a meeting. What's this all about?"

For the first time since I'd met him, Morton sounded like a man on the verge of giving up. "Before I met Mrs. Spadros, I worked as an investigator for many years. My business partner was a Miss Zia Cashout." He hung his head, face turned away. "My parents knew hers; I believe her parents hoped to match us." He straightened. "Just as I do with Mrs. Spadros, sometimes we had our own cases, other times we worked a case together.

"I had a case — the particulars aren't important — that I needed a bit of information to solve. A wealthy man had hired me; the information was worth a great deal of money. So when Zia told me she had an informant who could help, I was eager for the chance.

"She and I met in a restaurant in Clubb quadrant with a man calling himself Frank Pagliacci. He claimed he worked for the

District Attorney, and he invited us to discuss the matter at his office. When we arrived at this office, everything was as it should be. He offered the information if I helped lure Mrs. Spadros to a meeting with his informant."

Cesare frowned. "Lure?"

Morton's cheeks flushed red. "It sounds horrible to speak of, which is why I never mentioned it before." Morton sat, head down, for several seconds, then his head rose. "Frank said he'd hired a woman to say her son went missing, as a pretext to hire Mrs. Spadros to take the case. They would supply clues, then when Mrs. Spadros arrived to retrieve the boy, a meeting would take place with the informant. The man insisted on meeting with her before he'd give up the information. I never met him, nor learned what he wanted from her."

Morton leaned on the arm of his chair. "I felt the whole matter unusual, yet Zia and Frank felt this course of action to be best." Almost to himself, he said, "They seemed so sure of themselves."

Cesare said, "Go on."

"Mr. Bower came in claiming to be a Detective Constable. He said he'd be our support should any police entanglements occur."

Cesare nodded. "And?"

Morton's shoulders sagged. "It was a lie and a trap. The boy was known to Mrs. Spadros. The scoundrels planned to capture her for gods know what reason. We barely escaped with our lives. And they've hunted me ever since."

Morton had left out a great deal. But when Cesare turned to me, I nodded.

Cesare leaned back in his chair. "Good gods. Were these the men who tried to shoot you last year?"

"I believe so," Morton said. "Your retainer's death on my account still haunts me."

I said, "Wait. Someone died? Jon never told me this!"

"Think nothing of it," Cesare said to Morton. "The blame goes to those scoundrels." Then he turned to me. "Jonathan should never have told you anything!" Then he leaned forward. "Who have you told this to?"

I drew back, surprised. "No one!"

Cesare snorted. "You keep a great deal inside that lovely head of yours, it seems."

Was this a compliment or a threat? "What is it you really want from us?"

Cesare seemed surprised. "I? I want nothing more than peace for my quadrant."

"Nonsense. This isn't about peace and you know it. What will it take for you to stop this foolishness, let your father have his quadrant back, and allow your Inventor to join his peers?"

Cesare's eyes narrowed. "I want formal apology for the death of our manservant, and punishment for Peedro Sluff."

"The latter is unlikely, but I'll speak with Roy Spadros about it. Anything else?"

"I want restitution for those injured or killed during the Spadros-Diamond War."

"I think Roy may want the same, not to mention the Cathedral."

Cesare actually paled a bit at mention of the latter.

"What else? You didn't do all this for some cash and an apology." I leaned forward, pointing at him. "What do you want?"

He leaned back, crossing one leg over the other, hand to his chin, eyes far away.

We were close. "Cesare, look at me. WHAT DO YOU WANT?"

He pounded the arm of his chair as he spoke. "You damnable filthy Pot rag! Have you no shame?" Then Cesare gripped the arms of his chair, his knuckles a pale tan. "I am the Diamond Heir! How **dare** you speak to me in this way!"

What did I do to merit this reaction?

Then I realized my mistake: I had used his first name. Like he were my brother.

Sadness surged through me. "I understand. You see me as nothing. Yet through your nephew, we're tied together as surely as any accident of birth. I came here. You have control over whether I live or die. I trusted you with my life."

His eyes fell.

"I only want to help. But I can't until you tell me what you really want." This war between Spadros and Diamond would go on forever until I learned the answer.

Cesare's eyes closed, and he fell to the floor with a thud.

Gardena gasped. "Oh, gods." Then she called out. "Help!"

Cesare's men rushed in. They helped Lance and Morton move Cesare to the sofa.

Gardena said, "Get his family. And the surgeon. The surgeon this time, mind you. Something may be wrong with his wound."

A man about Cesare's age spoke. "But his father tried to —"

"I don't care. He needs to start acting like a father for once."

I leaned upon an armchair, completely taken aback by Gardena's sudden fury.

She paced. "I knew he was hurt worse than he claimed to be."

Morton took off Cesare's shoes and placed them to one side of the sofa, then sat upon the sofa's arm. Lance knelt beside Cesare and put a cushion under his head.

After a moment, Cesare opened his eyes. "What happened?"

Morton grinned. "Apparently you needed a rest."

Cesare's wife rushed into the room, the panic on her face vanishing when she saw her husband. Going to his side, she knelt before him, clasping his hand. "They never told me you were even hurt!" She put her forehead to his hand, then kissed it, tears streaming down her face.

Cesare smiled at her fondly. "It's not that bad." His eyes flickered to Morton. "Perhaps I just needed a rest."

A new man, not quite as old as the physician, came in carrying a black leather bag. Cesare's brothers followed him in. They hung back, surveying Cesare as he lay there. Gardena went to them, and they conversed quietly.

The surgeon moved the coffee table aside and placed his bag upon it. He began to remove Cesare's shirt so his left arm with its blood-soaked bandage lay bare. When Cesare leaned forward, another bandage, also soaked in blood, showed upon his side.

Cesare's wife gasped.

The surgeon pursed his lips, shaking his head. "This would be best done in my office."

I turned to Cesare's brothers. But before I might speak, Julius burst in. "Where's my son?"

I gestured to Cesare with my chin.

Cesare said, "I guess you didn't need to shoot me after all."

I believe Cesare was being facetious, but Julius suddenly looked ill. He moved to an armchair and slumped into it.

The surgeon said, "Your body has suffered a shock; you must do nothing more today."

Cesare said to one of his men, "Prepare rooms for our guests." To Lance, he said, "I suppose we must continue this tomorrow."

I said, "May I take Katherine Spadros into my rooms? The girl's probably frightened."

Cesare nodded.

His mother's old wheeled chair was found, and Cesare was taken away, the chair squeaking as it went.

When I got to my rooms, Katie was bathed and dressed in a nightgown. She'd been given the adjoining bedroom, but she begged me so much that out of sheer exhaustion, I let her climb into my bed.

I was just about asleep when she said, "Jacqui, are they going to kill me?"

Amused, I said, "Not tonight. Go to sleep."

***

Gardena loaned me the navy blue dress I'd worn the day of the zeppelin bombing. She'd worn it at Lance's yacht launch, but from its remarkably good condition, the dress seemed not to have been worn much since.

Breakfast was served in our room. Katie, now wearing one of Gardena's house dresses, didn't eat much, nor did it look as if she'd slept well.

I said, "How did you like Roland?"

She gave a one-shoulder shrug.

I sipped my tea. Katie might never see the boy again: after her invasion, it was unlikely they'd let her into their quadrant, even if this negotiation succeeded.

After our plates were cleared away, a knock came at the door. I said, "Come in."

Gardena poked her head in. "Cesare wanted me to bring you down to meet with him."

I said, "Katie, stay here."

Panic crossed the girl's face. "Please don't go, Jacqui."

Gardena smiled at her. "Octavia will be here shortly."

Katie stared at the rug, nodding.

I recalled her question the night before. "No one's going to hurt you. Just go with Miss Octavia and get to know your nephew." I felt sorry for Katie: she looked so young and forlorn. "I'll be back when I can."

Gardena and I returned to the same sitting-room, which had been cleaned and straightened. Apparently I was the last to arrive: Morton, Lance, and Cesare sat in their former places.

The glaze in Cesare's eyes reminded me of when Tony was medicated with opium after he had been beaten so badly by Frank Pagliacci's men. Cesare pointed at a chair. "Please, sit."

Surprised, I did so. Gardena again sat between me and Lance. But why was Morton here?

Cesare said, "I apologize for the delay."

Lance shook his head. "There's no need to apologize, sir."

Cesare moved a bit, then winced. He sounded tired, bitter. "I've had people in here for hours. You want me to help you. Everyone wants me to help you." He scoffed. "Yet you offer me nothing."

Lance said, "From where I sit, it seems Mrs. Spadros has agreed to a great deal." In his eyes I read the unspoken thought: *possibly more than she can deliver.*

Cesare might be medicated, but he hadn't missed the exchange. "Exactly. A Pot rag woman wants me to risk my cousin's life yet promises the moon."

Cesare was silent for a long time. "You want me to trust you." He sounded bitter. "You dare to talk to me about friends. Let me tell you about 'your people' and my friends." He leaned forward, elbows on his knees, fingers bridged. He gazed, it seemed, at nothing. "My friends and I were supposed to be in school. But we made our way to the Spadros Pot. We didn't realize how we would stand out."

High-card Diamonds wearing school uniforms in the Spadros Pot? Without meaning to, I chuckled.

Cesare gave me a disgusted glare. Sweat shone on his brow. "We escaped, hid. A woman appeared then, not much older than you, offering us safe passage to Diamond." He sounded furious. "We followed her. We trusted her!" Hate lay in his eyes. "She led us to Roy Spadros."

I gasped. "How did you escape?"

Shame flickered past, and I knew: he ran away. He left his friends behind.

He escaped, and they did not. And it was killing him inside. "You were only a boy."

Cesare lunged towards me. "I'll have no pity from you, you fucking Pot rag!"

Gardena cried out, "Cesare!"

Morton drew back. "Whoa, there."

Lance rose, carefully placing his hand upon Cesare's shoulder. "Sir, you forget yourself."

Cesare gave Lance a surprised glance, then retreated, crossing his arms once more. A spot of blood the size of a quarter appeared on his left sleeve.

Heart pounding, I tried to think. "Who was this woman?"

Cesare snapped, "How am I supposed to know?"

If someone had done that to me, I'd not rest until I knew. But saying that wouldn't help anything.

I almost offered to find her, then I thought the matter through. Would I help Cesare Diamond hunt down one of my own people?

Cesare leaned upon one arm, hand resting upon his forehead. "I think you remind me of her. But she was shorter. Her hair was black, and her skin brown. She looked like a Diamond."

I nodded. "Probably why you trusted her."

There were many in the Spadros Pot who looked like me, not as many that fit the description Cesare had just given. Could this have been my mother? The age would've been about right.

Why would she lead anyone to Roy Spadros?

But I could give him something. "You were recognized." I leaned forward. "He let you go, Mr. Diamond. He didn't dare murder a Diamond Heir. It's the only answer which makes sense."

Cesare nodded. But there was a tightness around his eyes: he hid something.

I didn't know what else to do. It all came down to trust, but perhaps I looked too much like my mother for him to ever truly do that. "Mr. Diamond, please. You say I've offered nothing. But I can't offer what you want if I don't even know what that is."

He sounded bitter, weary. "Do you even care?"

"Of course I do. It's why I'm —"

"I want my people back, that's what I want. I want my friends who Roy Spadros tortured to death brought back to their land so they can receive proper burial."

Our eyes met. *Another man Roy Spadros destroyed.* All the years of humiliation. The fear and sorrow. The guilt and regret.

I saw the blood on his sleeve, the sweat on his brow, the tightness around his eyes. He was hurt. He was in pain.

Then I saw something inside Cesare Diamond fold. He turned aside, sounding young, small. "I just want my friends back."

Morton put his hand over his eyes. Lance turned away.

Gardena rushed to her brother. "Oh, Cesare." She knelt, wrapping her arms around him, and he wrapped his around her as he rested his head on her shoulder.

My eyes stung. "Nothing is certain, sir. But that, we might be able to do."

The Inventors

Cesare lay his head upon his sister's shoulder for some time, then he sat up, rubbing his face with his hands. "I'll allow our Inventor to attend this meeting. But only if I attend as well."

Lance let out a sigh of relief.

Cesare abruptly stood, calling to his men.

They burst in, faces alarmed.

"Notify the Patriarchs we'll meet with their Inventors today. The meeting room atop the Opera House will do."

"But sir," one said, "it'll take time to get there. Not to mention gathering them."

Cesare considered this. "Tell the Inventors we'll meet for tea. But I have no way of knowing how long this meeting of theirs might take. Make sure dinner and rooms are ready if needed." He gave the man a weary smile. "You know what to do."

"Yes, sir." The men left, closing the door behind them.

Morton said, "You think they'll show up?

Cesare said, "They'd be fools not to attend." He turned to Lance. "It's a long drive. Why don't we take a few minutes' refreshment before we make the journey?"

Lance glanced at me. "Three Heirs will be there. It'll only anger the Spadros to put his woman in his place."

Cesare nodded, turning to Morton. "Take a carriage."

Morton left at once. Lance rose more slowly.

For several seconds, I could only gape at them. His "woman"? I wasn't Tony's "woman"! And the idea that they were settling for me all this time as some place marker ...

I pointed to Cesare's arm. "Your arm is bleeding."

Cesare growled and stalked out.

Gardena shook her head, wiped her eyes, then turned to me. "Thank you for helping him."

I grabbed her arm, dragging her into the toilet-room. "I don't think this is anywhere near over."

"Whatever do you mean?"

"Our enemies now know where you are. And they know my husband values you above all else."

"Jacqui, you can't mean that —"

"The longer you and my husband stay apart, the more you become a knife to his throat. Please, for his sake, for your son's sake, take Roland and go to him."

Gardena's face fell, and she shook her head. "Never in a million years would I have expected you to say this. I love my son more than life itself, but I've never regretted the night I lay with Anthony more than I do right now."

She didn't understand. I took her face in my hands. "I don't care about that. Nothing is more important than that boy's safety."

Tears lay in Gardena's eyes. "To abandon my home, my Family, take my child from the people he loves, break a good match, hurt Lance ... just to flee to the home of a man I don't love and a quadrant who would hate me? Even if Anthony divorced you, and you stood upon the Courthouse steps giving a speech in my support, no one would believe it. No one would understand it. I don't understand it."

"Dena, he's a good man. I know he hurt you in the past, but he's changed. Promise me you'll at least think about it?"

"No, Jacqui. I won't promise that." She rested her hand on my arm. "I know you care for my welfare. But please, trust my Family to keep us safe." She smiled, and sniffled a bit. "It seems it's what they're best at."

* * *

When we emerged, the carriage wasn't ready: a horse had gone lame and a footman was ill. Then the housekeeper stormed up, wanting "a word with the young Master."

(Being called this seemed to upset Cesare no end.)

According to her, by the time luncheon was made and packed, it would be time for luncheon. So the decision was made to stay and eat there.

In the meantime, everyone wanted to fuss over Cesare except, it seemed, his mother.

"He's a grown man and perfectly capable of tending to himself," Rachel Diamond said slowly. Other than a peck on the cheek, she barely acknowledged his wounds at all.

As time passed, Cesare became more and more restless. As soon as he finished eating, he stood. "I'm leaving now."

Lance rose. "Thank you for your hospitality." He followed.

For a moment, I felt astonished by Cesare's rudeness. He never even asked if I were done! Fuming, I wiped my mouth, stood, curtsied to Rachel and Julius, then ran from the room.

At the mansion's entryway, I grabbed my hat as I passed. The two men, who were much taller than I, walked quickly, and I had to run to keep up with them through the maze of corridors.

At the portico, a white Diamond carriage stood ready; the two men got in. Cesare sat in the midst of the back bench, Lance across from him. I followed, sitting myself in the smallish space next to Lance, who jumped a bit as if startled, then moved himself over.

Cesare stared at me. "What are you doing here?"

Had he not noticed me running behind him all this time? "I'm not being dealt out if I have any say to it. My people have just as much to lose as anyone."

Cesare and Lance looked at me as if they were seeing me for the first time.

The footman still stood there, door in hand.

Cesare growled. "Close the door, you, and be off."

Embarrassment and shame crossed the man's dark brown face as he closed the door. A few moments later, the carriage started.

"It's not his fault you're angry," I said. "Why do you quadrant-folk treat your servants worse than dogs?"

Lance said, "Gardena said you were outspoken, but ..." He shook his head, chuckling.

Cesare crossed his arms and turned his face away.

I put my hat on. "May I ask something?"

Cesare didn't move. "If you must."

"Where's your brother Jack?"

Cesare rolled his eyes, shrugging. "Who can make sense of my brother? Last I heard he was somewhere in the forest."

"You let him roam like an animal? Why do you not care for him? He needs to be in a ward."

Cesare snorted softly. "Our Family had this discussion many years back, with the same conclusions. Jonathan was adamantly against it, and somehow he has Jack's power of attorney, so we could do nothing. 'If this is how he wishes to live, why restrain him?'" Cesare shook his head. "I'll never understand it."

I didn't understand it either. But hearing Cesare agree with me on this made me feel a little less like I was the madwoman in this matter. The only real disagreements Jonathan and I ever had were over Joseph Kerr and Jack Diamond, and Jonathan was vehement in his opinions on them both.

Well, I suppose back then I was too.

The carriage drove slowly over the narrow forested road. After some time, we reached the Main Road, which was paved, and made better progress as the city proper approached.

By the time we arrived to Market Center, the sun hung low in the sky. We hurried up white stone steps past Cesare's footman to a dark wooden door.

Cesare stopped briefly to speak with the guard, then we went to a lift which took us to the top floor. Down a hallway paneled and floored in oak, across to a matching double door.

Tea had been set out. It seemed we were the last to arrive.

The mood inside was, in a word, contentious.

Brown-haired, pale-skinned and slender, the young Clubb Inventor Lori Cuarenta sat scowling, arms crossed.

Dumpy, auburn-haired, middle-aged Inventor Etienne Hart sat gloating behind his weird thick multi-lensed brass spectacles, a sheen of sweat on his pasty flat face.

The wiry ancient brown-skinned Spadros Inventor Maxim Call leaned over the table onto his fists, as if to dominate them all.

And a very young man with a thin face and skin so dark as to almost be black sat holding up a pen, mouth open as if caught in the midst of speaking.

This must be the Diamond Inventor, I thought. He seemed younger than I recalled, not yet twenty. I'd only had a glimpse of him at a Grand Ball over two years earlier.

The group turned towards us when we entered.

Tony stood across the room from Inventor Call, somewhat behind Lori Cuarenta. He stared at me, face shocked. "What's she doing here? Send her home at once."

To my surprise, Cesare said, "She represents the Pot. They built this city, and may bring insight to this proceeding we lack."

Tony stomped around the table, coming within a hand's width of Cesare. "This is **totally** unacceptable! **I** am her husband, and **I** say whether she's here or not."

Cesare frowned. "You can't send your wife into battle then claim she's made of glass. I would be dead twice over if not for her, and I won't send her away just because you don't wish to see her."

Tony took a step back, and our eyes met. I could see the struggle within him.

He still cares about me, I thought. And the relief and joy I felt at being able to read his emotions once more made me realize I cared about him as well.

And I felt ashamed at how I'd hurt him.

Then the instant passed. "Do what you wish," Tony said, loud enough for the room to hear.

He muttered under his breath. "She's probably seduced you, just like everyone else."

Shame and hurt stabbed at me; my eyes stung.

To my surprise, Cesare didn't call Tony out. "Please excuse our lateness. Where are we in solving this problem?"

Maxim Call and Lori Cuarenta glared at each other. Maxim Call made a dismissive gesture, as if allowing a child to speak.

The Clubb Inventor stood. "The problem is clearly electrical —"

Maxim Call snorted in derision.

"— yet the source of the fault is unclear."

Etienne Hart's voice sounded just like his father's. "I could have told you that without this meeting."

Cesare turned to the Diamond Inventor, who'd been tapping his pen upon a blank page. "What say you?"

Ignoring Cesare, the young Inventor stood, bowing to me. "Master Themba Jotela, Mrs. Spadros, at your service."

I curtsied low. "I'm honored, Inventor."

Inventor Jotela turned to Cesare. "The symptom is here in this room. I believe each wants what's best for our people." He held his hands up at chest height. "Yet we're divided, when the city," he clasped his hands together, fingers interlaced, "is built to function as one. A break in the system affects the entirety."

Inventor Cuarenta nodded.

He continued, "If the problem were in the timer, surely the clocks and lights would also be affected. So our Lady Inventor speaks true: the issue involves power. But —"

"I agree with Inventor Hart," Maxim Call said. "This meeting wastes our time."

"Let the Diamond speak," Tony said sternly.

The Diamond Inventor gave Tony a solemn nod. "Our task, then, is to find the break." He turned to Inventor Call. "Yes, this again is obvious, yet perhaps it's not, or else we would have found it already. I came here simply to ask each of you: what construction was in progress in your quadrant in the area around the train system shortly before the stoppage?"

Etienne Hart shook his head. "None."

"None in mine," the Diamond Inventor said. "Inventor Call?"

"There was some in Spadros, but for a month we've investigated and found no break in the lines."

"Very good." The Diamond Inventor turned to Lori Cuarenta. "And in Clubb?"

The young Inventor looked uncertain, a slight frown on her face. "Nothing ... except the day prior, we completed work on the zeppelin station —"

Maxim Call and the Diamond Inventor leaned forward.

Inventor Hart said, "What work?"

"Perhaps it was only mentioned in the Clubb edition of the news," Lance said. "We had a small ceremony. The last beam was moved into place to repair the damage from the explosion."

Everyone glanced at me, yet I ignored them.

"But the trains continued on for twenty hours afterward," the Clubb Inventor continued.

I recalled a ride in Jonathan's carriage a year or two past. "Could there be a battery? A mechanism to hold energy." I looked over at Cesare, who stood a step further away than he'd been. "Like in your brother's carriage."

Maxim Call began to laugh. "A battery? To run an entire train system for twenty hours? That would be some battery!"

Lori Cuarenta nodded slowly. "There could be. If you recall, the trains were slow for several hours prior to the stoppage." She hesitated. "It would take many batteries, yes. Very large ones. But we live in an exceptionally large dome." She sat silent for a moment. "The dome's builders must have designed this system to guard against sudden, short losses of power."

"There's something I don't understand," I said.

Etienne Hart snorted in derision.

After an irritated glance at Inventor Hart, Cesare said, "Go on."

"If something happened to stop the trains' power, and this is all one system, why is the rest of the power on?"

The Diamond Inventor smiled as one might at a child. "Good question. There must be separate power systems for each, so that a fault in one doesn't bring the entirety to a standstill."

Tony stirred. "What **exactly** was done up there? Is there some photograph, or drawing? It sounds as if something in the station's ceiling wasn't built right."

I gaped at him. "Could the **ceiling** be part of this system?"

Everyone in the room seemed struck silent.

Inventor Cuarenta's face turned red. "I'll have images sent up right away."

Lance stepped forward. "I'll have it done, Inventor, never fear."

She smiled at him. "Thank you, Master Clubb."

Cesare said, "While we wait, I've provided food, drink, and rooms if needed."

Pleasantly surprised murmurs all round, as men came in with tea, platters of food, and carafes of water.

I looked at Tony, and he at me. What he'd said to Cesare hurt. Yet it showed how much I'd wounded him. How much Gardena seducing then discarding him years ago still affected him.

I don't think he'll ever recover, Sawbuck had said. From Tony's haunted gaze, I believed it.

I never meant to hurt you!

But I had, deeply. I'd publicly humiliated him more than once, after betraying him in what his people thought the worst possible way. Not only had he caught me in the arms of another man, but it had been Joseph Kerr, a man he felt unworthy, a scoundrel.

I never blamed others, or pointed to my state of drink in excuse for what I'd done. What happened was my fault, and mine alone.

I took a chair from the many standing along the walls.

When I was shot in this very house, you didn't come here. You didn't even send a note to inquire after my health. Even after I worked tirelessly for months during the trial to save your life, you didn't give me a word of thanks, though it almost ruined me.

I took a deep breath, let it out, determined not to cry in front of these people. I retrieved my handkerchief, covering my face to wipe my eyes and nose at the same time.

Tony's voice startled me. "I don't wish to disturb you —"

I stared up at him. He came to me, after all I'd done?

He'd put his emotionless face back on. "But I wished you to know your people are safe. The maid and the footman. I know you care for them," he gave a tiny shrug, "for some reason. I didn't harm them."

A wave of relief swept over me. Amelia and Honor were safe. "Sit with me."

He did, perhaps two feet away.

"Cesare Diamond has Katie."

Tony's eyebrows raised.

"Frank Pagliacci persuaded her to attack their Country House."

"I heard. Of the attack."

How had he heard of it so quickly? "But she's unharmed."

Tony let out a breath.

I should let him know Dena and Roland are well, I thought.

"Your maid told me of your weapon," Tony said, before I might speak. His face softened, just a bit. "It was an ingenious plan."

I smiled in spite of how horrible I felt. "You should have seen Cesare's face when he learned of it."

Tony's eyes flickered past my shoulder. "I can only imagine."

Then misery descended upon me. *I've seduced no one. I never wished to. I was played a fool by the man I love.* But I couldn't say it. My eyes stung. "You and your father sent me off to die."

Tony flinched. Then he rose, his public face firmly set, and returned to his former place without a word.

A waiter approached. "Would you care for some refreshment?"

"Is there a room available?"

"This way."

I followed the man past where Cesare sat speaking with Etienne Hart to a small room with a cot and tea table in it. After he closed the door, I sat upon one of the chairs and put my face in my hands.

I regretted being here. I didn't want to see Tony. I hated listening to the Inventors posture and berate each other. I felt tired of Family troubles, tired of being a target. If I had a way home, I might have left.

After a few hours, the waiter returned with an assortment of foods upon a platter and a glass of water.

Did Mr. Hart lie to me when he said the year earlier that his wife was the least of my worries? I hadn't realized until then how much his failure to do anything about Mayor Freezout's allegations hurt. He hadn't so much as acknowledged them.

After a couple more hours, there came a knock at the door. "Pardon me," Lance said, "but I have the photographs, if you care to see them."

I forced myself to smile. "How kind of you!" He would've been within his rights to keep me from the discussion altogether. But I did like puzzles. "Yes, I'd like to see them."

The photographs were spread upon one half of the table. In the center of the table was a portrait of the ceiling, done in a skillful watercolor. "This is remarkable."

Murmurs of agreement went round the table.

Inventor Jotepa said to Lance. "Which were before the work, and which after?"

"Those taken prior to the work are on the left," Lance said. Then he pointed to one at the very right. "I had that one taken tonight, and rushed over."

The photographs were lovely studies in sepia and white. The newest one was still damp. At first, I didn't see any difference, and apparently the others didn't either, because they began to move away, talk amongst themselves.

I pushed forward. It was a puzzle.

If Tony's theory were true, some change must have taken place. But what?

I peered at the watercolor. I studied the newest photograph.

Then I surveyed the old photographs, some done over a hundred years past. One shot was ancient, taken as if the man lay upon his back. The angle of the photo matched the newest one.

I gazed at it, feeling weary, trying not to yawn.

I never learned to read the language of my homeland, but what looked like a word jumped out at me. I tried the word in my mouth. It meant — Ladies. "Wait."

Cesare and Tony both said, "What is it?" Then they peered at each other as if surprised.

"There's writing on the ceiling." I pointed to the old photograph. "I know that word. It's my mother's language."

It was in a flowing script, made almost invisible by the wild array of color, but brought forth once color had been stripped away. I ran my finger along the photograph. "It says, 'The Blessed Ladies Hold The Key'." I pointed to the top beam. "You see here? In the old photographs, the beams don't meet up. In the new, they do. And because they do, the sentence is incomplete."

Lori Cuarenta gasped. "It's a giant 'off' switch!"

Joining the beams had turned the train system off. I chuckled at the irony. Only someone who tried to fix the ceiling without consulting the "Blessed Ladies" — another name for the Dealers — would make this mistake.

Cesare said, "What amuses you?"

I turned round to face him. "Did you never once think to ask the Dealers about this matter?"

Everyone blinked at me, speechless.

A laugh burst from me. "Master Lance, Kitty is your **sister**. She's been with the Dealers for two years. Why **not** consult with them?"

Inventor Maxim Call had spent his entire life trying to fix the Magma Steam Generator. But he stood as a man completely baffled. "What do **women** have to do with this?"

Inventor Cuarenta's eyes narrowed.

I pointed to the ancient photograph. "Who else has knowledge from before the Coup? The Cathedral once had a whole department dedicated to understanding the city." Their faces were astonished. "You really didn't know."

"But it looked right," Inventor Cuarenta said. "My engineers and I never considered —"

"No one remembered." Those words were built into the zeppelin station ceiling five hundred years in the past. If I hadn't recognized the writing, no quadrant-folk would have remembered.

But the Dealers knew. They had to know.

Why hadn't they come forward?

Cesare said, "Well done, Mrs. Spadros!"

Tony's eyes narrowed.

Cesare said to the Inventors. "You must start work at once."

The room filled with chatter as people collected their things, preparing to leave. Etienne Hart rolled his eyes and gave a snort of derision, apparently unheard by anyone else.

This pretentious lump was an Inventor? The Heir to the Hart Family? I confronted him. "Why are you even here, if you feel fixing the trains is all so worthless?"

The man peered at me through his thick multi-lensed spectacles. His words held nothing but scorn. "Look at you bumblers rushing about, so important on your task. You flail from one symptom to the next." He shook his head. "What's needed is a change entire."

"What in the world are you getting at?"

And then it all came together. I raised my voice. "Stop. All of you. Just stop."

Lance said, "Mrs. Spadros, what's wrong?"

But then I had a dilemma. How much should I reveal?

I had all four Inventors here. At least two suspected that the Cathedral held some information which might help the city. I had no idea what information, but the Eldest banished me from the Cathedral simply for giving Inventor Call a drawing of the map to the Magma Steam Generators. "Can anyone overhear us?"

"No," Maxim Call said. "This room was built for meetings with that in mind. I made a report about the plans in my application for Apprentice." He chuckled. "Some time ago."

No waiters remained here. And I had everyone's attention.

I focused on Inventor Call. "First you recruited me to agitate to Roy Spadros for you four Inventors to meet together. For a long time, I've wondered why you chose me. Later on, you took my map of the Cathedral —"

All four Inventors twitched. They suspected something!

"— then you," I pointed at Inventor Cuarenta, "began making overtures to me about what I might know."

I then pointed at Lance. "Your mother tried to blackmail me in exchange for telling what I knew, then implied if I refused, she'd blackmail the Cathedral."

Tony and Cesare gasped. Lance turned pale.

The young Inventor Jotepa sat astonished, mouth open.

I turned to Inventor Hart. "Then there's you. You come here, mock these proceedings, and do your best to disrupt."

And then I realized the truth. "It was you, wasn't it. Not your mother at all."

Etienne Hart chuckled.

"That's why you stood beside your mother that day outside the Courthouse, so I'd think it was her that framed me. But it was **you**!"

He said nothing.

Lance stepped forward. "That's a serious allegation."

But Tony looked at Lance and shook his head.

Face chagrined, Lance withdrew.

Why would Inventor Hart do this? And why hadn't Charles Hart done anything about it?

I looked around. From their faces, some knew. Tony. Maxim Call. Lori Cuarenta.

But from their faces — not faces ashamed or afraid of some secret's reveal, but fear for me, for what it might do to me.

And it terrified me. I didn't know if I could take any more.

I didn't want to know.

So I struck back. "If any of what I must say leaves this room, you'll know he," I pointed at Etienne Hart, "revealed it."

Inventor Hart snorted in derision.

Fuck you, I thought. But even if this man were the worst possible sort, I couldn't say that. He was an Inventor. It was then I realized: if Etienne Hart was in on this, Mayor Freezout and the Red Dog Gang already knew everything.

Inventor Jotepa looked around. "Pardon me, but I don't understand. How is it you know anything about the Cathedral?"

I smiled, but didn't much feel it. "I was born there, the descendant of those brave women who defended the Cathedral during the Coup. I don't know what information they have, but if I don't tell you what I know, the trains are the least of our worries."

Themba Jotepa nodded. "The Magma Steam Generators."

So he did know about that. They all knew. Inventor Hart pretended not to care, but he seemed as interested as anyone. I took a deep breath. "Who suggested connecting the beams?"

Lori Cuarenta blinked. "One of my engineers." Her face fell. "He was killed during the melee at the train."

The only one killed. Could the Red Dog Gang have again eliminated someone who had outlived their usefulness?

My heart pounded. This might doom my Ma. But I had to speak, or I'd hinder the Inventors from helping this city. "My mother owns the Cathedral. She can help you."

Whether she would was an entirely different matter.

Tony blinked. "But —"

A great wave of grief came upon me, and not for my mother. For Tony, and how this would hurt him. "She's alive."

Not wanting to see the shock, hurt, and anger on Tony's face, I turned to Cesare. "Your mother knew something would happen. I don't know how. But she stopped my mother from getting on the zeppelin. She didn't have to do it. She didn't want me to know. But later," I glanced at Tony, "I figured it out. That's how I discovered the truth. But don't treat her with anger." My vision blurred. "Your mother is so brave. She saved us, sir. All of us."

Cesare stood there, mouth open.

Then I wondered: Was that why the Red Dog Gang killed Dame Anastasia by blowing up the zeppelin? Killing all those people ... just to damage the station?

Maxim Call stirred. "I fear we've handled this poorly."

I let out a breath, feeling grieved. But I couldn't yet bring myself to speak a reply. I'd been banished from my home for helping him, then he insulted me. I wasn't ready to forgive him.

Cesare spoke: "Thank you for telling us this, Mrs. Spadros. I think next we should make a plan amongst the Families as to how to approach the Cathedral for their aid."

I pictured the fury on my mother's face when she learned what I'd just done. "That would be best."

Maxim Call said, "Then I think we're finished here." He glanced at Lori Cuarenta. "If your people need assistance in restoring the station, let us know."

Inventor Jotepa nodded. Inventor Hart said nothing.

Everyone else rose, collecting their things.

I went to Etienne Hart. "You bastard. Why torment me? What hold do these people have over you?"

He snorted softly, shaking his head. "I don't know what my father sees in you." He waved me on. "Go, child, take your quick tricks. My people play the long game."

Something in his voice made me take a step back in horror. Was Etienne Hart the wild-card my informant spoke of?

Someone took my arm: it was Tony. "Come away from there."

When I faced Tony, he said, "All this time, I've berated myself for adding to your grief. Now I learn even your mother's death was a lie." He quivered, his face a mask of frozen anger. "How can I trust anything you say again?"

He was entirely right: I was completely to blame.

Tony let go of my arm and strode from the room.

Etienne Hart began to laugh.

What could Helen Hart possibly have seen in him?

But something about him frightened me: I feared to be alone in the room with him. I hurried after the others, who had held the lift.

Tony wouldn't meet my eye.

Inventor Jotepa said, "Doesn't Inventor Hart wish to join us?"

I shrugged. "I have no idea."

The Apology

We descended without him. Once outside, Tony didn't offer me a ride, going straight to his carriage and leaving. Lance and his Inventor returned to their quadrant in her carriage.

Cesare took me back to Diamond Manor. He'd gotten a note pad and pencil from somewhere, and scribbled the entire ride.

Cesare would of course learn that I'd investigated his brother Jack when he interrogated Mr. Jake Bower. But I no longer felt afraid of that. I felt certain Cesare would understand.

And to my great relief, Katie was at Diamond Manor.

Cesare let Katie go, along with the portraits of the dead and a large horse-truck stuffed full of the captured "Spadros" men. Katie never spoke during our ride into Spadros quadrant, appearing deep in thought.

Roy met us at the betters' bridge with a great crowd of his men. None of those captured men in the horse-truck were his, which pleased him immensely.

Katie was bundled off into her own carriage, while I rode back to Spadros Castle with Roy — who was not so pleased with me. "I sent you to find out what he wanted, not to negotiate!"

He'd lied to me, to Tony, to Jonathan and maybe even to Lance. "I did the best I might under the circumstances. You want a cease-fire? Or not?"

Roy glared at me.

"You can still talk with them. I don't think his demands are unreasonable."

Roy turned away, nodding. "His main concern was his friends?"

I nodded.

Roy sat quiet for a moment. "Then he's a fortunate man."

"What's going to happen to Katie?"

"We have a police artist on the payroll. A portrait of this Frank will help. Those who let her out of the house have been punished."

Her servants. I wondered if they'd been only whipped, or if they were now dead. "She wasn't fencing the jewels to anyone in the Pot. Someone's impersonating them. Someone, I believe, from the Red Dog Gang."

"I see now that we've been too lenient with her. That will change. Think nothing more of this matter."

"You don't want to know who knows about this? What information she might have given them?"

He snorted, his face amused. "We'll learn of it in due time. These sorts never can keep quiet."

I thought I understood. Roy had almost as many spies as the Clubbs. "And when they speak of it, you'll know."

Roy gave me a broad smile. "You're finally beginning to understand."

Looking back, I don't think either of us understood anything. But at the time, I felt the matter with Katie was over, and that she was safe — at least for now.

* * *

The next morning's news read:

INVENTORS SOLVE TRAIN MYSTERY

I rolled my eyes at the headline. But I always had enjoyed solving puzzles more than taking credit for them.

Apparently, it took several days of rearranging glass panels to move the beam back to where it belonged, but once done the trains began running again.

Jonathan received his medication and was never the wiser. Soon after, Cesare paid his youngest brother a visit.

I never learned what they discussed, but the next day, Jon moved back to Diamond Manor.

I don't know what Roy offered in exchange for not giving Peedro Sluff up to Cesare Diamond. But when next I saw the man who claimed to be my father, he seemed to be as well as ever.

After a huge fanfare, Roy Spadros and Julius Diamond sat together and made a deal: the bones of those killed in the first Purge would be returned to their people. They made sure to tell everyone that this was NOT an alliance.

And Mary had her baby, a little girl. Blitz named her Ariana, after his mother.

I think Tony felt badly about all that had gone on between his men, Blitz, and Mary, because after she recovered, he brought us to dinner in an entirely private room — with a door — at a little restaurant on Market Center.

And whilst we celebrated, Joseph Kerr showed up.

When the waiter brought me the message, I met Joe at the door. "What do you want?"

He'd grown a small beard at the end of his chin. "Please, I know you're at dinner, but I must speak to you and your husband."

"Wait here." I closed the door in his face and went to Tony. "Joseph Kerr insists on speaking with us."

Mary, holding her baby, peered up at me.

"For gods' sake," Tony said. "Here? Now?"

I shrugged.

Blitz looked over. "Is all well?"

Tony's cheeks flushed. "Let's get this over with." We went to the door, which Tony opened. "What do you want?"

Joe didn't look at either of us. "It's clear you no longer trust me as you did. But I'll make it up to you both."

I said, "What's going to happen with the loan sharks?"

Joe made a dismissive gesture, still not looking at me. "My grandfather's made a deal with Charles Hart: they'll be paid."

"Very well," Tony said, "good night." He drew me inside, closing the door in Joe's face. Then he turned to me. "You brought me out here for that self-serving nonsense?"

"He was trying to apologize. You didn't even listen."

"Joseph Kerr cares nothing about us. He's only trying to get back into our good graces. That's all."

I felt bitter. "You know what? Forget it." I went to my place at the foot of the table, the first time I ever relished doing so. I wanted to be as far away from both of them — Joseph Kerr and Anthony Spadros — as I possibly could.

But as time went on, the happiness of the table seeped in. Mary and her baby were well.

And I'd stopped a war. Surely that was worth celebrating.

Try as I might, though, I couldn't help feeling as if this dinner was only a small happy moment in the sun as a massive storm cloud approached, more terrible than any others before.

The Red Dog Gang was still out there. Roy had been right: the Hart Family was deep in it. Yet it seemed I was the only one who cared about stopping them.

~~ This ends Chapter 6 of the Red Dog Conspiracy ~~

The Two of Hearts:

Part 7 of the Red Dog Conspiracy

Coming October 2021

Acknowledgments

I want to thank Julian White, Lenka Trnkova, and Tasha Parks for beta reading. I'd also like to thank Erin Hartshorn for editing and proofreading.

Thanks also go to my street team, The Commission, without whom this book might not have made it into your hands.

Special thanks to my Patrons, whose monthly financial support helps make this series possible:

Julian White
Melissa Williams
Cristina
Michaelene Alston
Jennifer Eades
Eirlys Evans
Jane Kamvar
Phoebe Darqueling
Rachel Heslin
Aramanth Dawe
Toni Mcconnell
Jen Soppe
James Mallison, Sr.

Follow the Red Dog Conspiracy on Patreon
patreon.com/red_dog_conspiracy

About The Author

Patricia Loofbourrow is a writer, gardener, artist, musician, poet, wildcrafter, and married mother of three who loves power tools, dancing, genetics, and anything to do with outer space. She also has an MD. Heinlein would be proud.

You can follow her at:
- Her website JacqOfSpades.com
- Twitter @Jacq_Of_Spades
- Tumblr red-dog-conspiracy.tumblr.com
- The Red Dog Conspiracy Facebook page

Note From The Author

Thanks so much for reading *The Five of Diamonds*. If you liked the book, please contact me, or leave a review where you bought this!

For news, backstory, and more, visit JacqOfSpades.com

CPSIA information can be obtained
at www.ICGtesting.com
Printed in the USA
BVHW031711280920
589786BV00001B/14